Jump Into...

DEATH BEHIND
THE LILACS

Ivy C. Leigh

JumpRope Chronicles

JERSEY PINES INK

JERSEY PINES INK

Copyright © 2018 Jersey Pines Ink, LLC

For information, address the publisher at:
JerseyPinesInk.com

Cover art— Dar Albert, Wicked Smart Designs

ISBN: 978-1-948899-00-0

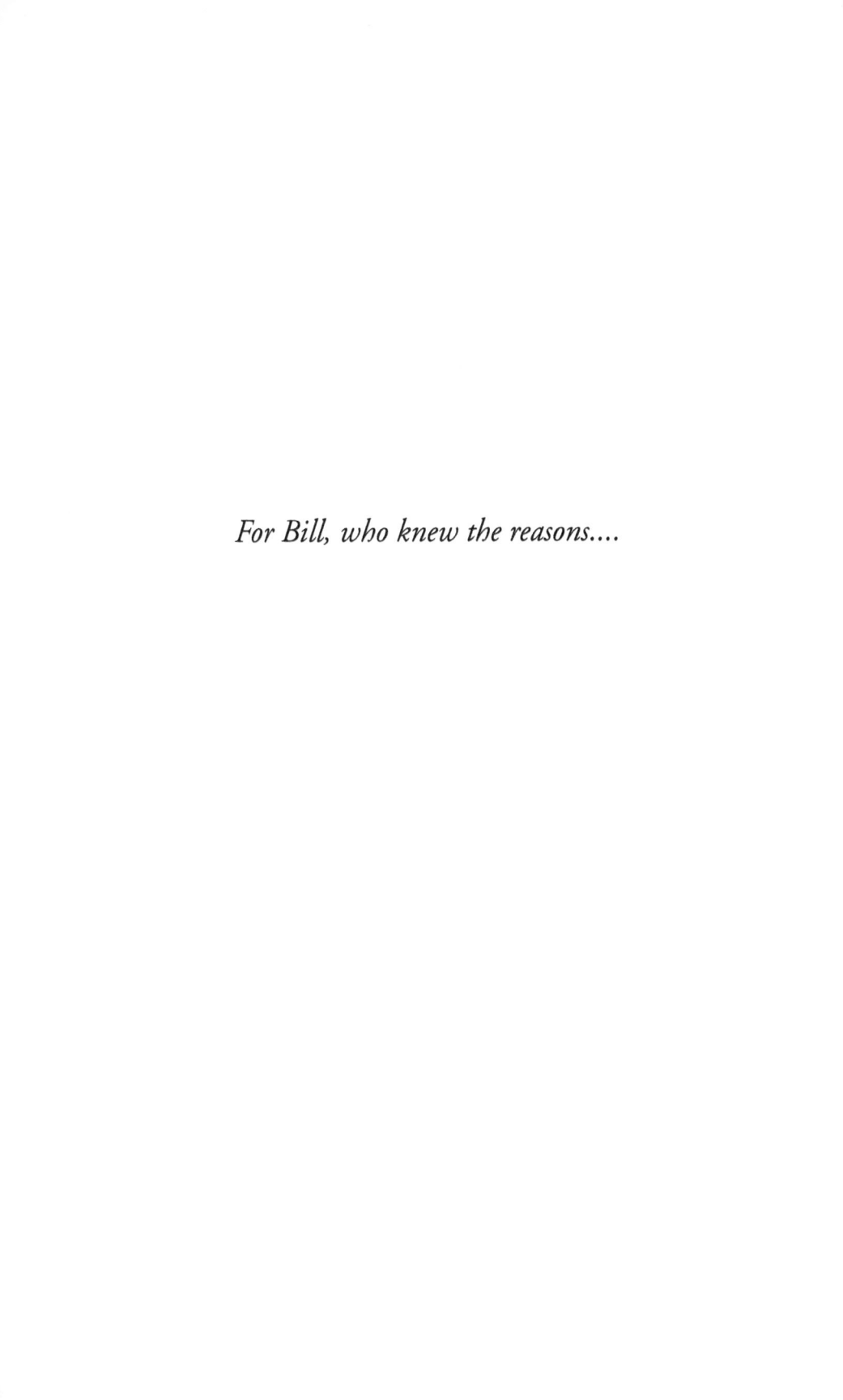

For Bill, who knew the reasons….

What is JumpRope?

JumpRope is a mythical New Jersey community, a small American town that everyone imagines remembering.

JumpRope is filled with romance, gossip, intrigues and of course, murder, with sufficient amateur detectives to solve any crime.

The personal loves, lives and dreams of the characters continue on with the next books of the series, as new characters step in to join the fun of the JumpRope experience.

Dear Readers,

When a friend became temporarily housebound I visited with library books (mostly mysteries) to read aloud. For fun, I started writing and reading a story of my own, a happy ending tale of a fictional town I called JumpRope. The story was set in modern times, but the title was inspired by a childhood jump rope rhyme that children once amused themselves with. (See one of the versions below.)

With my friend's encouragement, this story became the start of the JumpRope Chronicles, a book series about a small New Jersey town with people I hope readers will enjoy meeting.

Some of you might say, "I know people exactly like them!" or you might say, "Who could ever guess a person would think and act like that!"

Whatever it is for you, I hope you enjoy visiting JumpRope and following along with those who live there, sharing in their struggles, joys, adventures, romances, and yes, in the mysteries that they solve.

Best always and happy reading,

Ivy C. Leigh

Teddy Bear Rhyme

While jumping rope to this rhyme, jumpers mime the Teddy Bear's actions. The jumper either successfully completes the action or misses a step and a new jumper comes in.

Teddy Bear, Teddy Bear, turn around,
Teddy Bear, Teddy Bear, touch the ground,
Teddy Bear, Teddy Bear, touch your shoe,
Teddy Bear, Teddy Bear, that will do!

Teddy Bear, Teddy Bear, go upstairs,
Teddy Bear, Teddy Bear, say your prayers,
Teddy Bear, Teddy Bear, turn out the light,
Teddy Bear, Teddy Bear, say good-night!

Anonymous

When you love someone, all your
saved-up wishes start coming true.
—Elizabeth Bowen

To know that one has a secret is to
know half the secret itself.
—Henry Ward Beecher

DEATH BEHIND
THE LILACS

BEFORE

MAR-SEE-AH SPEAKS....

Her name was Mar-see-ah and she had the gift to see what was hidden from others.

Her concern was the intriguing community of JumpRope. That small town, so dear to her.

What was the origin of the playful name? No answer had ever come to her.

All thoughts of playfulness faded. There was only a sense of foreboding.

Death?

She closed her eyes as she saw a dark stairway.

Where did it come from, where did it lead?

Murder?

She saw an oak tree.

The perfume of flowers wafted to her.

"Lilacs," whispered Mar-see-ah.

It was a sign that whatever came to pass would end in joy.

The oak and the lilacs would be the start of everything.

CHAPTER 1

Holland Kingston Jr., known as "Holly," the thirty-seven year old, four-term mayor of JumpRope, New Jersey, was peacefully at work in his town hall office on a Tuesday morning. The month of March had gone out like the proverbial lion and the April breeze through the open window was as fresh and light as a childhood kiss. His duties that morning were light as well. There was no clue that his well-ordered life lay on the verge of chaotic change.

Francine Cramer Smithers, garbed in her stylish new spring jacket, stumped toward town hall with blood in her eye. Retired after forty years of pounding basic mathematics and first year algebra into high-schoolers' thick heads, she was convinced that nothing could thwart her. She was furious and demanded restitution. And like it or not, the mayor was going to help her get it.

Holly, neat-featured, with thick brown hair and warm blue eyes, contentedly continued with official correspondence. Finished signing grant requests for road work, he lifted a flyer for the rabies clinic. It had bright colors and cute clip art. He didn't know who had created it, but the date was wrong. He put it in a pile with a note to Susanna Washington, the competent town clerk, asking her to please deal with it. Holly next prepared a thank you to the JumpRope Ladies Civic Group for once again planning the community-wide May Day yard sale. It was the same thank you each year but handwritten anew. Holly took pride in doing a good job. He also liked pleasing people. As he had learned, however, accomplishing both could be as tricky as signing proclamations with a leaky pen.

Meanwhile, Francine had invaded town hall. The closer she steamed toward Holly's office, the more resolute she became. Projecting displeasure was her stock in trade—she was lucky to have that kind of face and to know how to use it. Years back, she had been engaged to Holly's widowed father, who had then been the mayor. He had jilted Francine to marry her younger sister, Peggy, a scandal that threatened his run in the next election. (In the small community of JumpRope, people enjoyed fierce loyalties and took other people's personal matters personally.) Francine had finally married and her husband, Bob, was a gem. Their elegant brick and frame Colonial style home on Centre Avenue was not only twice as big as her sister Peggy's, it had a dining room hand-painted by a New York City designer that encouraged guests to imagine themselves in a Greek temple with marble walls. In addition, Bob still had his hair while one-time beau, Holland Kingston Sr., was balder than an egg.

Five-foot one, with a square-shouldered, stubby frame, a fully-revved Francine marched into the mayor's office on her two-toned leather pumps and demanded:

"Why has that creaky old oak uprooted in a storm the day before yesterday, still not been removed? It's on the property right behind mine."

Startled, Holly started to say this was the first time anyone had mentioned the tree, but Francine, who never forgot that Holly could have been her stepson and would have been a lot better off for it, interrupted.

"And no nonsense about private property," she said. "The Mathers abandoned the place. Drove away and never came back. The house is boarded up, the lawn is knee high, and that toppled tree trunk draws kids like a carnival attraction. If somebody's Susie or John gets hurt, your inaction will never be forgiven."

After Francine triumphantly marched off with his promise of action, Holly sighed and smoothed his suit jacket, feeling he'd been in a tussle with a cyclone. He touched his necktie. His hobby was painting and he had a collection of art-themed neckties. Wryly, he wondered if he should have taken his neckwear choice that morning—Van Gogh's turbulent swirls of *Starry Night*—as a portent.

CHAPTER 2

On his route to the code enforcement office, Holly ran into his best friend, Allen "Slim" Parkerson. Slim, six-four-inches tall and rangy, was the town's police chief.

Learning Holly's mission, Slim grinned. "A tree down on private property? Sic the Empress on it. Keep her busy so she's not grousing to me about something."

The "Empress" was Darlene Gage, ruler of all things concerned with housing, property, construction and zoning. Slim was fun-loving and Darlene was a Grinch. They rarely saw eye-to-eye.

"Why didn't this person come directly to me?" Darlene challenged after Holly entered her kingdom and told her about the tree. She was fiftyish, exercised to bone-thinness and possessed of patrician features, intense blue eyes and shoulder-length ash blond hair. Her forehead was silk smooth (Holly had heard Botox rumors) but the grim and icy lines of her mouth prevented the beauty that should have been nature's gift. Holly had no quarrel with Darlene or how she did her job, but for the ten-thousandths time he wondered if she ever relaxed and smiled.

Narrowing her eyes, Darlene picked up a pen.

"The Mather house is on a dead end with woods all around," she said. "The place is no good to anybody. Owners up and disappeared.

However, neglect and damage cannot be tolerated no matter where it's found. Who complained?"

Holly had learned never to say who told what to who. He said, "We need someone in authority to document a possible danger to neighborhood children."

"Ah." Darlene's eyes went normal. Children were her only known soft spot. "Workers can't trespass without proper authorization. I'll start the paperwork."

"Perfect," Holly said.

He moved down the hall and outside to where Dewey Doyle, head of the town's four-man work crew, was preparing the truck to collect brush that residents set out along the streets.

He told Dewey about the fallen tree.

"Ain't heard nothin'. Nobody lives there," Dewey said. "Who cares?"

Dewey was the oldest of the work crew, tall, stringy, sour and always needing a shave.

"Children will be drawn to it," Holly said. "Darlene's writing it up as an attractive nuisance."

Dewey grunted. "Meet you there in a few." He turned to finish giving instructions to his helpers about the brush detail.

Holly checked with the zoning map. Francine's belligerent attitude puzzled him. She was always pushy but her indignation about the tree seemed personal. That usually meant she imagined somebody was trying to take advantage of her. Only there was no *somebody* because the Mather house had long sat empty.

The map showed a vacant lot directly behind the Mather house, but one rear corner of the Mather lot line touched a rear corner of Francine and Bob Smithers' property on Centre Avenue. That explained why Francine knew about the fallen tree when nobody else did, but it still didn't explain her outrage.

CHAPTER 3

Holly climbed into the municipal vehicle used by officials when on town duties. It was a former police car that retained the special lights but not the siren. As usual, he moved the seat forward. Holly, five-foot-seven with his shoes on, was stronger than he looked, but as a youngster he'd been so frail that his mother held him back from starting school. Then a truck knocked him off his scooter and put him in a body cast. He started first grade when he was eight years old and was still the smallest boy in his class.

Turning onto Main Street, he shot a glance at his watch, seeing he had time before he was due at the county. Holly's job as mayor was part time—his fulltime employment was as supervisor of Melton County Public Works. Enjoying the drive, he noted it was a perfect spring day. Scattered clouds sailed like swans across a Monet-blue sky. It had rained briefly at dawn and the leaves and petals of flowers in baskets hanging from the lamp poles along the wide street sparkled like jewels in the sunshine.

Leaving the business section of well-patronized shops, he passed through a residential area of Victorian style homes mixed with arts and crafts bungalows. The town website displayed antique photos of the community in bygone days. A brief description of the town's origin came from an elementary school writing contest. The winner had been selected by JJ Gilbert, a reporter for the county newspaper, the *Melton Monitor*.

Holly grinned, recalling wording that had made him wonder if some staid resident might find the tone irreverent. So far, no one had complained. The winning entry read, "The town is called JumpRope and nobody remembers why. Founded in the late 1600s by immigrants who came mostly from Northern Europe, it sits on eleven square miles of what used to be tribal land. The name is thought to be a mispronounced and long forgotten word in Native American. The only thing residents are sure of is that the "R" in the middle of the name has got to be capitalized because otherwise JumpRope is read as "Jum-prope," which is just plain stupid."

Smiling over the memory of the town's description, Holly increased his speed in more open country and slowed when making the turn that took him to the Mathers' paint-shy Queen Anne style Gothic, with its spindles and trims, a tower room and other embellishments. Not what one might expect from a farmhouse but it had been constructed in more fanciful times and now stood faded and sagging. Overgrown foundation plants climbed on the far side and on the right side, near the street, a lush wall of lilac bushes stood with branches heavy with buds that would soon burst into their annual display.

Remarkably, the tax payments on the deserted and forlorn property were current and paid by a corporation through a bank.

Holly remembered the buzz when the Mathers, a brother and sister who lived like hermits, stopped showing up at the market and post office—just about the only places people ever saw them. What had happened? Where had they gone? Some residents took it as an insult. One woman had said, "It's like they thought JumpRope wasn't good enough for them!"

Stepping from his car and hearing only a high breeze rustling through leaves and branches, Holly wondered about the children. School was in session but were preschoolers in the yard? Perhaps playing possum because they'd heard a car? He'd better find out. He threaded through the thick hedgerow of lilacs, the green scent of bruised leaves following as he entered the yard.

21

No children.

Relieved, he surveyed the toppled oak, its root mass pried up whole, as if tipped by a giant's hand. Fortunately, the tree had fallen away from the house. It angled toward Francine's property, the thick mass of crushed branches supporting the crown high off the ground. Other broken branches made it easy to clamber onto the upward sloping trunk. It was as Francine had described it, an attraction for children.

Holly moved closer, hesitated, and then on impulse used a broken limb to step up onto the trunk. Seesawing his arms for balance, he mounted the incline, rushing a bit when he reached intact branches near what had been the tree top. Grabbing on, he was surprised at how high he stood. He felt like a ship captain at the wheel, overlooking a sea of nothing much.

He realized he was having fun. When was the last time he acted simply for the joy of it? He couldn't remember. Involved in work and duty and making things right for the town, was he missing out on the zest of life?

Thrashing sounds came as Dewey shoved his way through the lilacs. He tilted his head up toward Holly's perch, "Jungle gym, huh?"

"Just about," Holly called down.

Nodding, Dewey stroked his jaw and laid out his steps of action. He'd cut the big limbs and saw through the trunk. He'd tip the roots back into the ground. Let the owners deal with the stump. Might rot before any of them showed up. Saw up the trunk and the big branches, clear away the brush. He'd use the new bulldozer for heavy lifting.

Holly inwardly raised his eyebrows. Bulldozer? From his experience at the county, he would have chosen the backhoe. From experience as mayor, he knew not to second guess a worker once a job had been assigned.

After Dewey left, Holly remained aloft, a gentle wind pleasantly lifting strands of his thick brown hair, airing the follicles he prayed he'd inherited from his mother's side of the family. Looking around, he became aware of a blurred line in the yard that might have been invisible except for his vantage point. It created the illusion of a long forgotten walkway. He visually traced a shadow path from the back door of the Mather house through the yard and out into the empty lot next to Francine's property.

Had the Mather back yard once run all the way through to Centre Avenue?

Impulsively, he pulled out his phone and took pictures. His days as an official could be wearing, with him always mindful of doing the right things for the people and the community. Being curious about a matter that had nothing to do with being mayor felt oddly liberating.

Lifting his gaze he noticed that one of the oak's crashing limbs had sliced off the top of a Colorado blue spruce in the corner of Francine's yard, leaving only a splintered shaft.

Ah-ha! Holly thought. That's why Francine was burned about the fallen oak. The tree wrecking her spruce tree had made it personal.

A suspicion struck. He looked back toward the Mather grounds. Where was the overgrown grass that Francine had complained about? He saw only straggly tufts poking through bare earth, moss patches and dead leaves. If children had made it a playground, where was the scuffed dirt, the scattered candy papers?

He'd been bamboozled.

Francine, outraged over her beheaded spruce, had made up a story about children in danger to prod him into cleaning up the fallen tree that had dared offend her. She was a piece of work, he thought, reluctantly impressed.

He clicked a shot of Francine's wrecked evergreen, his grin mischievous. If he ever heard more from her about the tree, he would tell her he had pictures for the insurance company.

She had made a big fuss, but really, what could come of it?

CHAPTER 4

Holly was too busy for the next few days to feed his curiosity about the Mather property. He had enough on his plate without poking a fork into a nonessential menu. His work schedule could be demanding, but it was manageable. He was at his county job as public works supervisor full days except for Tuesdays and Thursdays mornings when he was at his office as mayor. His evenings were usually free except for three Wednesdays a month at town hall. Two were for committee sessions and one was for the joint planning and zoning board. They all started at seven but ran late if residents turned out with questions and/or comments.

He considered again how routine his life had become. With no attractive alternative, he continued to plod along as if slogging through pudding. Maybe lightning would strike someday, but it wouldn't happen that Wednesday. After a day of discussions with designers and engineers about County Park landscaping, he was back at town hall that evening for a committee session with no surprises expected.

The police committee report from Committeeman Wilson "Reds" Burke was typically overlong. Burke, a retired plumber, had an imperious manner, broad shoulders, a huge belly and a similarly oversized ego. Cigar smoke was his signature cologne. The blazing hair that had earned him the nickname, "Reds," was now pure white, with a curling fringe across the forehead and long enough to touch his collar in back. The hairstyle and his increasingly haughty manner as he aged had earned him a new, behind-his-back nickname, "Hail Caesar."

Slim, garbed in his spotless police chief's uniform, sat lounging on his spine with his long legs stretched out. He nodded appropriately throughout Burke's tedious report as if in total agreement. Holly figured Slim's mind was really on his girlfriend, Lana.

Burke finally sat down. Holly thanked him for his report (thankful it was done) and it was time for the public session. First was a hot-headed neighborhood dispute about a front yard "butterfly garden," described by the opposing team as a "weed strewn disgrace." It was referred to the Property Department. Darlene would view the yard and decide if it complied with the ordinances or not. Either way, Holly thought, only half the parties would be satisfied.

Next, a resident stood to protest the destruction of the lilac bushes along the dead end road by the Mather property. Startled, Holly thought fast. He explained about the fallen tree and said he would look into the matter. What had Dewey done? The fact that Holly said he would look into the matter didn't keep three other residents from making protests about the same issue.

Finally, the meeting was over. Holly looked forward to his quiet apartment, a late supper, and the sounds of the meeting's squabbles fading into the woodwork. That's when Francine, her striped blouse broadening her squat form, barreled up between him and the exit.

"How do I contact the Mathers?" she said. "You saw my damaged evergreen. My insurance deductible is more than it would cost to replace it. The Mathers should pay."

Holly wasn't surprised at her attitude, but the glee he'd felt when snapping photos of her tree had gone as dead as a dodo.

"You should find the information you want at the tax office," he said.

Not bothering with a thank you, Francine called over her shoulder as she turned away, "You heard the complaints. Whoever wrecked those lilacs is a menace to the community."

CHAPTER 5

The following morning, with the notion of getting a pleasant start on his day before meeting with Dewey about the lilac complaints, Holly had breakfast at Krupple's Diner on Main Street. He chose a counter stool between two farmers wearing caps the right way around and ordered coffee and French toast with cinnamon apples. During an agreeable twenty minutes he chatted with the farmers and said hello to a few people who passed by, everything as relaxed as a meal on a cruise ship. Comfortably sated, he was in the line for the cash register when Oz and Mary McConnell appeared.

After exchanging greetings, Mary, a pixy of a woman, gave her husband a pointed look. Oz, normally blustery and high-tempered, shifted his feet and spoke with uncharacteristic hesitation. "Mary... she's been worrying about them lilacs."

Impatient, Mary spoke for herself. "Is work being done along that road? Is that why those bushes are being torn down?" Her delicate face tightened into a knot. "Those lilacs have always been a showpiece. If some developer's tearing things up, they could have at least waited until after the flowers bloomed."

"Developer?" Oz said, his wife's words clearly a surprise. Oz, who was on the planning and zoning board, reverted to his bombastic self.

"Mayor!" he said. "If there's a plan for new housing and the work already started, why didn't their application come before the board?" The skin around the man's eyes, seamed and sagging from years in the sun, drew tight. "What trick are you trying to pull?"

"What? No!" Holly was shocked. How had it leaped to this?

Finding an empty booth in which to talk so they weren't blocking the aisle, it took Holly several minutes to calm Oz down and explain that there were no plans for new houses. Mary explained where she'd gotten her idea. "I remembered the messy work for those other two developments. I thought this was the start of the same thing all over again, ending with new people coming in."

Holly nodded. JumpRope's two completed developments had drawn upscale buyers. Long-time residents still regarded them as "the new people."

Mary continued. "With the Pullen Farm, at least the developer kept a sensible name but the other—" Her Tinker Bell nose wrinkled in disapproval. "After tearing out acres of peach orchards that developer had the gall to call the place Peach Acres. I figured tearing out the lilacs meant we'd soon have something with a name like, 'Lilac Court,' filled with new people too snooty for us plain folks."

Relieved that the notion of new housing had started and ended with the McConnells, Holly left. Nothing good ever came from rumors.

A look at the Mather property told him why residents complained about the lilacs. Dewey had driven the bulldozer though the hedgerow, leaving a wide gap. The shrubs on either side looked okay, but the air was ripe with a green smell of plants that had been broken and plowed aside. Moving into the rear yard, Holly saw that the oak's root plate had settled back into its hole. The cut logs, the only remainder being sawdust, had been cleared, as well as a much of the brush. What remained had been heaped in one corner. Several damaged lilac bushes that seemed to have intact roots lay there, too. Could they be saved?

The job had taken a lot of hard work and it had been done well—except for wrecking the shrubs. Tracks showed that Dewey had apparently failed to negotiate the opening he'd made going in and he'd caused additional damage going out. The dozer had been a gift to the town when a heavy equipment company on the highway closed down. Had this been Dewey's first chance to drive it?

Holly reached town hall and caught Dewey before he started on his morning rounds. One look at Holly and the man scrubbed his scruffy chin and started making excuses. "That dead end street's drawing folks like flies. Blasted posy fans, burning up the phones."

Holly nodded, deciding that since the residents had already done the scolding, he'd keep it positive. "You solved the problem of the downed tree. There's nothing left to attract children. The wood has been hauled away and there's only a bit of brush left to deal with. But, lilac bushes were broken and some destroyed."

Another grumble from Dewey. "Folks yammering 'bout nothing."

"They were counting on seeing those flowers bloom."

Dewey's expression combined stubbornness with hopelessness. "There weren't no flowers when I did it. I wasn't thinking about them."

"They hadn't come out yet. What *were* you thinking?"

Dewey shrugged. "Maybe about that new dozer."

"First time you used it?"

Dewey's eyes brightened. "Nice machine. Made that wide space on purpose for the truck to haul out wood and brush. Abandoned house on a dead end. Who should care?"

Understanding, Holly finally smiled. "We guessed wrong about that."

He was relieved that the man had behaved responsibly according to his view of the situation. Remembering his own emotions when he'd climbed the trunk, he also felt a dart of kinship with Dewey's confessed fun with the dozer. But now, a solution was called for.

He said, "Once you're done with your rounds, see what you can do about the replanting any bushes left with roots, and tie them to the standing bushes. Let's hope they'll settle in the damp ground and bloom with the rest."

"Got it." Dewey hitched up his trousers and left, his grumble gone now that he knew what to do.

Holly sighed. He liked lilacs, but right now, they were as much trouble as poison ivy.

CHAPTER 6

Holly had finished a state report and was satisfied with how he'd handled the legal gobbledygook when Francine Smithers stamped in. The cheery light in the room seemed to dim.

Glowering, she proclaimed, "Kurt at the tax office is worthless. As worthless as that Dewey Doyle, rampaging that bulldozer like a wild bull. The engine roared, the back-up beeper beeped and the saw screamed. I thought my ears would never stop ringing."

Having no answer that he thought would satisfy her, Holly said, "Did Kurt give you the name of the bank?"

"Yes and that dolt of a banker passed me off to a snob of a lawyer who wouldn't speak a word except 'client privacy.' Wouldn't even confirm Grace's and Barry's names."

"Barry Mather," Holly said pleasantly, trying to coax a different vibe. "He drove a green Dodge. Your husband took care of it at his auto body shop. Bob does my car, too. A terrific mechanic. You can always depend on Bob."

"Barry always did," returned Francine, pleased by his positive words about her spouse.

Nodding, Holly said, "I remember the Dodge better than I

remember Barry. As for Grace, I only remember a heavy woman with big glasses and black hair screwed in a knot."

Francine sniffed. "Him so thin and her so fat. Like Jack Sprat and his wife, only they were brother and sister. The house was in the family for generations. Their parents were old people living there when I was young. I did chores for the mother when I was a teenager, but I was never around to see Barry or Grace. Wouldn't have known them if I fell over them. They went to boarding school, like the children of English lords."

Although brand name proud and liking the idea of an aristocratic life, Francine sneered at anyone in JumpRope actually achieving it—except for herself, of course. "Bob and I moved to Centre Avenue shortly before the old people left. When Barry and Grace moved in I went over to introduce myself, took cookies. They said their parents had died. If I hadn't visited, I would never have known who they were. They never socialized, never got involved."

Holly said, "When did they leave? I didn't know they were gone until I heard people talk about the house being boarded up."

"That's when I found out." Francine gave a disapproving sniff, not liking to admit she'd been out of the loop. "I saw that their car wasn't there, but they were always going someplace. Next thing, a crew sealed the doors and windows as tight as a drum. That was about four years ago. The place is a disgrace to the neighborhood. Somebody should tear it down and put up something new."

She marched out, fiercely vowing that her attorney would get payment for her tree from that bank lawyer no matter how long it took.

Updating his frequent self-reminder to never get on Francine's bad side, Holly consulted the jottings on his calendar and called the president of the Ladies Civic Group to confirm his requested attendance to their upcoming meeting.

Iris Roundtree came in with a letter for him to sign. Plump and cheerful, Iris was a floating town secretary and the sister of Committeewoman Azalea Roundtree. Although dependable and able to take directions accurately, Iris was slow on the uptake and a tad gullible.

"Have you seen what's on the Internet, what Pilar Fanshawe has in her *JumpRope Jive* page?" she asked. Pilar and her son, Alexander, not only sporadically published a four page newsletter (a gossip sheet as far as Holly was concerned) called *JumpRope Jive*, they also had a blog of the same name where other residents could contribute memories, experiences and opinions.

"I'm afraid I don't have much time for that," Holly said.

"It has photos of how the lilacs looked last year," Iris said. "So pretty. And now, how ugly the bushes look this year. People are saying Dewey did more damage than the fallen tree."

Holly clicked on the site and cringed. He was thinking that only a few people even knew about the lilacs in the past, and now everybody had an opinion as if they were life-long members of some lilac club.

"I'm getting a weird feeling about the Mather house," Iris said in a troubled tone, placing the letter for Holly to sign. "You know Mar see-ah the Psychic?"

"I've heard of her." Holly knew that Francine and her friends went to dinner at Teddy's Bar and Grill restaurant where a psychic named Mar-see-ah was featured. Francine called it amusing twaddle. Did Iris take it more seriously? If so, he wouldn't be surprised.

Iris said, "At our last dinner at Teddy's, Mar-see-ah mentioned lilacs. She talked about a stairway, too, but that didn't make sense. Those flowers could be a symbol."

"Oh?" Holly said, touching his necktie, a multicolor Kandinsky shape against a pale background. Wild, like his day so far. He should find ties with soothing artwork. Maybe cows standing in water.

Iris's gaze went far away. "There's trouble at the Mather place. I feel it in my bones."

Holly knew he shouldn't ask, but he did. "And that trouble is?"

Clasping her chubby hands, she refocused and shuddered. "I'm not sure. I heard it was going to be torn down. That would be good. But as it is now, just be careful, will you, hon?"

"Thanks. Being careful is smart advice."

With the signed letter in hand, Iris departed, cheerful again now that she'd warned him. About what, Holly wasn't sure. Francine and Iris were long-time friends. He suspected Iris had heard Francine say that the house "should be" torn down, and wishfully upgraded it to "going to be" torn down.

It was time for Holly to leave for his job at the county. On his way out through the building he stopped at the police department end to see Slim.

Slim was back from checking to make sure traffic was moving okay around a temporary detour set up for the removal of a buried oil tank. He sat in his desk chair with his feet propped on a half open desk drawer, studying a report as he snacked on corn chips. Slim was always snacking, which could result in crumbs yet he somehow kept his uniform neat.

"Hey," Holly asked. "You hear anything new around the Mather place?"

Slim looked up. "Nothing new since that lilac fuss."

Holly told Slim about his run-in with Oz McConnell at the diner.

"What did Oz think?" Slim laughed. "That you were in bed with a developer, getting your palm greased to slip through a deal?"

"Just about." Holly remembered the scorn in Oz's voice. A disheartening moment.

"Sounds like you explained it away." Slim extended the bag of cheese snacks. "You worry too much, bud. Eat something and cheer up."

Holly couldn't help chuckling at Slim's light-hearted response. "Guess you're right," he said. Besides, the talk of the Mather house had reawakened his curiosity about the phantom walkway.

CHAPTER 7

Contrary to the bumpy morning, Holly's afternoon at the county ran like cream. Last thing, he went to the court house to drop off legal papers. Remembering his curiosity about the walkway, he stopped at the County Clerk's department to see what he could learn about the Mather property. He wanted to see the old land description. Did it once run through to Centre Avenue?

He was directed to the section of the building he'd never entered before, one that held deed and mortgage records, a long narrow room, gloomy despite tall windows, constructed in a time of architectural history that saw a supposed relationship between sanctified temples and places of business. It smelled of some sort of cleaning preparation, possibly for the black and white tile floor, a likely update in the 1940s. Holly's awestruck gaze moved across walls with racks jammed with hefty bound books that reached from floor to ceiling. He then saw the long counters where the oversized volumes could be spread flat and documents examined. People standing at the counter copied information, many typing directly into laptops, all clearly knowing which way was up. After Holly spent useless moments pretending that staring blankly was a hobby, he broke down and questioned one of the researchers and learned that there were computers where grantee and grantor names or block and lot could be entered to identify whatever book was wanted.

At a computer, Holly stood before an old-looking screen that was blank except for a bouncing green cursor. There were instructions, but when he typed in what he understood was the correct command, the screen went dead. Feeling the cream of his day curdling around him, he shifted to the next computer and another mocking cursor. He re-read the instructions, lifted his hands to the keyboard and then paused, feeling helpless.

"That other computer doesn't work," said a timid sounding voice at his side.

Holly turned to see a county employee with an ID card hanging from a cord around her neck, Victoria somebody. Her photo made her look even more out of focus than she appeared in reality.

"I need help," Holly said, afraid she might evaporate. He told her the block and lot of the property he was interested in and stepped back and to one side, making the path clear to the computer.

Not looking at him, she hesitated and then stepped in. Compared with her diffident manner, her hands on the keys were steady and sure. Welcome green letters of information appeared on the screen.

"Is that the property you're researching?" she asked.

He said it was.

Continuing to look at the screen instead of at him, she said, "The book that has the deed information is here—" She pointed at the screen with a neat fingernail and then indicated a pencil on a string and a pile of blank cards he hadn't noticed. "Copy this information…" she tapped the screen again, "then go to the records room and find the book with the number you copied, turn to the page number and find the deed."

"I need to search backward, I don't know how far." Holly explained he wanted to find out if the empty lot behind an old house had ever been a part of the main property.

She finally looked at him. "We have books on the lower level that go back to the early eighteen hundreds."

An image flashed of a coal mine filled with books and him leafing through pages by the light on his hard hat. "I'll have to come back."

She reached for a pencil and a blank card. "Let me copy down the book number and page. You'll at least have the place to start."

He watched as she wrote. She was taller than him, no big whoop. Rare was the man who didn't top him and many women were taller, too. That didn't bother him—what got under his skin was women thinking his size made him "cute." He'd had a number of pleasant relationships with women over the years but never with anyone who was exactly right. And he hadn't met anyone recently who seemed even remotely possible. The woman who had last approached him, a company union rep from Trenton, had cooed that she wanted to pin him to her lapel and show him off around town. He grimaced at the memory.

This woman wasn't sending off signals either way, which was perfect. Her ID photo was blurry and she looked blurry as well, her pale complexion showing uneven coloring, as if she blushed in patches, and her brown hair was so fine-textured it seemed adrift even in the still air of the room.

Thanking her, he placed the book and page number card she'd handed him into his pocket and headed for home feeling relieved. He had the information he would need if he wanted to follow the matter further, but he didn't have to.

He could do as he pleased.

A good feeling.

CHAPTER 8

The reported home burglary late that afternoon seemed no big deal.

The homeowners, who lived in Peach Acres, a collection of luxury single family "Carriage Homes" in the eastern section of the township, came home from work to find their back door ajar. (They swore they'd locked it.) All shaky and scared, they went through the house with two officers. The only thing they found missing was the dog mat from inside their back entry. The dog was a St. Bernard, the pride of their sixteen-year-old daughter, and the mat sopped up water that the dog tracked in when it rained.

The police wrote down the information and the homeowners vowed to burglarproof their windows and doors—can't be too careful, dog mat one day, wedding silver the next.

"A prank," said one of the cops back inside the police car.

Later on the evening of the same day, a frantic teenager called from her ground floor Peach Acres bedroom to report that her reality star sponsored cosmetics kit had been swiped from the dressing table by her window.

The teenager said the window wasn't locked and she blamed a

schoolmate for the theft. "She was jealous because I got invited to a birthday party and she didn't." The schoolmate claimed she was at the mall and the movies with companions and they all had shopping receipts and ticket stubs to prove it.

"Somebody playing pranks," Slim said when talking to Holly later.

The next morning, the county newspaper, the *Melton Monitor* gave it a one inch headline:

JumpRope Jumping With Petty Thefts

The article was barely longer than the headline. Holly was glad the newspaper didn't play it up big—except for the headline—and thank goodness the thefts were nowhere near the Mather property. Otherwise Iris would claim it had proved that her premonition had been right.

CHAPTER 9

By the following week the puzzling Peach Acres thefts as well as the questions about the Mather property had dropped into the background of Holly's thoughts. A reminder of the latter came when Shirley DeGarmo visited his office accompanied by her live-in companion, Ruth Wilson. A lifelong resident, Shirley had two sons, Donny, a JumpRope police officer, and Kurt from the tax office.

As was her habit, Shirley brought in cookies and fudge to be shared around in town hall. She'd been famous for her cookies until she'd gotten older. Now that she had Ruth, a terrific candy maker, she'd started making cookies again, with Ruth adding her chocolate treats.

"Mr. Mayor, I wish to thank you," Shirley said after they were seated, her manner its usual Sunday school teacher formal. "I learned from Kurt that you arranged to replant and prop up damaged lilacs out by the old Mather place. Ruth likes to drive me around. We saw them when they looked so dreadful." She nodded as she spoke, her gray curls freshly poodled by the local beauty salon. "We drove out again yesterday. The undamaged ones are already flowering and the ones you saved have taken hold and may bloom almost as well as last year. Isn't that so, Ruth?"

"Indeed," confirmed Ruth. With her prominent brown eyes and thin frame, Ruth, who could perform simple nursing duties as well as serving as a companion, had a faintly anxious manner and oddly enough, looked less fit than Shirley, who had a serious heart condition.

After a bit more community chit-chat the two women had started to leave when Shirley glanced back. "Kurt says there are no plans to extend that dead end road for a new housing development, correct?"

"Correct." Holly tilted his head. "What brought up the question?"

"Someone overheard Oz McConnell asking you about it. Mary told me it was a misunderstanding on her part because of the damage at the Mather house. But then, when I heard something again…." Her words trailed off.

"So you decided to check it out?" Holly was thinking that Oz might as well have used a loudspeaker that morning in the diner.

"Well, I didn't like it that people thought something sneaky might be going on. It didn't sound like you. Kurt said there are no large plots of land for sale and there have been no questions from anyone who might be interested. So it's all a big nothing. That's what Ruth and I will be sure to tell people."

Ruth nodded. "We certainly will."

Holly thanked them for their concern and the ladies left. He sighed. Maybe Iris had a point about the Mather property—if empty gossip was trouble, that empty old house fit the bill.

At his county job, county planners had wanted him to attend a meeting with a financier named Acer Wolfgang, who was interested in a solar farm project, only the meeting had been canceled. Glad to have the extra time, Holly skipped lunch and left early enough to revisit the County Clerk's department. Thanks to Shirley DeGarmo, the subject of the Mather property had moved forward in his mind. He'd check the old property records. This was the day to finish what he had started.

He found Victoria in the county records room standing near a desk with her nameplate. Seeing him, she blushed. Not quite meeting his eyes, she moved to the desk and lifted a pad with neat jottings written in ink. "I found information for you. I thought you might not have the time. Being mayor and all."

That startled him. "You knew who I was?"

She examined her shoe. "I live in JumpRope."

"I'm sorry. I didn't realize." The municipality's population was near five thousand so it wasn't possible to have met each person, still he illogically felt negligent when faced with a resident he didn't know. He looked at her notes. "Is that the research?"

She darted a quick glance at him. "I enjoy research projects. If...if you would like me to go through what I found..." Her words trailed off.

Cheered that he might be able to find his answer and be satisfied, he said quickly. "I'd appreciate it."

With him seated by her desk, she ran her pencil down neatly printed notes as she spoke, her manner confident now that the focus was her work. Efficiently she took him back through the recording of a series of deeds. "This one is dated 1926 and it's here that we have our answer. Leon Mather, et ux, which means "and wife," sold off property at the rear of their long lot to people named Curry. It's still in the Curry name, probably descendants. And it's still apparently a vacant lot."

"Yes." He took out his cell and found the photos. "This shows what looks like a path. That started my interest." He handed over his phone.

She squinted at the small display and angled it.

"Hard to make out," he apologized. "I should have printed them."

"You didn't know you'd be trying to show them," she said with a hint of a smile.

"I guess it no longer matters." He accepted his phone back. In retrospect, his curiosity seemed silly, but at least it was satisfied. Hallelujah! He'd been right, the Mather property once ran all the way through to Centre Avenue. He was glad the whole business was done with. He gave Victoria a grateful smile. "I appreciate your research and your time. Thank you."

"I'd like to research a bit deeper," she said. "See what deeds to surrounding properties might reveal."

Not prepared for this, he fumbled. "Well...if you want...I guess."

Her attention had returned to her notes. She spoke without looking up. "I'll let you know when or if I have something more."

Glumly, Holly drove home. Now he still wasn't done with the Mather place. That fallen oak and resulting smashed lilacs had started a string of nonsensical events. Would he ever be done with it?

It was like getting nibbled to death by ducks.

CHAPTER 10

At the monthly morning town hall staff session, department heads, plus the mayor and the police chief and whatever committee person wished to attend, met over coffee and Danish around a table in the judge's chambers. It was also the day for Holly to attend the Ladies' Civic Group tea and cookies session.

As usual, the town agenda was keeping employees on the same page regarding the goals and objectives that maintained JumpRope's reputation as "Best Living Little Town." (The slogan had come from a contest run by the Joint Fire and Emergency Auxiliary.) There was also discussion of the June primary election. Holly had previously been elected to a four year mayoral term, but Committeepersons Reds Burke and Azalea Roundtree were running for re-election of their three-year terms that November. Since they were running uncontested, the voting turnout was expected to be light.

Reds cared about the town, and he did his job well—he was committeeman in charge of Police and Public Safety—but he had an irritating habit of needling people, especially since he'd gotten older. This time, as he turned toward Holly and spoke, he sounded unpleasantly snide. "Good thing you're not running again this year, Mayor. There may be no truth to the tales of you and a secret land deal, but even if there was, by the time you're up for election again, it won't matter. People have short memories. So either way, it amounts to nothing."

The room had gone silent. Holly, caught off-guard, couldn't decide how to respond. Darlene Gage stepped into the void, snapping, "If it's nothing, why bring it up?"

"Moving on," Holly said. Darlene and Reds had bumped heads several times in the past on zoning issues—no telling where this would go if allowed. As for himself, he would ignore Reds' comment. "Next on the agenda is a report from the Police Chief."

Slim, who sat slumped in his chair, long legs stretched out, looked ready for a nap. Meetings bored him and he didn't care who knew it. Not bothering to straighten up, he said, "Sycamore Shades Cemetery got a complaint about a rabid rat. The animal was an opossum. I saw it, a young one, come from its hole in the brush." He roughed his streaky blond-brown hair as he talked. Holly hid a smile, thinking that Slim would rather be stalking opossums than be trapped with squabbling officials.

"Opossums are harmless," Slim continued. "They hiss to protect themselves and rarely contract rabies—something about their body temperature. I reported this to the secretary at Shades, and then stopped to see the people who thought it was a rat. Turns out the family is from Europe and never saw an opossum before." He glanced at Holly. "It's all in my written report. I should be out on the street. If that's it, I'm out of here."

Slim stood, nodding all around as he stretched to his full height and turned to leave.

"Excellent job of community policing," approved Reds.

His words of praise fell on Slim's disappearing back.

CHAPTER 11

Holly left for his Ladies' Civic Group meeting, which coincidentally was at Sycamore Shades Cemetery. The ladies assembled each month in the cemetery trustees' meeting room, which was in the former home of the farmer who donated land for a private cemetery in the late eighteen hundreds. Now, perhaps forevermore, the location would make Holly think of opossums.

Arriving early, he chatted with several women on the well-groomed front lawn and then followed them into the meeting room already set with rows of chairs. At the head of the room was a podium. Next to it sat a lace covered table arrayed with fancy china and decorative dishes of cookies, nuts and candies. Holly winced to see a vase of lilacs as the centerpiece. He hoped he wouldn't have to hear where they'd come from. The setting and genteel hubbub lent the suggestion of old-style hats and gloves although the attire was mostly slacks and blouses. Shirley DeGarmo was there, the second time he'd seen her that week, as well as her companion, Ruth, who wore slacks and a sweater set with pearls.

Darlene Gage, having escaped from the staff session ahead of Holly, stood pouring tea. A long-time Ladies' Civic Group member, she took time off from her housing and property job on Group meeting days.

Holly's father, as mayor before him, had encouraged town employees to be involved in community work. Holly had continued the practice.

Marge Santos, the cemetery manager and current Group president, called the meeting to order, greeted the mayor and requested that members respect his time by keeping the meeting moving. She turned the program over to the activities chairperson, Cindy Hoyt, who spoke of a new event for the following year: a town-wide beautification project that would include prizes to the town's best looking houses. Holly said he thought it was a good idea. It was to seek his approval that he'd been invited.

"I know houses that need beautification," Darlene gritted. "That or a citation and a fine in court."

"We're thinking positive, Darlene," Marge admonished.

"Sorry." Darlene flipped her long hair. Despite her stringent diet program she reached for one of the candies—fudge dipped in dark chocolate with a little design on top that was one of Ruth's specialties. Holly hid a smile. Darlene was excellent at her job, but adding some sweetness would be good for everybody.

As the plans for the new event continued, some at cross-purposes, Jessi Spellman's name rippled a series of groans around the room.

"Who's Jessi Spellman?" asked a new resident.

"You don't want to know," Marge said. "She's a cute little thing, but she's always making trouble."

"She's vindictive, too," said Amy Newton. (Amy and her husband, Chuck, the cemetery caretaker, lived in another part of the house with their young son.) "We went to an Auxiliary event and heard Jessi arguing about a pie she'd donated to the baked goods table. It had a flat crust and was tagged at five dollars while the others were seven. I guess she felt insulted. She probably made it herself instead of her husband, who's supposed to be a good cook. Jessi said the ingredients had cost five dollars and she wanted her money back and the Auxiliary would still make a profit if they priced it right."

"She makes a donation then wants to be paid back?" cried the new girl.

"That's Jessi," Amy said. "The woman at the bake table didn't know what to say. Chuck was afraid she would give in to Jessi, hand over the money and then be stuck with a pie nobody wanted so he said, 'I'll give five dollars for it.' The woman at the table said, 'Sold!' and shoved that pie over so fast Chuck figured it left skid marks. After that, Jessi had it in for us."

"Tell how she called child protective services on you," Marge said.

"What?" yelped another member, who hadn't heard that part of the story.

"We couldn't be sure it was her," Amy said, "but it probably was. A day or so later, I met her at the market, and snippy-like, she said, 'Getting hubby more pie?' I ignored her and that afternoon a child protective agent was at my door checking an anonymous tip that I'd left my son locked in the car while I food shopped. It wasn't true. He was in day care. But it could have created a lot of trouble if I hadn't been able to prove it."

More stories about Jessi started flying. Holly knew it was time to leave. Sitting still for negative gossip made it appear he condoned it. Besides he'd had his own bad Jessi experiences that he didn't like remembering. Offering his thanks for the invitation and repeating his approval of their future May Day plans, he started working his way toward the door through a forest of feet with purses scattered like land mines. As he did so he heard the conversation turn to the recent thefts at Peach Acres. Shirley was saying that if the thefts began again, police should patrol the troubled location. Ruth spoke in agreement, saying it made complete sense.

As Holly slipped through the alcove that led to the front door, somebody mentioned it had been nice that most of the Mather house lilacs had been saved. The last thing he heard was Darlene sardonically returning the topic to event planning when she said, "Maybe the Mather place could win our award for the tidiest ghost house."

CHAPTER 12

Jessi Spellman sat in her car searching the *Melton Monitor* for news about the rumored new development. Unaware that she'd been the subject of gossip at the Civic group meeting (she would have been flattered by their recognition of her shrewdness), she was disgusted to find nothing about the development in print. Making spitting sounds she crumpled the paper and tossed it out the open car window like the piece of trash it was. Hadn't those news idiots ever heard that phrase about inquiring minds wanting to know? Wasn't there something about that in the Second Amendment? Or was that gun rights? In any case, she was being denied information.

Jessi was parked in Apple Corners across from the dump she'd bought six months ago. The Apple Corners house was providing some back and forth devilish fun with the Botox blonde property inspector, Darlene Gage, but it was time to unload it. Jessi had applied a few cheap fixes and cast her line on the Internet. A fish took the bait and that's who she was waiting for.

Posing for the visor mirror, she admired her up-tilted green eyes, thinking, *what a pussycat!* (Her husband called her Kitten.) Jessi shifted her thinking to how smart her husband was. Arnie might not look like much, kind of plump and ordinary, but there was nothing ordinary about his brain. He performed title searches for area real estate brokers, most frequently for an old coot of a sharpie realtor called Pastor, thanks to an ordination certificate issued online by the Church of God's Grace and Sparkling Waters. Pastor never lied about having an actual congregation, but if his collar influenced anyone favorably, so be it. Jessi considered Pastor a weasel, but she admired his cleverness. By working with Pastor's tips, she and Arnie were able to jump ahead of the crowd when it came to property investment. Arnie felt they owed Pastor a lot. Jessi figured it was just business.

Now, she and Arnie were selling off stuff for extra bucks because of a possible deal he got wind of at the county records room. He had seen the mayor wandering like a lost lamb and getting rescued by that limp rag who worked off and on at the library—Victoria Dahlgaard. Long name, short personality. Library bookends had more spark.

Always on the alert for an opportunity, Arnie had taken a glance over their shoulders when they'd been together at a computer. He saw the address they were discussing and looked it up himself. The old house on the dead end road, the Mather place. It was held by a corporation with an address in New York.

Interesting.

Arnie had filed it away.

He was in the records department often enough to have an idea of the employee schedule and a few days later he saw Victoria researching deeds at a time when she would normally be at her desk with her bag lunch.

When she left a deed book open to help someone, he managed a peek at the open page. Again the block and lot for the Mather property. When she put her books back in place and went down to the basement where the scabby handwritten records were stored, he waited a minute and then followed.

Pretending to be doing his own research he pulled a book at random and spread it on the opposite side of the broad table where she examined a yellowed page with spidery handwriting. Busy making notes, her attention was focused on the page before her.

Reading upside down, Arnie noted the page number. When she

reshelved the book and went upstairs, he took it down again. Hmmm. Not the Mather property where the house was, but the adjoining property.

That's when he started his own research project and hot damn! Way back there had been a huge Mather farm, later divided up into lots owned by different corporations, all with the same New York address. Old handwritten deeds contained details and Arnie read that eighty years ago, the Mather property that was now all wild woods had been a working farm.

Still flirting with her visor mirror reflection, Jessi remembered that after Arnie had gathered his information, he and she put their heads together. She told him of rumors about a new development near the Mather place and also that the mayor was denying it. In recent years JumpRope had two new housing developments, Peach Acres, and what was called the Pullen Farm. They became convinced that a third one was in the works.

"Hey, Kitten," Arnie had said, "Look here—" He showed her on a map the area owned by the corporations. "See this triangle shaped strip along the highway that butts against the old Mather farm? That's where there is a broken down gas station and the ruins of a big old barn."

He then had outlined a plan.

"I don't know if the mayor and committeemen are in bed with the principal of this corporation or what, but this triangle is accessible to both a future development and the highway," he said. "A great spot for somebody who sees the advantage of something commercial near a bunch of houses. It's been for sale for a dog's age and the price hasn't budged, so word hasn't gotten around. We can get rid of that ruin at Apple Corners and add that money to what we got from the two houses we sold last year and buy this." He jabbed at the map again, his eyes glistening. "As soon as that development gets started, the price of this will shoot through the roof. We'll flip it and make a killing."

Jessi left off remembering and straightened in her seat as a red convertible parked in front of the Apple Corners dump that Jessi had landscaped into a showplace. She had spiffed up the tiny front lawn with a few bucks worth of turf, put new paint on the stoop and decorated it with two pseudo Chinese vases planted with spiral evergreens. The cracked foundation was hidden behind bushel-basket sized impatiens.

A blonde woman dressed in a smart looking pantsuit got out of her low slung car. Jessi didn't know much about cars, but it looked like money and that's what her line had drawn in.

"Here fishy-fishy," Jessi whispered. She stepped from her car and went to meet the future owner of what Jessi would claim, with tears in her eyes, was a house that was precious and dear to her. She had a terrific story ready, and when she told it, she would sound so heartfelt she would almost believe it herself.

CHAPTER 13

April and May swept themselves away in a glory of spent spring blossoms and then it was June, with its sweet riot of roses perfuming the lengthening days and ushering in vacation time.

Holly's vacation was spent at Sunshine Shores, a small seaside resort along the Atlantic Ocean. The community had begun as a religious retreat in the 1800s with the "Sun" in Sunshine spelled "Son." The name was changed sixty years later, but the resort maintained a family atmosphere. Holly vacationed with friends he'd made when attending Rutgers University. The friends were there with their wives and kids— the kids regarded Holly as an honorary uncle. The time sped by quickly and then Holly was heading home again late on a Saturday afternoon. The vacation had underlined his feeling that life was passing him by. Would he ever have a family of his own?

As he neared JumpRope, a concern that he'd struggled not to stew over returned to his mind—that jab from Reds Burke about suspicions that he was involved in an underhanded land deal. He wanted to think that Reds was just being Reds, but he'd heard whispers that made him fear that the unfounded rumor was spreading. Discouraging. Holly felt that a man's good reputation was a treasure. Keeping it clean was a duty he owed to himself and to those whom he knew. For a mayor, that duty extended to the residents he'd been elected to serve. Could Mary McConnell's wrong-headed conclusion about the wrecked lilacs leading to a new housing development be on the verge of going viral? If so, like opening Pandora's Box, the mistaken notion couldn't be locked away again. Trying to deny it would only make it worse. Holly knew the only cure was time, but it was still blasted frustrating.

His cell phone rang, a welcome interruption. The number was Slim's. Slim knew he was returning that afternoon. What news couldn't wait? Now, Holly was worried. It couldn't be anything good.

He pulled over to the gravel shoulder of the road to answer. His forebodings were proven when Slim said in a heavy voice, "There's been another robbery in Peach Acres, only this one turned deadly. I wanted you to know before you got in and picked up your messages."

As Slim explained it, the couple who owned the robbed house were asleep. They heard nothing until the thieves were outside with their loot, yelling and arguing. The automatic garage light came on. From the window, the owners saw two males tussling. One gave a yell and collapsed. The other one tried to lift up the fallen man, but failing, he jumped into a passenger seat of a car that sped off. The police answering the call found the male on the ground dead from a knife wound.

"Who was it?" Thinking of the previous thefts which had seemed like pranks, Holly was braced to hear the name of a local student—a teenage stunt gone horribly wrong.

"Nobody we know, if that's your worry," Slim said.

Holly blew out a sigh of relief, but it didn't remove the seriousness of the event.

"Meet you at the station and we can chew it over," Slim said and Holly agreed.

The two men had been best friends since second grade. Because of Holly starting school late, he was two years older and because of genetics, Slim was a foot taller. An odd pair perhaps, but by middle grades Slim was playing basketball with pals built like him and Holly was always included. He was quick and agile and learned great moves. It probably helped him to be at ease later in life when he was the shrimp in the room.

At the police station at one end of the town hall building, Holly learned that the stabbing victim had been a criminal from New York State. Also the theft was different from the previous Peach Acres incidents. This time, items of value had been swiped—sterling silver from the dining room and a framed gold coin collection from the husband's first floor study.

In his small office with the nameplate, *Chief Allen Parkerson*, weighing down the open flap of a bag of cheese puffs, Slim said, "Nothing about this crime matches the earlier ones." As he spoke, his light-blue eyes slitted so dangerously that the color disappeared. Slim wasn't as skinny as he'd been when he first earned his nickname, but he was otherwise much the same, including the laid-back manner that turned fierce when the occasion called for it.

"You mean the previous jobs seemed like mischief."

"Yeah." Slim rubbed a hand though his streaky hair, making an even bigger mess of it. "Except, the house owners thought one of the guys was angry because the other guy had taken 'good stuff.' It almost makes it sound as if this job was supposed to be a prank as well."

"And the dead man was a known criminal? That doesn't add up."

"Exactly." Slim lifted his rawboned shoulders in a shrug.

Having learned all he could, Holly went to his office and returned messages left by people who had heard about the crime, glad he could tell them that no one from JumpRope had been injured, that the dead man was a stranger and that the police were on the job. Done that, he realized it was near to five o'clock and he was hungry. His first thought was to go to Krupple's Diner until he realized he'd be bombarded with questions about the killing.

Slim unexpectedly came to the rescue by rapping on Holly's door frame and poking his head in. "If you want to eat, how's Sean's Pub sound?"

Holly exaggerated surprise. "A Saturday night and Slim Parkerson is at loose ends?"

Slim grinned. With his easy-going good looks (and a uniform didn't hurt) he was rarely without weekend companionship—always casual until recently. "Lana is off on a girls' weekend."

"And you're cooling your heels?"

"Well…" Slim looked sheepish. "Lana's a bit different."

Holly didn't see it. Lana was blonde and curvy and giggly like all the rest, except she seemed to think Slim needed improving and that she was the one to do it. She also had Slim thoroughly wrapped around her little finger—not that Holly was going to point any of this out.

CHAPTER 14

On Sunday, Holly had dinner with his dad and stepmom, Peggy, at the bungalow where he had grown up. Holly's dad from his own experience as mayor, as well as in life, agreed that the only action Holly could take with the unfounded rumor was to let time take care of it. They then briefly acknowledged the other troublesome subjects, the prank thefts and the robbery with its murderous consequences, and moved on to relaxed conversation.

They ate in the backyard, his dad sporting a Greek fisherman's hat. He had an assortment of wigs that he called "head covers" for indoor occasions. They were different colors and styles. He wasn't trying to fool anyone, he just didn't like looking bald. Peggy didn't mind either way. After traveling when they were first married, she had gone back as a secretary to the law firm where she was still employed and he, at age sixty-five, ran an accounting and consulting business out of their home. The couple now spent their leisure time together on hobbies. Their latest was geocaching.

"Always wanted to hunt for treasure as a kid, so this new craze has satisfied it," Holland Sr. explained over dessert—Peggy's scrumptious chocolate cake—telling Holly they used GPS devices to find hidden items, with successes and adventures communicated with other players, mostly online. Peggy enthusiastically joined in about a recent adventure that took them roaming through the scrub pines of Southern New Jersey.

Curious, Holly asked, "Sounds like you're having fun—have Francine and Bob ever gone along?"

Peggy smiled. "She's probably waiting to see geocaching outfits on a fashion runway. Or until someone she admires adopts it as a hobby." Her smile broadened. "That person not being me."

Holly chuckled. It was hard to imagine relaxed Peggy and up-tight Francine as sisters. And even harder to imagine his dad ever being attracted to Francine.

Looking at his father, he said, "Tell me again why you started dating Francine." He'd found that the "tell me again" line increased the chance of an answer.

Wise to the trick, Holly's dad gave him a look, but answered anyway. "Francine taught math and I was an accountant so I guess we had numbers in common." Then he grinned. "And maybe she was sexier back then. I can't recall."

Peggy gave him a teasing swat on the shoulder. "Better not recall."

Then she said to Holly, "My sister liked it that your dad was the mayor. She always liked being on the inside of things. She's no different today."

CHAPTER 15

Because of anxiety about the latest robbery and the murder, the scheduled Wednesday committee meeting became a special public session. The TV reporter on the 6 o'clock news showed an aerial photo of town hall and announced it as the location of "an emergency meeting to help residents deal with their tiny town's alarming increase of violent crime."

As if such a statement would do anything except get people even more upset, Holly thought, displeased. He was at town hall early. Dewey had wanted to take chairs out of storage and set them up to accommodate the expected crowd. Holly had nixed the idea. Standing would provide more room for a crowd and fewer places to sit. Less comfort would discourage people from staying late. They wouldn't get many answers because there were so few answers to give. The longer they stayed the more they would work themselves up, the last thing anybody needed.

He was looking over the arrangement in the still empty meeting room when Iris Roundtree came in. Susanna Washington, the super-sharp wiz of a registered municipal clerk, with her warm brown complexion and Nefertiti profile, was on vacation and the deputy clerk was recovering from knee replacement surgery, so Iris was filling in.

"It was smart to arrange this special meeting, hon," Iris said. "People are scared about the murder, and now some say the early thefts were more violent than reported." Her round face showed concern. "One caller said a dog in a Peach Acres house was wiped out trying to protect the family home. The caller even knew the dog's name. It was Matt."

Holly sighed. Talk was running wild, the stories more confused with each retelling. "It was a door mat that was stolen," he explained. One of those super absorbent mats for the animal to drip on when it came in wet from outside. To wipe its feet. The caller was mixed up. Nobody or nothing was wiped out. And the dog, a St. Bernard, is just fine."

"Oh, that's so good to know." A bit airy, but always well-meaning and reliable with paperwork, Iris fluttered a hand on her full bosom in relief. "Did the caller have the dog's name wrong too?"

"What?"

"Is it really Matt?"

"I think it was Wookie," Holly lied, not having the slightest idea.

The meeting went better than Holly had expected. Slim's laid-back, competent manner was almost as reassuring to residents as the clear evidence of increased police patrols throughout the streets and cul-de-sacs of Peach Acres. There were more comments of appreciation than there were complaints—a gratifying result.

Holly went to bed that evening confident he would have a good night's sleep.

His phone rang at three in the morning.

The caller was Francine.

"There's something bad going on at the Mather house!" She sounded more excited than alarmed. "I don't know what woke me, but I looked outside and saw a light. I thought I was dreaming, but I got Bob up and he saw it too, on the second floor where there's a chink in a boarded up window. We dialed 911."

"The right thing," Holly said groggily. "You did the right thing."

"You need to get over there and find out about it. After I called, a police car came out making a big commotion. It came out quick, I'll say that. The car had searchlights, lighting up the sides of the road like the Fourth of July. More cars came and the police were running around like chickens with their heads off. Now there's an ambulance. Somebody's gotten hurt and you need to come find out who."

When Holly arrived he found not only police and the ambulance, but also people from TV and the *Melton Monitor*. The news helicopter hovered like a spy drone, adding its noise and searchlight to the scene. It was otherwise a pleasant spring night, the air clear, the stars twinkling, with nothing to discourage a crowd from gathering and standing around.

Slim spotted Holly and yanked him off into the shadows by one side of the porch, saving him from the attention of a TV guy roving with a camera capturing pictures of everything.

"Francine called me," Holly said, shouting to be heard over the chopper. Slim nodded like he could have guessed it. He was garbed in a ratty T-shirt and jeans, probably what was handy when he'd been dragged out of sleep.

The chopper veered off and they didn't have to shout anymore to be heard as Slim said, "We might have got them if we'd been cagey, only Donny DeGarmo caught the call and decided sirens and lights were proper procedure." Slim made a face—Donny could be a trial. "He saw them run through the Mather back yard and across that vacant lot toward Centre Avenue. The front door is secure, but boards were pried off the back. Whoever was here probably left their ride on Centre. By the time backup arrived, they were gone."

Holly gestured to the ambulance. "Who was hurt?"

"Nobody living."

"What?"

Slim ran a hand through the mess of his hair. "When my men stopped trying to chase the break-in guys and got inside, they found a body on the steps half way between the first and second floor."

Holly blinked, trying to take it all in. "Another falling out among thieves?"

Slim's smile was weary. "I should have said they found human remains. Probably male. At this point there's no clue as to what happened. From the condition it's not recent. And it's not pretty." Slim sighed. "It's common knowledge this place had been boarded up for about four years. From the looks of it, this guy, whoever he is, has probably been lying dead in the house for all that time."

CHAPTER 16

After calling Holly, Francine had stayed at her window, watching the uproar at the Mather house. Bob had gone back to bed. How could he sleep with so much going on? The TV helicopter that had made the neighborhood sound like a war zone finally zoomed off, but there was still an army of people and lights around. That's when she pulled on her new slacks, lightweight cashmere top and latest design ankle boots and trudged through the dozer ruts of the Mather back yard to get a piece of the action.

Lights made the place as bright as high noon.

Nobody would tell her anything except that the back door was broken in (thanks to the lights, she could see that for herself) and that the bad guys had run off. What a surprise. Ha! Where was Holly? If that boy had shown up, he was invisible. Chief Parkerson, looking tense, directed his men. He was a lamb but he grew teeth when he got busy. No sense getting snapped at. She made her way through the opening in the lilac shrubs to the road out front. A TV news van was driving away but a newspaper van sat parked. A tall, skinny woman with a pony tail and a *Melton Monitor* T-shirt stood with a notepad in her hand. Francine recognized her—Joyce Jane Gilbert, called

JJ. Francine read her articles in the paper and back when she'd been teaching, she'd known JJ in high school. The girl had a bunch of older brothers built like storks who played high school basketball. Was she looking for someone to interview? Francine marched forward. Who better to talk with than the sharp-eyed neighbor who'd called 911? She would explain she'd been able to see the light in the house because of a gap when a tree got blown down that spring.

She'd just about captured her target's attention when somebody yelled from the van, "Yo! JJ! Saddle up! There a fire in that Chevy place on the highway."

Francine grabbed the reporter's arm. "I'm a neighbor and I—"

"Call me tomorrow," JJ said, shoving a business card in Francine's direction.

You bet I will, thought Francine, anticipating her fifteen minutes of fame.

But the next morning, those fifteen minutes counted down to zero when the *Monitor* plopped on Francine's doorstep with a headline so screaming she didn't even have to lift it to see what it said.

Skeletal Remains Found in Old House

Francine glowered. Waste of time to call the newspaper now. All she knew was as stale as old bread. One good thing, this story would take over for what was being whispered around about Holly. Foolish tripe. Holly would never be involved in anything shady—no almost stepson of hers would. Once people saw no new housing being started, they would realize there had been nothing to it.

Her mind returned to her resentful thoughts. When she'd known something was wrong, she'd called Holly, hadn't she? He should have had the courtesy to let her know what the police had found. Being cut out wasn't right. Nobody would have even known about the break in—or the body—if it hadn't been for her. That made her a central figure.

Why hadn't she been kept informed about what was going on?

She should do something about it—only what?

CHAPTER 17

Acer Wolfgang sat at a table in his favorite Manhattan restaurant with luncheon spread before him. Later, one of his corporate jets would take him to a meeting in Boston. A handsome man of fifty, his carefully styled dark hair showed only a slight feathering of grey at the temples. His exquisitely tailored suit fitted a tall, powerful body that was only slightly broadened by good living. His menu selection that noon was an example: sauerbraten and potato dumplings, as delicious as the home cooking he remembered from his youth. He reflected that home cooking meant sharing and companionship yet the right companion had so far not presented herself. The desire to find her had come to him only recently. He would know her when he found her. She would be a challenge. He smiled at the thought. And what a splendid thing to have a trusted female perspective on matters such as the news he had learned from the *Melton Monitor.*

The reporter, JJ Gibson, had called for information about the solar farm. With regret, he said his company had decided the project wasn't currently feasible. He complimented JJ's past articles and they discussed the township of JumpRope. With a charming manner that probably had her saying more than she had intended, he learned that a damaged lilac hedge in JumpRope had inspired rumors about a coming housing project. In one of life's coincidences, the hedge was on property that was part of a large parcel of land that attracted Acer for sentimental as well as practical reasons. He had made his fortunes in various ways, including land development. Trained as an engineer, he had been involved in a number of housing projects, but he wanted to create his own, one in which he could feel special pride, and he wanted it in that particular location. The problem was that one of the three land owners, a woman he referred to fondly as "Auntie," was definite about not selling. He didn't understand her reluctance.

His attraction to the area was the reason for his subscription to the *Monitor*. In reading the news, it had struck him that Holland Kingston Jr., holding his fourth consecutive term as mayor of JumpRope, might be persuaded to further his interests. Especially when he'd seen a photo of the mayor standing in a group and realized he was at least half a head shorter than his companions. Comfortable in his own six-foot tall domain, worldly-wise Acer had learned that little men often harbored a thirst for attention and power. If he offered a community benefit that would make the little mayor shine, would the man then find a way to make Auntie take a fresh look at her property?

With this in mind, Acer had made arrangements with people at Melton County to meet the petite politician, using a solar farm proposal as the topic. Only then, he learned that Holly, as the mayor was called, was a confident man who was highly respected and considered an excellent manager. Acer decided not to waste his time on what seemed pointless. He returned to his original plan: finding an argument to persuade adorable old Auntie to see things his way.

Acer's thoughts returned to the recent disturbing happenings in JumpRope. He could accept the prank-like thefts and even a robbery and stabbing death as anomalies, but the discovery of the dead body in the Mather house had shaken him deeply. Were the remains those of his friend, Barry Mather—supposedly lying in that house since it was boarded up four years ago?

When Acer first became a part of the Mather family, an informal adoption of sorts, he had looked up to the older Barry, an electronics genius with successful patents. Then there was Barry's sister, soft, pretty, fragile Grace, a lovely brunette, who married a man who had treasured and protected her. Acer had been saddened some years later when he'd heard her husband's sudden death had shocked her into a near fatal decline. Barry, retired by then, moved them both to the ancestral home in quiet JumpRope. Acer had visited, enjoying Barry as always, but he'd been pained at the decline in Grace. When he'd been fifteen and she a young adult, he'd been admittedly moony-eyed over her, but now, for lack of better words, she had let herself go. She'd gained weight and her dark hair was pulled back tight and twisted into a knot at the back of her head. She'd always worn glasses, but now they were thicker, with unattractive heavy rims. Even worse was the loss of her fey humor that had been so appealing. Not at all the type of woman who drew his eye as he matured, but he remembered the past fondly and grieved at the changes that sorrow had brought to her.

Four years ago, Auntie had told him that Barry and Grace had left the Mather house, which she had boarded up. She confided that Barry and Grace were in seclusion at an address they insisted on keeping private. But now, Acer thought, if the body in the Mather house was Barry's, Auntie's story about the siblings' relocation was a lie. And if Auntie had known Barry's body remained in the house, no wonder she wouldn't allow the property out of her hands.

It also meant that he, Acer Wolfgang, as much as the *Monitor* and the police and anybody else in JumpRope, wanted the answer to two burning questions:

How did Barry Mather die?

And where in the world was Grace Mather?

CHAPTER 18

Tuesday morning, Holly was ready to leave town hall for his county job when Iris handed him a phone message. Before he could read it, his phone rang. It was a resident, Mrs. Kroll, calling because of a dead person lying in a ditch by the road. She'd already told the police and was calling him to ask, her voice trembling, "What's going on in our town?"

Holly gave what he hoped was a soothing answer. Putting the unread note into his breast pocket he went down to the police station. Turned out the so called "dead man," was actually a dead drunk Nero Gibeau, an Afghanistan War veteran in his late twenties.

Slim said to Holly, "Donny went out on the call and just reported back. Nero must have holed up somewhere with a bottle last night and couldn't make it home. Mrs. Kroll and others are edgy because of the thefts and the stabbing." He scrubbed a hand through his hair. "Can't say that I blame them."

Holly said, "I can swing by and see Mrs. Kroll on my way over to the county."

The location was out in the country, green trees, freshly plowed farmland. It didn't take much imagination for Holly to think he was seeing a pastoral scene from years ago, and then to imagine it as a painted landscape by Monet or Manet or other French Impressionists. The name Gibeau was French, the "G" pronounced with a j" like in "just," and the "beau" pronounced like "bow." *Gibeau.*

Holly's route took a turn to a lonely stretch of road where there were only two houses. Parked near Mrs. Kroll's, Donny was maneuvering tall, broad-shouldered Nero into the rear seat of the police car.

Holly pulled his four door blue pickup truck to a stop.

Nero, who couldn't hold a regular job, lived on his family's farm with his grandmother. A skilled mechanic before he entered the service, he now did chores on the farm and pick-up jobs at Bob's Auto Repair and Towing, where he'd once held steady employment. Days would go by when he'd be okay and then he'd get loaded and stumble around until he found someplace to sleep it off.

Holly remembered how Nero had seemed fine when he'd first been discharged. The town had held a welcome home parade in his honor. Then something bad happened to a service buddy and Nero had gone off the rails. Seeing Holly through the open car door, Nero, who under better conditions, was noticeably good looking, gave Holly a bleary smile that showed a flash of white teeth and then he sagged back in the seat and closed his eyes.

Donny, red-haired, his uniform neat as a pin, his shoes shined to a glare and a stickler for what he considered proper protocol, gave Holly a brisk salute. "Taking him home, Sir. His grandmother is probably worried."

"Good man," Holly said, returning Donny's salute but feeling foolish about it.

Donny *was* a good man, Holly thought, the type of officer the term "Community Cop" had been invented for—good with kids, old ladies, drunks and keeping injured people soothed while waiting for emergency services. Trouble was, he was inclined to swallow hook, line and sinker any words spoken with authority and let independent thinking fall by the wayside. Like when Kiki Vera called the police because she feared a roof repair guy might be a scammer. When Donny answered the call she expected him to ask questions and check the man's documents and tags. Instead, Donny, fresh from a racial profiling seminar, sent the roofer on his way and explained to Kiki that the town could have been sued if he had "racially profiled" the guy. The irony was that Kiki, a native of Jamaica, had the same skin color as the roofer. She'd stormed into the police station mad enough to spit tacks. (Or roofing nails.) Slim had finally calmed her down, but Kiki was right. Donny should have checked the guy out and Slim made sure Donny knew it.

Holly walked to Mrs. Kroll's white frame house. The paint job her late husband had done on the shiny black front door and matching shutters was holding up good. Mrs. Kroll, who must have been watching from the window, opened the door before he reached it. She was tiny, with blue tinted white hair. Cuddled in the crook of one arm was a dark grey cat—clearly a good friend in uncertain times.

Holly set her mind at rest by explaining about Nero and that Donny was taking him home. She thanked him and then shook her head. "His grandmother is a lot older than me," she said. "She never tells her age, but she has to be at least ninety. What's going to happen to that boy when she goes?"

Holly said he didn't know. She invited him in. He thanked her but said he'd take a rain check—he was on his way to his county job.

Holly's afternoon was hectic, filled with lawyers and state regulations about matters that should otherwise be straightforward. It was late in his day when he remembered the note. He took it out and saw it contained a phone number and a message that read: "Victoria at County Records has information that you want."

He winced. The bad penny of the Mather place again. Crushed lilacs and curiosity about musty deeds and even the rumors about him keeping secrets about a development seemed minor compared to a burglary gang, a stabbing death, and now a mysterious dead body. In a city, it might be no big deal, but in JumpRope it was capital letters, BIG DEAL. He wished he could ignore the note, but he'd told the woman, this Victoria, to go on ahead with her research and she'd spent time on it. The image of her soft, out-of-focus face floated up like mirage, doing nothing to increase his desire to punch in the phone number.

His sigh was heavy.

The right thing to do was to call and invite Victoria to an early supper as a thank you, accept the information she'd gathered and be done with it. He imagined sitting across from her at the table, neither of them having anything to say. Okay, then, he would dash home and print out those photos. They could be conversational topics.

Besides, she was a JumpRope resident, so he had a responsibility.

CHAPTER 19

Victoria was waiting for Holly on a bench in the entry of the agreed upon place, a quirky casual restaurant in Melton near the County Court house called the Giraffe's Neck. Holly had chosen that particular eating place because it was near Toria's workplace, making it reasonable to meet there instead of them traveling together. Also, the oddball décor was a surefire topic for conversation.

It had a first floor bar and dining room and also a dining area on the railed balcony, where he'd reserved a table because it was interesting. The Hoof Bar had a giant toy giraffe standing on the end of the bar counter. With the five-foot stretch of the long neck, the toy, with its large eyes, appeared to look at diners seated at tables on the balcony.

Holly escorted Victoria inside and past a sign in front of the giraffe that announced, "No Animals Were Harmed in the Making of this Restaurant." When he saw Victoria's smile at the sign he figured she was a newcomer, but he played it safe by asking, "Have you been here many times?"

"With a girl from work for lunch, never for dinner," she said softly.

It was early and not crowded, and not noisy, but Holly could still hardly hear her.

The hostess appeared. Recognizing Holly, she dazzled a greeting and nodded pleasantly at Victoria and then led them upstairs to a wooden table painted with giraffe spots. It was close enough to the railing to see the giraffe's large-eyed placid gaze, but not so close that it was creepy. The waiter came with menus shaped like cut out giraffe hooves, recited the specials and asked about beverages. After a hesitation and hearing Holly order a beer, Victoria decided on a white wine spritzer.

They looked at the menu. The waiter returned with their beverages and left after taking their orders. Holly, sensing the possibly of an uncomfortable silence, said, "When I called your number the woman who answered called you Vicky. I guess that's what I should call you, too." He figured that was safe enough assumption.

A flustered blotch rose up her throat and colored her cheeks. "That's what they all call me at work, but it's not what I like."

Caught by surprise, he said, "That's okay...there's no need for a nickname. The name Victoria is very pretty."

"It's not because it's a nickname." Unexpectedly, she laughed. A light, pleasant sound. "It's that Vicky reminds me of that mentholated ointment."

That struck him funny but he kept his face straight. "What about the name, Holly?"

"The Mayor of JumpRope," she answered her face equally straight. Unexpectedly, her eyes twinkled. "Did you think I would say Holly reminds me of a Christmas wreath?"

He did laugh then and it went through his mind to quip, as long as you don't say a lapel pin, but that would make no sense to her and besides, this woman was nothing like the pushy union rep who had said it in the first place. She was—well, he didn't quite know what she was like, so instead, he said, "I don't get it. They call you Vicky even when you don't like it?"

"I've never said anything." Her complexion blotched again. "If they had asked, I would have said to call me Toria."

"Oh, that's easy. Hi, Toria."

She smiled into his eyes. "Hi, Holly."

Whoa, he thought, mentally backing off from the threatening breeze of what felt like a more intimate mood.

He was glad when the waiter appeared with their meals.

From then on their chit-chat maintained a friendly, but impersonal level. There was a brief mention of the robbery and the shock of the one man being killed, and then there was general conversation, with him finding out innocuous tidbits like she volunteered for the JumpRope Free Library and she found out things like he had graduated from high school five years ahead of her.

Over coffee, their meals finished, (he'd had blackened tuna and she'd had chicken with sun dried tomatoes) he spread out the photos he'd printed from his phone and she took out her research notes.

He pointed out the area in the photo where it had looked to him that the path had extended to the property behind, which she had confirmed the other day.

"What's this?" she asked, indicating a spot in the Mather's current back yard.

"I thought there might have been planting beds in the past," he answered. "The yard was shady, so the pictures don't show up as well as in real life. If I'd taken the time, I could have played with them on the computer."

"May I borrow them?" she asked hesitantly.

"Sure, you can even have them if you want." He pushed the photos toward her as he glanced at her notebook. "Your research is probably going to be a lot more interesting."

"It might be," was her answer. As he'd noticed before, once she got into her field of expertise, all signs of hesitation dropped away.

She said, "You came first with the question of whether or not the Mather property once included the lot behind it. We learned that it did. Now, I can tell you that in early 1900s, the Mathers owned acres of tillable land. The existing Mather house—" she tapped one of the printouts— "had to have been an extremely elegant farmhouse. What's now a dead end road was likely the lane to the house. Over time, the strip behind it and on Centre Avenue was divided into lots and sold to various individuals, as I mentioned before. The acres of farmland in front of the house were divided, too, but it was put into the names of various corporations that still exist today. Some old deeds, all longhand, contained what now would be considered improper—like a family sold a property because the patriarch had gone insane."

"No political correctness back then," Holly said, amused, wondering if Donny had attended a seminar on *that* yet.

Toria smiled. "Some of the oldest deed books have damaged pages, so I couldn't trace an unbroken backwards path, but I suspect that the original corporations held blocks of property inherited by Mather siblings. There were no individual names, just the bank name. Time has passed so the blocks of property would have been inherited by descendants. The property remains under what's called the Mather Corporation and only the bank can reveal who now actually owns it."

She closed her notebook. "I drove out there the other day. Most of everything I saw was scrubby woodland, making no money for anyone." She met his gaze with brown eyes that were innocent yet surprisingly direct. "It's near the town and bordered by two major roads, one of them being a highway that leads to the New Jersey Turnpike. As they say, location, location, location. If the Mather Corporation land were developed by someone really smart, that property would be a gold mine."

CHAPTER 20

At her home on Strand Street Jessi Spellman, having given up on the newspapers, had been watching the TV news and still coming up empty. Glaring, she flounced about her living room in her pretty little skirt and her pretty little sandals on her size four feet. Why was information being held back? Nothing new since that interview with the JumpRope police chief that had been so dull she almost fell asleep reading it.

Stinky dead body from the Mather house. Who cared?

No clues about who broke in and if they stole anything or not.

Who cared about any of that stupid stuff?

What she wanted to hear about was the Mather property.

Was the development nothing but a rumor? It couldn't be! How were she and Arnie going to make their big bucks if it wasn't true?

So there had to be a housing development in the works, Jessi thought, making another flouncing spin in her living room. There had to be because that was what she wanted and that's all there was to it.

Over on Centre Avenue, Francine was feeling as shut out as a stray cat. She was the one who had called the police about the break in and what was her reward? Getting cold-shouldered. Neither Holly nor the police chief would give her a scrap of information. Barry and Grace Mather had been her neighbors. The authorities were fooling around with identification, but of course the body was Barry's.

All these years, she and the few others who had known Barry and Grace assumed they'd moved someplace else. Now to know that he had never left. Was Grace lying dead in the house, too? Old houses have plenty of hiding places, attics, cellars, nooks and crannies. Had the police really looked? Francine had been in the house before and could give them some ideas. She didn't have much respect for men thinking they could find things. Bob would stand like a dunce staring into a cupboard. "If it had been a snake it would have bit you," she would tell him when she picked up the very thing he'd been too blind to see.

It was probably the same with the police.

Right in front of them, only they don't know how to look.

Making the bed, cleaning up in the kitchen, Francine's thoughts tangled in frustration. Would there be a smell in the house after all that time? Maybe the police would bring in those smart nose dogs like on TV when they searched for bodies. Being such a close neighbor and all, she certainly knew more than anyone else. She clearly remembered the time she'd seen them food shopping at the market. Barry was so shaky his legs would hardly hold him up. She'd helped Grace get him to the driver's seat of their car and then he'd seemed okay. Just to make sure, she had followed them home in her own car. Their driveway, all overgrown now, was on the side away from the lilacs, handy to either the front door or the back. It was all Barry could do to get inside the house, so she had helped poor heavyweight Grace, who'd been huffing and puffing, carry grocery bags through the house and into the kitchen. The couple was so reclusive she was willing to bet she was the only neighbor who had ever been invited inside.

She had known Grace and Barry better than anyone else, so the police should be begging to interview her instead of brushing her off.

That's when it stuck her. She had been trying to wheedle information from Holly and Slim but had never suggested she had information they needed. From what it said on the TV, the police were speculating that the missing car meant Grace had driven off alone. Did they know what they were talking about? Francine knew Barry drove, but she'd never seen Grace behind the wheel. Did she even have a driver's license? Had the police checked that?

Francine hated to admit it, but she had gone about things all wrong. Instead of asking questions, she should have presented herself as the individual with the facts. But it was too late now. She'd already been too much of a nuisance.

Glowering, she knew she needed a fresh approach. Her household chores finished, she reread the old article that first reported the finding of the body. She had gone over it a dozen times and it still had the power to make her boil.

"Thieves found more than they bargained for when they broke into an abandoned house in JumpRope and stumbled on a long-dead male body. Whether they made off with anything before they fled from the alerted police is not clear."

The phrase "before they fled from the alerted police" still had Francine steaming. Who had alerted the police? She had, that's who. And where had it gotten her?

Nowhere.

A thought struck. For the first time Francine ignored the offending phrase and paid attention to the words written around them: "Whether they made off with anything is not clear."

A long abandoned house. Who would know if it contained anything worth stealing? Did the police know? Of course not. Not a one of them had probably set a foot in the house before that night.

But *she* had*!*

When she was a teenager she'd earned money caring for people's pets. She'd done it for Barry's and Grace's parents when they had lived in the house. She took care of their indoor cats for a few summers before she gotten a real job.

Time passed. Francine married and moved into the house where she lived now, catty-corner behind the Mather house. Sometime later the parents left and eventually Barry and Grace moved in. When Francine had been in the house with them, she had noticed that everything seemed the way it was when she'd taken care of the cats—the dark old furniture, the sterling silver on the dining room sideboard, the gilt framed pictures on the walls. The place was a time warp, a museum to their parents.

This was the angle she needed to approach the police!

It had been right under her nose.

She applied to herself what she'd said when she scolded Bob: If it was a snake it would have bit her!

Her chuckle was one of triumph.

CHAPTER 21

It was Friday and Francine had been working the phone all day, each completed call another one of the eggs she was hatching.

Unaware of Francine's plot, Holly had his hands full with Darlene Gage. He'd left his county job early in the afternoon to stop by town hall and sign a grant application to go out the following Monday but he had barely gotten seated when the Empress charged into his office.

"Here's something you're not going to believe." Exasperation tightening her matte finish, artfully tinted complexion, she waved a letter.

"This is from that rabble-rousing Jessi Spellman. It's about that foreclosed Apples Corners wreck she bought this spring and the fine china restoration business she's been saying she wants to run out of it."

Apple Corners was a JumpRope 1950s era group of homes so-named because the four one block long streets between Apple and First Streets all had apple variety names, Cortland, McIntosh, Baldwin and Winesap.

"What's she know about china repair?" Holly couldn't imagine flamboyant, flashy Jessi sitting still long enough to fit together fragile pieces of broken china.

"She knows nothing except making trouble and scheming to make money. She and her husband, Arnie, flip houses like burgers. She has this place for sale on the Internet, but there's no sold sign out front. I guess she's wanting to see which works out for her." Darlene's voice rippled with annoyance. "This has been going on for awhile. First she wanted a Certificate of Occupancy to make the Apple Corners house a rental, but there were violations, one being that raccoons crawled into the attic, tore out the insulation and crashed through a bedroom ceiling. But now, that menace, Jessi, not the raccoon, says she doesn't expect anyone to live in it. She says she wants to establish it as a commercial location for this repair business, complete with signs and parking."

"Apple Corners is zoned residential," Holly said. "She needs to apply to the Land Use Board for a change of use."

"Ha! She claims the business is grandfathered in because she's been already been running it out of her residence on Strand Street."

Holly frowned. "A home business is different than setting up shop. And that's not what the term grandfathered means."

"You think I don't know that?" Darlene sputtered, insulted. "Grandfathering is continuing a use for a property as it was before zoning ordinances were adopted, but the two locations Jessi's talking about have been zoned residential since they were constructed." She waved another paper. "And get this! To prove she's been running the business, which has nothing to do with change of use for Apple Corners, she includes this letter, a thank you to Jessi for her excellent repair of a royal bone china ornament belonging to the Queen of England. "

"What?" Holly reached out. "Let me see."

"Sure, but it's bogus." Darlene crossed her arms after handing it over. "I don't know how the Queen's stationary is supposed to look, but this is on ink jet paper you can buy by the ream. Plus, I recognize Jessi's loopy handwriting. She didn't even try to disguise it."

Holly saw that the paper had what appeared to be a clip art picture of Buckingham Palace at the top, and under it, in a scrolled blue font, the words, "From the Desk of Elizabeth II, Queen of England."

He read the salutation aloud, "Dear Jessi," and said, "Whoa, first name basis, huh?" He saw a smiley face in place of a dot in Jessi's name. The supposed signature of the queen, 'Her Royal Highness, Elizabeth II,' had another smiley face over the "i" in Highness.

"Incredible," Holly said.

"Told you," Darlene said in disgust. "Bogus. Jessi's name with a smiley face for the dot is her usual signature."

Holly thought of his past bad experiences with Jessi. She would tilt her little face and sound one hundred percent credible while she told outright lies, spouted contradictory statements and flashed suspicious looking documents. Her technique was constructed to be so confusing and illogical that folks gave in because she simply wore them down. What Holly didn't get was the point of this current stunt. Jessi wasn't stupid. That letter was deliberately obvious. Only, why?

Sitting back in his chair, he asked, "You received this today?"

Darlene nodded. "Too busy to read my mail until just now.

"Okay," Holly said slowly, giving himself time to think, realizing there was no perfect answer. He settled for, "Run it by the others in your department on Monday. Come back after you've kicked it around. If there's anything I can do, I'll do it."

He didn't think he'd done much, but Darlene gave him a grateful a smile as if he'd really helped. He noticed she was dressed in a silky looking outfit and high heels instead of the usual slacks, jacket and low heels. She would look glamorous if her bristly attitude didn't keep breaking out and ruining the impression. He said, "That shade of blue looks wonderful on you."

She gave him a suspicious look, as if the compliment might be poison tipped, then she relaxed and smoothed her skirt. "Thanks. Friends are taking me out for dinner tonight to celebrate my birthday."

"Well!" He said it as if it was news to him. "Happy birthday!"

What Darlene didn't know was that her friends planned a surprise party and Holly was one of the guests. His invitation had included a note: *Gag gifts only for a fiftieth birthday*. He didn't think Darlene was fond of surprises—she liked to be in control—but he and the other guests would be waiting in a private dining room at one of the area's nicest restaurants, the Teddy Bear Tavern and Grill.

But he wasn't sure about this age fifty business. He seemed to remember it was more than ten years ago that Darlene had celebrated her fortieth.

CHAPTER 22

D arlene stepped into one of Teddy's party rooms and stopped dead, confused to see a room full of eyes all staring at her.

Then everyone screamed, "Happy Birthday!

For a split second Holly thought Darlene might cry. Then she tried to hide how flustered she was by laughing. Still laughing, she started greeting and hugging the friends who rushed to her.

Slim, who sat next to Holly said, "That was good, nobody tipped her off. If they had, instead of being taken aback, she would have put on a big, Oh-how-surprised-I-am, act."

"You're good at reading people," Holly said.

"Goes with the territory and in this case a pleasure," Slim said. "She's a far cry from my kind of woman, but she gets full credit tonight. Imagine, Darlene Grumble Gripe with a smile on her face."

"Her neckline's too high and her skirt's too long for your kind of woman," Holly said.

"Yeah, and the Empress is all skin and bones, what you'd see in some society rag."

"That's your reading fare these days?" teased Holly. "I thought Miss January on a calendar was more your style."

"Not when I can look at the real thing." Slim laughed and then he looked serious. "I think Lana might be a keeper, you know?"

No, Holly didn't know. And he didn't want to be asked his opinion. "Your own Miss August," he said.

Slim grinned. "Yeah, you've got it, bud. Hot."

By the time the two men finished their appetizers, the crowd flocking around Darlene had thinned. They went over to express their good wishes.

Holly saw that she wore a triangular black and white pin she hadn't had on earlier. It had a big letter V, a little letter "d" and what looked like four eyes. A novelty birthday gift? Then he saw that Francine, standing nearby and talking to someone, wore a similar pin.

After a few minutes he and Slim separated to talk with others. Holly walked around chatting with people and enjoying the old world ambiance of the restaurant. Even though they were in one of the private rooms, there was still the beamed ceiling, creamy-color plaster walls and richly stained plank flooring. Theodore Baird, the owner/chef, was a hefty, fuzzy-haired young man, nicknamed Teddy Bear, a name he not only gave to the tavern, but by making the restaurant's emblem a bear jumping rope, he had tied it in with the name of the town.

It was Teddy's pictorial theme that especially delighted Holly. Instead of the tapestries that might have hung on English Tudor walls, the tavern's rooms had picture book style murals that showed a medieval-looking thatched roofed town where small bears, barefoot, but otherwise dressed, jumped rope. Lettered on the wall under each mural was a stanza of a children's jump rope rhyme, Teddy Bear, Teddy Bear, Turn Around… The aim of the game was for jumpers to mime the named action without tripping on the rope. The art had inspired Holly to buy a necktie depicting a 16th century Bruegel painting called, *Children Games*. The murals were a wonder. No matter how many times he'd looked at them, he could always spot details he'd swear he'd never seen before.

Wanting to take another shot at the appetizers before returning to his table, Holly ran into Iris. She wore the same kind of black and white pin as Darlene and Francine. He asked her about it and she happily explained.

"It's for our club. There are six of us. We come here for dinner on a night when the psychic is here."

"I knew you and Francine and some others regularly met for dinner," Holly said. "I didn't know Darlene was in it, or that it was an actual club."

"The Voodoo Club, that's us. See—" Iris angled her head to peer down at the ornament pinned to her plump bodice. "It spells out the name, the letters V and d and the four o's for each part of the name. The o's look like eyes because Mar-see-ah sees everything."

"Clever," he said, which was true. He'd only heard a few things about Mar-see-ah, and that from Francine and Iris.

Iris giggled. "The name was the Colonel's idea, although he didn't intend it. He doesn't have a high opinion of psychics. He calls it 'voodoo.' I told the others. We had a good laugh and decided to name ourselves the Voodoo Club."

Holly could imagine Iris's colonel, down-to-earth widower Colonel Herman McDuff, U.S. Army, Ret., pooh-poohing anything that verged on the supernatural. Idly, he wondered who the other three club members were, but he didn't feel like asking. It was a pleasant gathering, with Darlene clearly having put Jessi's latest scheme, whatever it was, on the shelf, and nobody was in the mood to bring up town troubles, including anything about him. He recalled his inner reaction when Toria's research on the Mather property had her saying the land would be valuable to a developer. The word "developer" had zinged through him like an electric shock. His first thought was, had she heard the rumors? Did she think he wanted the research as a cover story, so he could claim his knowledge of the land was brand new?

Then he'd realized how paranoid that was. And now, darn it, he was thinking about it again. What he should do was set it aside and concentrate on this harmless puzzle of voodoo club membership. Enjoy a relaxing bit of intrigue that had nothing to do with anything.

By the time he had returned to his table for dinner, he had found two other women sporting the pins. That was five of the six.

The main meal had been cleared away and it was time for the cake when Holly glanced at his watch. He had a seminar scheduled for seven the next morning and Slim had already left on a police call. Time to bail. The seminar was in an hotel, forty minutes away.

He had reserved a room for the night to save an early morning drive through traffic.

He was crossing the lobby and almost to the outside door when a woman burst in, her light brown hair flying.

Toria.

"Well, hi, there," Holly said, as startled as she. She froze and the closing door would have caught her if Holly hadn't caught it first.

"Sorry," he said. "I didn't mean to surprise you."

"I...I wasn't paying attention...I was in a rush because I was so late to the party. I had to take over at the library when someone was sick and I just got out now."

Her face was a bloom of red blotches and the whole time she talked, words running together a mile a minute, she never met his eyes.

He nodded. "The party is still going strong in the 'Turning Bear' room. You missed dinner, but you're probably in time to see Darlene cut her cake."

"That's great." She darted a glance in his direction, then veered off again. "I'd better get in there."

"See you around," he said and watched as she flung herself in the direction of the party room. "Whoa," he murmured to himself, marveling at his unexpected discovery.

Fastened to the front of Toria's mouse-gray blouse had been a black and white pin that identified her as the sixth member of the Voodoo Club.

CHAPTER 23

The following Tuesday was an A-plus day for Francine Smithers. First, the newspaper announced that the dental records of Barry Mather matched the body found on the stairs . That settled it. It wasn't some stranger who broke in and died or whatever people were wondering. Barry had been a resident, someone people actually knew. They would demand that the mystery of his death be solved. And she was the one who could help get the job done.

Second, Holly had called and invited her to stop by his office.

She had given a triumphant hoot as she replaced the phone.

Her scheme had worked!

She set off for Holly's office, swathed in confidence. As the long-term president of the Fire and Emergency Auxiliary she had called in favors. The volunteer squads, which included police force members, knew how much they owed to the Auxiliary's fund-raising abilities. It had taken a bunch of phone calls, but Francine had managed to put fleas in people's ears, the word being that she knew something helpful. Not only in solving the crime of the break-in but in also determining what might have happened to Grace Mather. It had created a buzz, as she had known it would, and word had obviously reached town hall.

After greeting her, Holly said, "I've heard you might have information."

Francine hid a smile. The mayor wouldn't give her the time of day when she was begging for answers, but now that she was offering answers, out rolled the red carpet. She launched into her spiel, making it sound as if her familiarity with the Mather house had come from frequent visits with Grace and Barry rather than her far more frequent visits when it had been the home of their parents.

When she had finished, Holly said, "I didn't realize you knew Grace and Barry so well."

She preened. "I was their closest neighbor."

"Yes. I see." Holly had already discussed the matter with Slim, who had also been hearing through the grapevine that Francine knew things. The investigation seemed stuck so they both figured they might as well listen to what Francine had to say.

Standing, he said, "Let's go talk with Slim."

"That would be wonderful." Her grateful tone disguised her usual forceful manner. She had decided that if she was going to get anywhere with Slim, she should park her pushy self.

After they were seated in the police chief's office, Slim gave her a long, steady look. "I understand from some of my men that you know a lot about the Mather house."

"About things that could prove helpful, yes." She wore a lightweight knit blouse and a denim skirt. Casual dress, nothing like a power suit. Miss Passive, that was her name today.

Slim said, "The mayor probably told you that the investigation has stalled."

She gave him a prim look. "He didn't tell me anything that was police business. That wouldn't have been right."

Slim's lips quirked at the thought of Francine being a stickler for protocol when it stood in the way of something she wanted. He asked, "How do you think you can help?"

"Since I was close with Grace and Barry and so familiar with the house, I would recognize what's missing, what someone might have taken to sell...is fence the term?" *Always let the experts believe they were the ones with the knowledge*, she thought to herself. "As far as Grace being missing, if she went off on her own, she would have taken her purse. I know what purse she was carrying around the time she disappeared. If her purse is still in the house, then something else must have happened to her."

Slim stared. "Four years ago and you remember her purse?"

"It was a Louis Vuitton bag! Of course I remember." Francine bristled like a stick-poked porcupine. "Grace dressed plain, not a hint of style. She had nice things in her house, but they were from family. But Grace herself? No! Except, she did have a beautiful cream-colored calf leather bag, and when she opened it to get something and I saw that cream and black stripe signature lining…well! You could have knocked me over with a feather!"

Slim still looked incredulous, but perhaps he was trying to imagine Francine's sturdy form being knocked over by a feather.

Seeing that things were going well, Francine felt it safe to ask a question. "I never saw Grace drive. Did she have a driver's license?"

Sighing, Slim lifted an opened package of corn snacks from behind the barrier of papers on his desk. "If she did, we haven't found proof of it."

"That doesn't mean she couldn't have taken the car, anyway," Francine said. "She and Barry were always driving off somewhere. The car would be gone, one, two weeks at a time. That's why it didn't seem odd at first when they disappeared."

Slim was quiet for a long moment and then he said, "This has been dragging on and the *Monitor*'s been on my tail. I've given their reporter an update that I might as well share."

Francine listened eagerly. She didn't like him telling her after he'd already told a reporter, but at least she was in on it before the whole world saw it in print.

According to Slim, the autopsy found nothing to indicate foul play. The break-in that brought the body to light was the only apparent crime. There was nothing to indicate the death was anything except natural. As far as the break-in, the investigators from the county had gone over the scene with the JumpRope policemen and found no leads.

Continuing, he said, "Our police force doesn't have the training for heavy investigative work, but the county sent a detective over to talk with neighbors on Centre Avenue—"

"What!" interrupted Francine. "They didn't talk to me!"

Ah-ha, thought Slim, *At last the real Francine.* But what he said aloud was, "My officers knew you were the individual who had alerted us to the entire situation. If you had known anything more than you had told us then, they were well aware you would have already come to us with your valuable information."

"Exactly right!" she said. Realizing she had vaulted forward in her chair, she forced herself to relax and lean back, folding her hands sedately in her lap. Meek and mild Francine.

Hiding a smile, Slim continued, "Our only clue came from a woman walking a dog late on the night in question. She saw a dark colored car parked near the vacant lot that's behind the Mather house. Her dog called her attention to it by running over and lifting a leg on a tire." He allowed his smile to creep out at that. "She thinks it had a New York State license plate." Not mentioning the speculation that there might be a connection between the Mather house break-in and the one over in Peach Acres where a New York State thief had been stabbed, he said, "Maybe someone will see mention of the car in the newspaper and provide more information."

Slim's glance at Holly indicated the two had discussed what he was about to say next. "There's something screwy about the Mather setup. It looks like the people just up and left, yet the house held no personal documents of any kind." His glance sharpened on Francine. "You say you knew them, you were in the house. What did you see? Mail on a table? A calendar with notes pinned to it the way people do? Anything?"

She had to admit she had seen nothing of a personal nature. Annoyed that she didn't have a good answer, she huffed and said, "It sounds weird."

"That's the word for it. We don't even know next of kin. The body's still in the morgue."

Francine blinked. "I heard something about that, but I wasn't sure it was true."

"It is. The story about a dead man found on the stairs was picked up and spread all over, but no one's come forth to make a claim. The lawyer for the corporation that pays taxes on the house says he never heard of Barry or Grace. We had a lawyer on this end examine the property documents and Barry's and Grace's names don't appear."

"That makes no sense!" Francine blurted, forgetting about meek and mild. "It's their family house. If Barry and Grace didn't own it, who did?"

"The corporation principals are an elderly woman in a nursing home, demented, unable to speak with authorities, and a younger woman whose last address was in a foreign country. Nobody knows where she is. So, there's a mystery on both ends. Since Barry and Grace were mostly away in boarding school when the parents lived here, who really knew them? The pair who took up residence could have been squatters. Maybe they read the obits of the old couple and simply moved in with a pretty story."

"Squatters! I don't accept that for a minute. The body was *identified* as Barry!"

"No, the body matched dental records of a person *calling* himself Barry Mather. Could be a false identity." Slim shrugged. "Whatever the truth is, we're only left with guesses about the persons you knew as Barry and Grace. Let's stick with those names for simplicity's sake." He ticked off possibilities on his fingers. "One, Barry died a natural death and Grace simply packed up and left. Two, she bailed because she was in some way responsible for his death—maybe he was found dead on the steps because she shoved him off the top. Three, a third person is involved. In that case, Barry is dead by fair means or foul and Grace either goes with or is taken by the third person. Which leaves us with the same question we started with—where's Grace Mather?"

Leaning forward, Francine asked, "Do you think she was murdered? Because that's the only explanation. Grace would never do such a heartless thing like leaving Barry's body. I saw how they acted together. They had their tiffs, but who doesn't? They enjoyed each other's company."

Holly spoke up. "If the person we're calling Grace is dead, who had the house boarded up? It must have been done to hide the body. If she didn't order it, who did?"

"There's that third person theory again," Slim said. "Francine, you've pointed out you were the closest neighbor. Were you home the day the house was closed up?"

Her jaw took on a determined set. "No, I was not. It might even have been several days before I noticed, but my familiarity with the house may tell you what's missing. If the house was robbed, knowing what's been taken might eventually lead you to the thieves."

Slim cracked a smile. "So the bottom line is, you want to get inside the house and play detective."

"Oh, my." She sat back. Shy little her. "I surely can't aspire to detective work, but I still might be able to see something that would help."

"You understand," he said, "that you won't be wandering around on your own. You'll be accompanied and you're not to take anything."

"Oh, of course," she said, not letting the trumpets of triumph ring in her voice. "All I want to do is help." She also wanted to pump her fist, but she did nothing of the sort. She was quite impressed with the success of her performance. She was so gentle and agreeable that Slim might have mistaken her for timid sister, Peggy.

CHAPTER 24

At the appointed time on a sunny summer morning, Francine arrived at the rear of the Mather house accompanied by two JumpRope officers.

She had to freeze off a grimace when she saw that one of them was red-haired Donny DeGarmo.

When she'd been teaching, Donny had been in one of her high school math classes. He'd been like a light in a refrigerator, bright enough to do the job but not turned on full time. And then, there was his irritating manner of speaking as if he copied the words from something he'd heard or seen. She'd thought he'd gain confidence and grow out of it, but he was now in his early twenties and still hadn't. He irritated her worse than ever. It wasn't fair, but she found herself wanting to find fault with every little thing he said or did.

The other officer was Ed Lakewood, a steady fellow who seemed able to think for himself, she thought approvingly.

Together, the officers unscrewed a sheet of plywood that had been installed over the broken back door.

Donny said, "We have to go in the back way, Ma'am, because the front door is still sealed off. I'll go first to make sure the way is clear."

"Thank you." She said it politely because it wasn't to her advantage to blurt that he sounded like a TV cop entering a building full of drug dealers. It's a wonder he didn't have his pistol out in that straight arm, two fisted grip they sometimes showed on TV, sweeping the weapon back and forth before shouting, "Clear!"

The first space they entered, the enclosed back porch, was neat except for splintered wood where the thieves had worked their way in. To one side was a stack of plastic tarps. Francine wondered if Grace and Barry had intended to have painting or other messy work done. If they'd planned to update anything, she thought, it would have been a first.

She cautiously moved into the house proper, at first taking shallow breaths, expecting the worst, but there was only a musty, closed-in smell. The kitchen and living room showed nothing interesting, but in the dining room she could point with confidence to something missing on the top of the sideboard.

"There was a silver set here, coffee and tea server, sugar, creamer and waste bowl all sitting on a footed tray, all sterling silver and all very heavy. You can see from the dust where it sat."

"That's a help," Ed said, writing it down. "We knew something had been moved, but didn't know particulars."

She opened the silverware drawer in the sideboard. "A set of sterling flatware is also missing. It's called Francis First," she added with authority, indicating to Ed to write that down, too. "It had details of different fruit clusters in the design. It was made by Reed & Barton."

She made sure she was giving the impression she knew all this from close association with Barry and Grace. She had seen it on their table, which had been set, but her detailed knowledge came from when she took care of their mother's cats and she had *not* been snooping. It was simply that she liked examining nice things and imagining that someday she would have nice things in a house of her own.

She stepped toward the hall and the front stairway.

Donny put up his hand like a traffic cop. "Sorry Ma'am. The back steps will be best for ascending. The front landing is where human remains were located. They cut a big piece of rug out."

For once she thought Donny might have a point. Still, she had gone far enough to glance up the stairway and wonder if Iris would ask if she had seen Barry's ghost.

The back steps, narrow and mean, led up from the kitchen and opened directly into a bedroom that had been made into a sitting parlor with a TV set so old it had rabbit ears sitting on top. The trio proceeded into the adjoining bedroom. From the men's clothes in the closet, the room had been Barry's.

"The bedding was removed by the county team," Ed said, noticing her glance at the stripped bed.

After poking around and finding nothing interesting except an empty suitcase in a funny little cupboard, Francine moved to the hallway and a view of the front stairs where Barry have been found.

Shuddering, she turned quickly and gave a brief look around the bathroom and then entered the bedroom that had been the mother's, and then, clearly, had been Grace's. The bureau and nightstand matched the bed. The plain wooden chair, painted green, matched nothing. She found the well-remembered Louis Vuitton shoulder bag in a drawer. She unclasped it. Nestled against the distinctive lining was a playbill and several ticket stubs from a New York theater.

"New York City," she said to Ed, motioning that he should write that down. She lovingly stroked the designer bag and then reluctantly replaced it.

Finding nothing more of interest in the bureau she went to the closet. She found a number of name brand plus size outfits. She realized she should no longer be surprised. Obviously, the Grace she knew had a fancier side. In one section of the closet there were dresses that still had their tags, Bergdorf Goodman, Bloomingdales, Saks... "These are from upscale New York stores," she remarked, caressing the quality fabric. On the bed table was a pair of Grace's big old-fashioned eye glasses. Aloud she said, "She always wore these glasses. I wouldn't think she would go far without them."

Donny, standing as if at attention, his stance wide, his hands behind his back, said, "She probably had several pairs, Ma'am."

Francine scowled, deciding she liked Donny better when he was a dependably consistent dimwit.

There was luggage on the closet floor. She moved it to look inside.

"Examining items for possible clues and latent fingerprints was part of the county investigation," Donny said.

"Then you won't have to worry about fingerprints I might leave," she answered shortly. The suitcases were empty except for more playbills and ticket stubs—all from theaters in Manhattan. Francine had a hard time imagining the Grace she knew attending a Broadway show, but she surely had the clothes for it.

"New York City, again," she said, waving a hand imperiously toward Ed and his writing pad. She started to return the luggage to the closet, but Donny was there. "I'll take care of that, Ma'am."

"Thank you." The words threatened to stick in her throat, but she squeezed them out.

There were only a few pieces of costume jewelry in the nightstand drawer. Judging from the name brand clothing she would have expected Grace to have good jewelry, but since she never remembered seeing her wear any, there was no way of knowing if anything was missing.

Frustrated, she searched through all the drawers while the two officers watched impassively. A manila folder lay in the nightstand top drawer. Inside were a collection of canceled stamps from all over the world and a white envelope. Francine felt a start of excitement. Slim had asked if she had ever seen any mail—perhaps this would be a clue.

There was no address on the envelope because it was torn across, probably to save the canceled Asian stamps that were pictured with red monkeys. Disappointed, she was about to return the folder to the drawer where she saw penciled letters on the reverse side: IBBI.

What was IBBI? She cast around for thoughts. Law firms used abbreviations like that—she made something up...Irving, Brown, Baker and Ingham. Slim had talked about a lawyer for the principal of the corporation. Would their firm's name fit the initials? Or maybe IBBI was the name of some foreign place, like a city in Arabia or some other Middle East country. That would tie in with the canceled stamps. Slim had said one of the corporation principals was in a foreign country. Were some stamps saved from letters this person mailed to Grace?

Francine's excitement bounced back with a satisfying thump. The theory about Grace and Barry being squatters was nonsense, and if someone in the corporation, lawyer or family individual, had been writing to Grace, it would prove it. It would make a direct connection despite the wool the lawyer was trying to pull over everyone's eyes.

"Slim should see this folder and the contents," she said, waving the folder in the direction of the two officers. "And those playbills and ticket stubs, as well."

Donny, still standing at attention, spoke, "Ma'am? Excuse me. We have orders that you are to remove nothing from the premises."

"I'm not removing them, I'm asking you…" She trailed off in exasperation and directed her attention to Ed. She spoon-fed it out. "You have the notes of valuable silver items that are missing—that may help track down the thieves. Have someone come in and look at the New York City store tags on those dresses in the closet. Make a note of that. The ticket stubs and playbills indicate New York theater performances Grace attended. All that should be followed up on. Someone in the city might know more about Grace's life outside of JumpRope than we know now, especially if the tickets were bought for the season. The foreign stamps and the initials IBBI might also provide information to anyone smart enough to put it together. Check with Slim, if you have to."

"I'll consult the Chief," Donny said smartly, as if the notion had originated in his brain. He strode off, the heels of his polished shoes rapping with purpose as he stepped into the next room to make the call. Slim must have given the OK, because within the next ten minutes, the ticket stubs, playbills and the folder of stamps had all been collected and placed in labeled bags. Donny did the gathering, Ed the labeling.

"Evidence bags, Ma'am," Donny informed her importantly as he dropped the last items into the bag Ed held for him.

"Very good," she said, her thoughts elsewhere.

When she first got the idea of getting inside the Mather house she had intended to call the *Monitor* reporter whose card she had kept. Now, however, she felt she had made discoveries of such importance that her consultations would better be made only with the police. But it might be good to wait until the morning paper and see exactly what Slim had told the reporter. More or less than he had told her? Something different?

The next morning, the newspaper had everything Slim had told her, nothing more, nothing less. *That's going to change fast*, she thought and smugly called Slim at the police station to learn what had been done with information she had helped gather.

She itemized the things she'd found and how she thought he should proceed, which included someone going to New York City.

Slim told her that chasing down a shopping spree from four years ago didn't sound practical. "Besides," he added, "There's been no time yet to investigate anything."

"But someone must have traveled to mail all those stamps"

"Look Francine," Slim said. "I'm going to tell you something I didn't tell the reporter. You could be right about the stamps. We've been told that the Mather relative who is currently out of the country, Vivian Mather, is something of a world traveler. But since nobody knows where she currently is, we don't know if there's a connection between her and the people we knew as Barry and Grace."

"You're still insisting Grace and Barry had no right to be there?"

"We've got no proof that they did. I told you, the lawyer for the corporation that pays the taxes on the house never heard of them."

"There has to be *somebody*."

"Who knows something? Yeah, sure, I told you there was an old lady in a nursing home that we can't even talk with. Senile or too sick, I guess. That's what the lawyer said."

"Do the initials IBBI match the law firm?"

"They do not."

"But if you follow up on what I gave you about the New York connections, that should lead to something."

"Sure. I've got to hang up. I've got another call."

Yeah, yeah, Francine echoed to herself as she slammed down the phone. She didn't have to be a bloodhound to smell another brush-off.

CHAPTER 25

In another part of town Jessi Spellman had also looked at the *Monitor* and come up empty.

It was all dumb stuff, like the dead guy's stinky body still unclaimed. Like anybody cared.

Hold on! Her shrewd little mind started turning.

Why was nobody claiming the body?

Arnie said a New York outfit owned the property.

Didn't they have a connection to the dead guy? After all, he and his missing sister had lived on a piece of it.

So why was the body unclaimed?

Something wasn't hanging together.

There must be secret problems.

Was it these problems that were holding up the land development?

She bit down on a shiny little fingernail with her shiny white teeth.

She shouldn't be bird-dogging for news. She should be taking action before word about the development got out. That's when the price on that adjacent property with the old gas station and barn would go through the roof. But she and Arnie didn't own it yet.

Arnie hadn't even found a way to speak to the owner and find out if the gas tanks were still there. He'd been too busy to follow things through.

So *she* would.

That was the ticket.

She could do anything better than anybody else.

It was a proven fact.

She showed a feline smile.

When Jessi Spellman made up her mind to do something, she thought, it was as good as done

Because of vacations and a lack of business to attend to, there was no joint planning and zoning board meeting that Wednesday evening. Holly was at his desk in town hall finishing paperwork he'd set aside because of answering people's concerns. Questions about the long-dead body at the Mather house seemed to have faded, but the Peach Acres thefts and the fatal knifing were still viewed as present dangers. He had several appointments coming in. He expected the issue to be the thefts. Once he was free, Holly planned to stop by Krupple's for dinner. Wednesday evening was their meat loaf special. If they had any left he would have it with a side of onion rings.

When he heard a light rap on the frame of his opened door he glanced up and to his surprise, saw Toria. She had not been one of his appointments.

"Hi," he said, rising. "Come on in…take a seat." He gestured to the chair in front of his desk as he spoke.

She hesitated, as if on the brink of skittering away. Then she stepped inside. She was dressed as she probably had been for work, a brown straight skirt that seemed a trifle too long and short-sleeved patterned top, beige against an off-white background. She wisped her way to the chair and sat, keeping her woven straw purse clutched tight in her lap as if someone might snatch it away. She gave him a quick look then directed her gaze down to the purse. He could see blotchy color rising from the scoop neck of the blouse.

As he resumed his place behind the desk he saw something in her almost painful discomfiture that struck a chord. She seemed to vibrate with the same anxiety that he had struggled with years back when he was first thrust into the position of mayor. His father had won reelection even after the scandal of jilting Francine to marry her sister, but then he'd come into an inheritance and surprisingly resigned so he could take off with his new bride on a world tour. He'd suggested that Holly take his place and the flustered committee members had gone along with it.

Holly, who'd been taking a break from college, had accepted the appointment, but he'd been filled with a stomach-churning certainty that he was in deep water way over his head and no amount of arm flailing would bring him safely to shore. To his amazement, he'd done fine.

At the next election, he was voted to a full term and, as they say, the rest was history.

He rummaged for a thought to put Toria at ease and could only come up with, "Were you in time to see Darlene cut her birthday cake? I bet it was delicious."

She darted a smile. "It was angel food with a strawberry whipped cream filling."

"I'm sorry I missed it," he said. She was looking down again, fiddling with the purse handles, so he was speaking to the crown of her downcast head.

He said, "I understand you're in the same club as Darlene and Francine. They've both mentioned it, but I really don't understand what it's all about." He figured he'd better ask a question or the conversation would stall again. "Are you all psychic?"

She dared look up. "I knew you were going to ask that."

For a second she had him and then he caught the twinkle in her eye. He burst out laughing. She could be a surprising person. "I guess I walked into that one. But honestly, I don't get it. Is it like fortune telling?"

"In a way, I suppose, but not really," Toria said. "I think the psychic—her name is Mar-see-ah—reads people and catches clues from behavior. She knows when to back off and try something different and when to press on."

Holly saw that Toria was more comfortable now that she was talking about someone else. He said, "Is she a member of your group, then?"

"Oh, no. The group members all live here. Some are older than me, some younger, but we all get along. Three of us are Auxiliary and three are Civic Group, like me. Mar-see-ah is from Rancine."

Rancine was the next town north. JumpRope might have the stupider name, but Rancine was considered the stupidest town. Like JumpRope, it was roughly halfway between Philadelphia and New York City and about an hour from the Atlantic Ocean, but the Rancine three-term "farm girl" mayor boasted she had never dipped a toe into salt water and never saw a building higher than three stories. Rancine voters loved that she'd never gone anyplace or seen anything outside their community. They bragged she was "down–to-earth," just like they were. The town was also known by local jokers as "Rancidville" so maybe its name was stupid after all.

"So the psychic is simply good at reading people?" Holly asked.

Toria looked thoughtful. "She says a lot and every once in a while she hits on something that has real meaning, but mostly it's just for fun. We're at the dinner table over coffee and dessert and we go see Mar-see-ah individually."

"Crossing her palm with silver?"

She grinned. "Yes, but we're regulars and get a group rate," She now seemed totally at ease. "The last thing she told me was that I was about to embark on a great adventure."

"Ah! And so—here you are."

The moment the words left his mouth he recognized the error of shifting the focus back to her. His error was confirmed when the color flamed into her face and her composure fled.

"No! I...I came to give you this. Because of what you showed me."

She started rummaging in her purse. At the same time, Holly heard the sound of voices in the hallway. Residents arriving for their appointment.

"Look," he said impulsively to Toria, "have you had supper? Wait for me and when I'm done with the people who have just come in, we can go to Krupple's and—"

"No, no. I can't." She scrambled to her feet. "This is my regular night to volunteer at the library. Francine's coming in. She has research she wants me to do. Here—" She thrust a folded paper at him. "My number's on it. You can call if you want."

She was out the door just as three people, a woman and two men, appeared, stepping back to make way for her.

One of the men whistled and said, "Sort of a whirlwind, there."

"She just remembered an appointment," Holly said. "How may I help you?"

The three people were neighbors in Peach Acres and their problem was items missing from their respective homes. The man who had made the whirlwind comment, apparently the spokesperson for the trio, said, "We tried to see the police chief earlier today, but he was at a meeting. We decided to see you this evening."

Their report was about the gardening gloves and a trowel that a high school girl had left in the side yard mysteriously disappearing, a decorative ceramic elf statue from an adjacent yard also disappearing and a hanging pot of geraniums taken from the third individual's front porch.

"It sounds like the pranks we had earlier in the season, not what was done by real criminals, but it still can't be ignored," said the spokesperson. "We're convinced it was done by kids, only this time they had the sense not to sneak inside houses."

"Up on the porch, that's close enough," corrected the woman, who had lost the flowers. "Those geraniums decorated the porch for my daughter's sixteenth birthday. And that sweet little elf belonged to her best girlfriend next door. Who knows what's next?"

"Well, there you have it, Mayor," the spokesman said. "Look at the situation. Peach Acres has suffered minor robberies, then a break-in where items of value were taken plus a man was stabbed to death and now the minor robberies have started up again."

"Peach Acres used to be so peaceful," wailed the woman. "What's happening to us?"

Holly advised them to follow through on a talk with the police chief about the resurgence of prank thefts. And even though there was no proof who was behind the thefts, he said he thought it was time for the police to seek cooperation with the school. He assured them that the patrols at Peach Acres would be increased.

When the residents finally departed, Holly found his appetite for dining out had vanished as completely as the garden elf. He decided to head home and hunt for something to eat out of his refrigerator.

That's when he picked up the folded paper Toria had thrust at him as she ran off. Smiling again at the memory of how she could catch him by surprise, he unfolded the page. He saw the photo of the Mather back yard that he had given her. Abruptly, Holly's smile faded. Toria had made a ballpoint pen X on a spot that was vaguely rectangular and with one end possibly squared off. She had drawn a line from the X out to the white margin. There she had written in a neat cursive:

Everybody's been asking what's happened to Grace Mather. Could this be Grace's grave?

CHAPTER 27

Toria drove from town hall to the library chewing her bottom lip and counting telephone poles, anything to stop from thinking what a fool she'd made of herself. Reaching the library she walked straight to the return desk and the filled cart and started putting the returned books back on their shelves. She worked swiftly and efficiently, refusing to think, unable to bear the thought of thinking. But finally alone in the bathroom, she stared at her miserable reflection, words scourging through her mind.

Ninny. Idiot. Twit. Geek.

All those descriptions fitted and one hundred more, words to describe the fool she had proved herself to be. She couldn't even hold a decent conversation. The mayor was always one hundred percent put together while she couldn't manage two words without stumbling all over herself like a drunken stork. What must he think of her? He was calm and collected, with a cosmopolitan flair. The tie he had on that evening went so perfectly with his cream-colored suit jacket and dark trousers, a Toulouse Lautrec poster design, black and cream silk with delicious touches of hot orange red.

She closed her eyes in misery.

And she towered over him.

And the way she blushed. She must have looked like a lobster.

Oh, dear Lord. Why had she fantasized that such an attractive man might look at her twice?

She wasn't even someone he could respect.

By the time Francine came into the library, Toria was reasonably composed and fortunately what her fellow clubwoman wanted enabled her to put her mind on something else entirely.

"I need you to research this on the computer," Francine said importantly, as if speaking to an office assistant. "I think there's a connection with Grace Mather." Francine showed Toria the letters she had written down—IBBI. She told Toria how she had come by her information and about the fancy department store dresses, the theater stubs and play bills and finally about the stamps and the cryptic initials on the folder.

"I found out that the police aren't bothering to seriously investigate my clues," Francine huffed indignantly. "They won't check any of the New York connections because it was too long ago. As to this—" She poked a finger at the paper she'd handed to Toria. "I thought they might be the initials of the law firm handling the corporation, but Slim said it's not. I need you to check on the library computer and see what the letters might mean."

It went through Toria's mind to share with Francine the thought that an area in the Mather back yard might possibly be a grave, but that would lead to her remembering her idiotic behavior with Holly. Best to concentrate on something she was comfortable with—like research.

On the Internet, Toria found several commercial companies with the initials IBBI but nothing seems to apply to the stamps Francine had found. "Maybe the writing was put on the folder at some other time, before it was used for the stamps," Toria said. She got another blip on her computer search display. "Look. There was an Ibbi-Sin, a king in 1940 BC who was taken captive from the city of Ur.""

"Ur? That's a city in the Bible."

Toria's fingers moved over the keys. "Yes, in what we know as Iraq."

Francine looked pleased. "I knew there was some connection with the Middle East."

Toria was following a different line of thought. "King Ibbi-Sin, that's a name. Is Ibbi a name, or a nickname?" Another moment and she pointed to the computer screen. "Look, Ibbi can be a nickname for Isabel. Is either of the corporation holders named that?"

"One is an old lady in a nursing home. I didn't ask about her. She's infirm or something. Anyway, they can't talk with her. I was concentrating on the one who travels. I thought she might have sent the stamps. Her name is Vivian."

"Suppose she has a middle name and that's what she prefers?" Toria suggested. "Or it could be the name of the lady in the nursing home."

Francine looked thoughtful. "You've made a good point. Trouble is, I've worn out my welcome. I've given the police good leads about possibly stolen silver. I think they will follow up on that, but it will take time. As far as the New York connections and the stamps and IBBI, they think it's nothing. If I try to go back again to ask the other corporation owner's name, they're going to blow me off." She wheeled on Toria. "You should go."

"What?"

"Yes. Not to the police, to the mayor. He and Slim are buddies. Holly knows everything the police know. I saw them exchanging glances when I was with them. I think they're holding something back. Men try to keep the upper hand. The point is, what I probably can't get out of them, you could."

Toria was stunned. "Why do you think that?"

"One, they don't run when they see you coming like they do with me. Second, you're young, at least younger than Holly, and not all that bad looking if you'd fix up a little. You've got a light frame, like you should be petite—too bad you're so tall. But you'll do fine. You'll go walking in there, a new face."

Toria bit her lip. What she was to Holly was a red, blotchy, foolish face. And although she understood it was just Francine's blunt way, the comment about her height had stung. She didn't need to be reminded that she was taller than Holly.

As if Toria had already agreed, Francine ran on. "The information I want is simple enough. You can handle it. Nursing home or not, all I want to know is, what's the other woman's name? We can discuss our plan tomorrow night with the others at our Voodoo Club meeting."

CHAPTER 28

The Voodoo Club met, as usual, on Thursday in the evening in the "Touch Room" of the Teddy Bear Tavern and Grill. It was an intimate space where its storybook wall mural showed a bear with one little paw stretched toward the ground as his back feet cleared the jump rope, depicting the "touch the ground" stanza of the jump rope Teddy Bear rhyme.

If it hadn't been their regular meeting night, Francine would have called a meeting anyway. She wanted them all to hear about her conversation with the police chief and her subsequent tour of the Mather house and how irritated she was that the police were ignoring the importance of her finds. During the meal, Francine addressed the other members, Iris, Toria, Darlene, Amy Newton and Nancy Lou Withers, a nurse at the Melton County Hospital, and brought them up to date on her involvement with the mystery. She concluded on a note of confidence. "I know the police chief and the mayor are holding something back. Toria's going to meet with the mayor to learn the name of the woman in the nursing home. That should solve what the letters, IBBI, mean on that folder in Grace's bedroom."

Listening, Toria felt guilty. She hadn't decided if she would see Holly or not. And she still hadn't told Francine her idea about Grace's possible grave. If the police didn't want to follow up she'd just look stupid. She also hadn't said anything about the Mather house being only a small part of a larger property. She suspected that's what the police were holding back. There was gossip about a secret development that hinted Holly was involved in something unethical. She didn't believe it—not only because she didn't believe it of Holly, but also because he hadn't known about the extent of the property until she'd told him. So she was keeping quiet because any mention of the size of the property would only add to the gossip.

When Francine finished speaking, Amy, who earned extra money cleaning for people, said, "One of the places I go, Shirley DeGarmo's, has a framed sampler on the wall. A little girl in the 1800s did the work. She signed her name and it was, Ibbi."

"Hoo-Ha!" Francine trumpeted, with a glance at Toria. "A girl's name, like we decided." She looked back at Amy. "A nickname for Isabel, right?"

Amy shrugged. "I'll ask, but since Ruth has moved in to help, Shirley hasn't needed me much."

"Shirley's little yes-woman," Darlene said. "Ruth seems nice, but she's so quiet. Shirley runs the show."

"Sometimes Shirley just thinks the ideas are all hers," Amy said. "Like taking her medicine on time and eating right. Ruth has a polite way of making suggestions that makes Shirley think it's what she intended to do all along."

Francine huffed. "What I want to know is, how Shirley could end up with a son like Kurt, who can hold a sensible conversation even if you don't get the information you want, compared with that numbskull Donny, who talks like a TV script. But, enough of that—" She clapped her hands. "Iris has something to say about our evening events."

Their customary routine was that after everyone had finished meeting with Mar-see-ah, each would report what she had been told. Because Mar-see-ah could say so much, someone, usually Toria, capsulated the possible meaning into a few pithy words, like, *Look before you leap*, or *Don't take candy from strangers*. The members would then put their heads together to find messages in the words.

That night, however, Iris, her pink flowered blouse as bright and cheerful as her manner, offered her new idea. "We're all dying to figure out the Mather house, right? Who broke in to rob it? How did poor Barry come to be dead? What happened to Grace? So, we'll each fix our minds on the Mather house when meeting with Mar-see-ah." She clapped her hands in delight, as if her idea would solve everything. "When we discuss the messages, we'll expect answers to the Mather mystery."

"Worth a try," said someone, and the others agreed.

As they went out one by one for their private consultations, the conversation among those remaining at the table drifted to the August Banquet and Penny Auction, although nothing cost a penny anymore. It was an Auxiliary endeavor, but Ladies Civic Group members pitched in. (Years back, it had been a street fair, introduced by Irish families from County Kerry who remembered a three day event, Puck Fair, held in early August.)

When the last member returned from her session and they were together again, everything else was set aside as the revelations were reported.

Francine, in her outspoken way, had once deemed the sessions "fortune cookie hog slop," but she always had as much fun as anybody. When the only word Nancy Lou came back with was 'snowball,' Francine hooted. "When it comes to solving this mystery, the police don't have a snowball's chance."

"In hell," added Amy, who was more plain-spoken.

"Exactly," agreed Francine. "Everything I told the police to look for is exactly right, only they're too dumb to see it."

"What Mar-see-ah told you," said Nancy Lou to Francine, "was something about a doorbell ringing. You said she repeated it twice."

"How do you think that fits in?" Francine said.

"That the police are as dumb as a doorbell," Iris piped up brightly

"That's doorknob, not doorbell," Amy corrected.

"Oh," Iris said. "Then Mar-see-ah meant they're as dumb as two doorknobs."

There was a bit of a silence, then Darlene, who had a brandy instead of dessert and was feeling unusually relaxed, intoned in a spooky voice, "*The doorbell rang.*"

"Or doorknob," muttered Amy.

Nancy said to Toria, "What Mar-see-ah told you tonight is about the same as the last time—that you're going to have an adventure. Maybe that means your meeting with the mayor to ask about the name Isabel."

The memory of how she had messed up with him earlier had Toria blushing in embarrassment.

"What's this?" asked Nancy Lou. "Something cooking with you and his honor?"

"No—no," Toria stammered. She thought furiously. "I think it's about me spending the weekend at a friend's house at Sunshine Shores."

"A friend?" probed Nancy Lou.

"A girl friend," Toria said emphatically.

"But the two of you are set up for dates, right?" Amy demanded. "That's what all the blushing is about. Some guy. Is he cute?"

Toria's cheeks blossomed hotter. It was true she would spend time with her friend Kay at the shore, but that wasn't why she was coloring. Giving a false impression was the same as lying and she hated to lie.

Fortunately, Darlene unintentionally came to her rescue by jumping in. "What I was told has nothing to do with the Mather house. But 'wealth doesn't always mean happiness' exactly fits my cousin's situation. She won a lottery and now her teenager is driving her crazy, thinking she should have everything she wants."

Darlene didn't mention that Mar-see-ah also said something that might be misinterpreted as a man coming into her life. She jeered to herself. Empty nonsense. Men were always coming into her life— every time she issued warnings about poor property upkeep or work being done without a permit, there would be some man. Scofflaws and operators, every one of them.

There was general agreement that nothing Mar-see-ah said really had anything to do with the Mather house.

Iris said, "I guess the theme idea didn't go so well, but—" she shot a happy little smile at Francine, "—at least Mar-see-ah doesn't make up stuff and just tells us what she thinks we want to hear. She may not be right all the time, but her abilities are genuine."

Francine sniffed. "What about her great revelation to you? A tall, dark-haired young man will come to the rescue."

Iris giggled. "Maybe it's a boy holding the door for me at the supermarket. Everything Mar-see-ah says isn't necessarily important. It's just what she sees."

CHAPTER 29

Later that same evening, Holly and Slim stood in the back yard of the Mather property. Although the pale moon through the over-shadowing trees made a gloom of the space, there was still a little gap in the lilac hedge that hadn't yet completely filled in.

Holly made some comment and Slim said, "I don't think I ever told you that the department got complaints about the damage. What we were supposed to do about snuffed lilacs wasn't clear. One lady didn't like my attitude and said I was probably the grim reaper in another life. Or that's how I'd be reborn. One or the other." He shrugged and then chuckled. "At least nobody called 911 to report the whole mess as an emergency."

"The way some people felt, it's a wonder." It seemed in that moment Holly could almost smell the heady, sweet fragrance, although of course, by that time of the year, the flowers were only a memory.

Returning to their purpose for being at the site, Slim indicated an area with rocks that had to have been deliberately placed. "The photo you took made this look more like a grave than it does in real life. It was probably a little marked-off garden, maybe a flower bed, but I've talked to county detectives and they're hot about checking it out."

"With a cadaver dog?"

"You've been watching too much TV, bud. The county could get a K-9 team with a specialty dog, but this isn't like locating a fresh body for an arrest. Regardless, the judge will sign to go on private property and they're going to do it next Wednesday or Thursday when they've got some expert to help. There will be hand-digging. I suspect the disturbed surface won't go deep. The expert will be able to tell when they reach what's been solid for a lot more than four years. They'll sift what's loose, probably find nothing and that will be the end of it." Slim, who used to be a smoker, pulled a miniature pack of corn snacks from his pocket and dipped in. After a moment, he added, "This Victoria Dahlgaard who saw the photo and got the idea of a grave. Does she know how to keep her mouth shut?"

Whoops, thought Holly. It would have been so easy to pick up the phone and ask her to keep mum, but he hadn't thought it necessary. Toria seemed ... well, discreet. A desirable trait. Aloud, he said, "You know this town. If she had talked, do you think we would be standing here alone?"

"You're right," Slim agreed. "The way people are, creeps would be nosing around for souvenir bones." He folded the half empty snack package and tucked it back into his pocket.

He and Holly had come together in the police car, leaving Holly's truck at town hall. "Before going back for your ride, let's go for a game of pool at the Spyglass," Slim said, making a reference to a local restaurant that had been an inn and tavern during Revolutionary times. It had once been a place of fine dining, but now was mostly a pool hall offering liquor and short order food.

Holly nodded. "Sure. Haven't been there for a while."

"I've got a reason. It's at the far end of the Pullen Farm near the Gibeau farm. I hear Nero's been going over and I'm curious."

"That's a shame about his drinking," Holly said, remembering the last time he'd seen Nero, with Donny pouring him into the back of the police car. "He's a nice guy, but messed up."

"Yeah, but lately I've heard he's off the sauce. He's been playing pool with Colonel McDuff and other old war vets. They've taken him under their wing. You've probably heard Nero lost his license—got picked up for DUI. A few weeks back I was headed to New Brunswick and saw him hitchhiking so I gave him a lift. He said he was meeting a friend for the weekend. I asked him if he didn't have any women around here and he said, 'Maybe, but nobody my grandmother would approve of.'"

Holly chuckled. He'd heard stories about Nero and a widow in town.

Together, the two men walked toward the police car. Slim added, "The Colonel's got him helping at the historical museum. Your father's been working with him, too. He saw him picking up aluminum cans along the road awhile back and they started talking. Now your father's got him interested in geocaching."

"The things I don't know about my own town."

"And your father," Slim added.

Holly grinned. "He's been catching me by surprise ever since he bailed out and plugged me in for mayor."

The county crew showed up at the Mather house the following week to examine the back yard for a grave. Holly, who had been at town hall, went over to the Mather house to observe. He was ambushed by reporters from the *Monitor* and the TV stations. Lucky him. He told them there was a police investigation in the yard and he didn't know anything more, but that he would tell them when he did. The JumpRope community depended on the news for coverage of their events, so it was smart to cooperate when possible. Glad he could escape at noon to his county job, he left Slim to the mercy of the-public-needs-to-know protectors.

Slim called Holly at four o'clock at his county office.

"The Mather yard is clean except for a little cat cemetery," Slim said. "That's what the rocks were for—not to mark off a flower bed, but to mark off where cats were buried. The county guys also examined the rest of the yard, front and back, and even took a look at the vacant lot adjoining the rear and saw nothing suspicious."

Afterward, Holly thought about it and then put in a call to Toria at her job and made plans for dinner after they were home from work. Although her suggestion about Grace's grave hadn't panned out, it could have, and he wanted to thank her.

CHAPTER 30

Holly and Toria had agreed to meet at Teddy's Bar and Grill. There, the mural with the jumping rope bear was pictured reading a newspaper. The bar had become known as the News Room/ Booze Room and it was the hang-out for *Melton Monitor* reporters. Holly had already given the reporters what was learned from digging at the Mather property earlier that day. They were a good bunch and he could trust that they would now let him eat in peace. A peace he would be unable to find at a restaurant where family groups and seniors would approach him with questions.

He had arrived first and was surprised when Toria came in wearing a red blouse tied over a white silk T and jeans. And red high heels. What had happened to her shy-wren costumes? He stood as she approached his table. She had a tan. It looked good on her. In fact, terrific, but he was too cautious to say so. He'd learned it didn't take much to throw her into a muddle.

As she slid into the chair he held and then resumed his own seat, he said matter-of-factly, "You've gotten some sun."

"My friend, Kay, has a shore house. I spent last weekend with her."

Toria felt her face flame as she spoke, but at least she wasn't stumbling over her words. This is going pretty good, she told herself. She was comfortable talking about other people. She could even talk about herself as long as she led the conversation. It was answering other people's questions that got her flustered. She remembered how she'd told Kay how she'd made a fool of herself with Holly and how her hair, so fine and flyaway, only made it worse—she not only sounded foolish she looked foolish too. How hair products made the fine strands stick to her scalp and whether she had it long or short or tried to pin it back, strands always escaped with a mind of their own.

Kay had laughed and said, "Your hair is brown with gold sparkles and if that's not good enough, wear a wig and shut up about it." Kay also scolded her about her clothes, said it was time she stopped hiding in old lady browns and grays. She had dragged Toria out to shop for cute summer attire. Including red high-heeled shoes.

When Toria had protested about the shoes, Kay had said, "So you're taller than him…if you wear flats aren't you still taller? Go for the sexy walk in heels. If he doesn't like tall girls, better you know now than be wasting your time."

Kay hadn't understood that Toria didn't have a relationship with Holly—it was just that she'd finally promised Francine she would talk with him only she kept shying off. She wasn't comfortable with any man, but she was especially uncomfortable with him. Because he was so important, she guessed. He was nice, too. Somehow, that only made it worse. Her constant stupid blushing! But even if she couldn't control that, her brains shouldn't fly off like fireflies every time she opened her mouth.

Then he had called her before she could work up the nerve to follow through on what Francine wanted and call him. Her first reaction was panic, but she was sick of acting like a ninny. If she was going to do it, she was going to do it right.

The waitress came.

Toria and Holly each ordered Teddy's "famous" blue cheese burgers. She had a side of fries and he had onion rings.

When the waitress left, Holly said, "I was going to have Krupple's meat loaf special with onion rings last Wednesday, the night you came in with the photo, but Teddy's are better."

"And is that what you finally decided on at Krupple's?" She dared look at him directly. As long as she asked the questions, she felt could keep a handle on herself.

"No, it was when you were leaving and those other residents came in." He hesitated because he didn't usually air what went on in his office, but then he continued. "You've probably heard there have been more prank thefts. These homeowners were worried. The police stepped up patrols and Slim talked to the high school principal. It's got to be kids, but nobody has seen anyone. It's disturbing."

"And that killed your appetite?" The moment she spoke she realized it had been a forward thing to say. Feeling her face go all hot again she was about to apologize, then she saw him nodding in agreement.

"Yes." He was thinking it was neat that she understood. She seemed different, less skittish. She sure looked different. Her soft-looking chin-length hair was the same though, seemingly spun from something lighter than air. The color was light brown, with pale amber streaks. He wondered how it would feel to touch it.

He reached for his beer mug and took a long sip. She was having a light beer, one pretty hand with its short, unpainted nails curved around the pilsner.

He cleared his throat. "What I wanted to tell you was that everyone agreed about the photo—that plot did look like a grave. The county investigated." He made a gesture toward the *Monitor* reporter's table. "They're from the news crew that showed up when the county crew worked. I wanted you to know before you read about it in the paper. Your tip was taken seriously and I want to thank you for not talking about it around town. It was good that nobody heard ahead of time and decided to investigate on their own." He showed a small smile. "And, in a way you were right. There was a grave—two in fact. The stones were markers for two cats."

Toria felt a pang. "Someone's pets."

"Yes. They were buried with what had been balls of string—cat toys. Slim stayed there after I had to leave. He said that the workers recovered the graves. They weren't doing any harm."

"That was nice." Toria imagined a group of workmen standing silent for a moment, touched by long gone devotion for pets. "Francine said when she was a teenager, she cared for the elder Mathers' cats. I guess that spot was a little pet cemetery for them."

Holly smiled. "There were several larger rocks with remnants of worn paint, probably grave markers. One of the cats must have been white. The paint was flaking but Slim said he thought the letters would have spelled, *Snow*."

Or *Snowball*, Toria thought with a funny little chill, remembering that was a word from the Voodoo Club's last session with Mar-see-ah.

Holly took another sip of his beer. "So that's what we discovered, but it left us not knowing anything more than we knew from the start."

Toria saw her lead-in to discuss the Mather mystery and what Francine wanted to know, but she suddenly felt herself losing it, her skin flushing. Trying to give herself a chance to regain control, she looked around the room and caught sight of two people at a corner table she hadn't noticed when she first came in.

Talking about other people was the ticket, she reminded herself.

"I see Pilar Fanshawe and her son sitting over there. Do you think they're trying to scoop the *Monitor*?"

Holly chuckled. Pilar, whose outfits were theatrical, looked Bohemian that evening. She was a successful interior designer who had to be in her forties, but appeared too young to be the mother of her bearded, twenty-something son, Alexander. (God help the misguided person who called him Alex.) Their sporadically published four page newsletter, *JumpRope Jive*, was a mishmash of Alexander's tortured playwriting efforts and Pilar's decorating advice. What made the publication a draw was the section written by "Madam Jive" and called, *News and Noose*. Illustrated with a drawing of a child's jump rope twisted into a noose, it was a combination of innocent local news and scandal-mongering, such as "Why is that electrician truck parked so often on Maple Street? Are there sparks in a room of a certain blonde homeowner? Want to guess which room?"

Holly said, "I don't think hard news is their specialty."

"Not with Madam Jive, anyway," Toria said, feeling back on solid ground.

"Who everybody knows is really Pilar," Holly said.

"In her lemon colored Mazda," Toria said.

"Her yellow journalism ride," Holly said.

Toria smiled. "Anybody who sees that car touring their neighborhood, they've got to be quaking. It must be about time for another issue."

"Last one was in March," Holly said. "Town Hall always gets at least one victim complaint. The next issue will probably have wild speculation about the Mather house."

This was it, Toria thought, a second chance to ask for the information Francine wanted. Quickly, before she could lose her nerve, she said. "We talked about the corporations that owned the properties. Did you ever learn anything about the principals?"

He hesitated and then decided it wasn't a secret. Besides, if he could tell anyone, he could tell Toria. She was involved.

"There's a Vivian Mather, only nobody knows how to reach her because she apparently travels all over the world. The only other one is an elderly woman in a nursing home."

"What's that one's name?" Toria asked, inwardly begging to hear him give the right answer. *Isabel*, she silently urged, *Say her name is Isabel.*

"Her name is Elizabeth," Holly answered. "Elizabeth Mather."

CHAPTER 31

On Tuesday at town hall, Holly ordered out for lunch. He had a busy afternoon at the county and decided to eat early so he could go non-stop once he got on the job. A tropical storm, too early for July, but there was no reasoning with the weather, was scheduled to move from the Caribbean and up the Atlantic Coast. People hoped it wouldn't hit New Jersey on the weekend and spoil planned events. To be on the safe side, Holly scheduled culverts to be cleaned throughout the county to prevent road flooding. Instead of eating at his desk he decided to relax in the lounge, a comfortable space between the municipal offices and the police department where there was a kitchenette, a table, chairs, a couch and two matching easy chairs.

Since it was early, no one else was present when he started on his roast beef sandwich and coleslaw from Sean's Pub, which had some of the best deli food in town. He was thinking about Toria, belatedly deciding there had been something odd about her questions the other night at Teddy's. She'd acted cool—surprisingly cool for someone who had always been so vague and jumpy, still there had been something intense in her manner. He couldn't figure it out.

He was still pondering when Darlene came in and sat down at the table with her own so-called lunch, a cup of plain yogurt and two rice cakes.

"Did you ever notice," she begin in a testy tone, unscrewing the top of her club soda bottle as she spoke, "that no matter how obnoxious a person is, they always have a least one friend?"

"I hadn't thought about it, but it sounds right," Holly said.

"Well, that insufferable Jessi Spellman has at least one friend, Pilar Fanshawe, but she's not her best friend because she confided something about Jessi. Remember Jessi's claim of a china repair business?"

"And the fake Queen of England thank you that was supposed to prove it?" Holly said. "How could I forget?"

"Well," Darlene huffed, "Pilar said the whole thing was a joke. She and Jessi sat together on Jessi's patio with a pitcher of margaritas and dreamed it up. A joke! Can you imagine?"

With a fierce move, Darlene smoothed her poker straight hair, ash blonde except where the slightest hint of roots showed silver. "Pilar said Jessi was mad about not getting a certificate of occupancy for her Apple Corners landfill-on-a-foundation so she decided to get even. Her payback was keeping me riled. Like claiming she had a business against ordinance and that bogus thank you. She thought winding me up was hilarious. Every time she received one of my responses trying to explain the rules and regulations of why she had to go before the Land Use Board for approval, Jessi would laugh like a lunatic. It was just a joke with her. A joke! When I have so much to do. You know how hard I work for the town."

Holly agreed that she did. She always got the job done even if she never left her by-the-hour appointment calendar lying around. There'd been a time when he'd wondered if she was faking the hours she worked but he'd come to realize that if she was, it was because she was working more hours than required. It was as if she didn't have any life outside the job.

Donny DeGarmo stepped into the lounge, his police uniform meticulous, shoes shined, red hair slicked flat. "Sir, Ma'am," Donny greeted as he walked to the soda machine. "Any item I can obtain for anyone?"

"We're good, Donny," Holly said.

Nodding smartly, Donny frowned at the vending machine, probably trying to puzzle out which soda or snacks were most appropriate for an officer of his caliber.

"So," Darlene said, biting into a rice cake with a venomous snap, "Pilar isn't as much a friend as Jessi thinks or she wouldn't go tattling to me."

"Unless that was part of the plan."

Darlene jerked her head up and glared at Holly with narrowed eyes. "What's that mean?"

"The whole object was to annoy you, which it did. And now that you've been told it was a sham, you're madder than ever."

"You're right! Oh, I could just wrap my hands around that Jessi's neck and throttle her." She clenched her fist, crushing what was left of a rice cake into fragments. "Thank God I'm taking some time off and escaping this madhouse."

Darlene was going to Pennsylvania, to visit her daughter who had a new baby.

"It's too bad there's no one from Melton who can cover for you," Holly said, picking up from a previous day's conversation, "but the inspector who will come over from Rancine is fully qualified."

Darlene's mouth set in a line as straight as her hair. "Yes and I already told you what I think of that jerk. He may be qualified according to regulations, but he doesn't care a rat's behind about this town. When you look at properties in Rancidville, you'll see he doesn't care about them, either. I'm going to come back to a gigantic mess. It will take me longer than I've been away to get things back in shape."

Holly felt helpless to say or do anything constructive, so he settled for sympathetic comments and murmurs as he disposed of his napkin and the papers that had been around his sandwich. He dropped his soda can into the recycling bucket and brushed nonexistent crumbs from his blue suit and his necktie, which was printed with Andy Warhol multicolored dollar signs against a sunny background.

He wished Darlene a good visit with her daughter and wished the baby well, said goodbye to Donny, who still hadn't made his selection, and fled.

CHAPTER 32

Thursday evening Francine and Toria were sitting at a table on Francine's back terrace on her new-that-season teak outdoor furniture. They discussed Toria's disappointing news that the other person associated with the corporation paying the Mather house taxes was not named Isabel.

"All right," Francine said, "the name on the envelope of collected stamps isn't the woman in the nursing home. And it isn't the woman they can't get in touch with, the one who travels, because Slim said her name is Vivian. However, this Vivian could have still sent letters to Grace from foreign counties, with of course, foreign stamps."

"And why did Grace clip out and save the stamps?" asked Toria. "And what about the name Ibbi on the envelope?"

"Trying to figure that out is useless." Francine looked at Toria as if it was her fault they'd wasted time on it. "Grace probably saved them for somebody who has nothing to do with this. It's no longer important. We have three names that *are* important. Vivian Mather, who travels, Elizabeth Mather, who's senile, and Grace Mather, who's missing."

"If the missing one is truly Grace Mather and not an imposter," Toria said, ignoring the dirty look that Francine gave her. She didn't necessarily agree that the stamps and the name, Ibbi, weren't important, but she wasn't going to argue. She grew up with a father who ran his family as if he was the general and his wife and daughter were recruits in need of constant training. In her quiet way, Toria was never cowed by Francine's blustering bossiness.

"The fact that Grace is missing is a mystery that was literally dumped in my back yard," Francine said. "If the police can't solve it, I will."

"Only, how?" Toria asked

"I don't know yet. That's why you're here. To help me figure it out."

"But the other club members—"

Francine cut her off. "Iris is a dear and I'll love her forever, but for something like this she hasn't got the brains God gave a grape. Darlene is off to Pennsylvania, and the other two are involved with young families." She gave Toria an appraising look. "Now, you—you've got a gift for research."

Toria made a face. "The county records only list the corporation. From what you told me, the corporation lawyer denies that Grace and Barry even exist. What more can I research?"

There was a silence while they each sipped iced tea, the glasses from Francine's lead crystal monogrammed pitcher set. The threatened storm was still off the coast of Florida. And still predicted to eventually sweep on up the East Coast and hit New Jersey, but presently, the town of JumpRope was enjoying a lovely evening, the air clear, the humidity low. Sounds of crickets came from the grass and somewhere in the trees a couple of birds were saying goodnight to one another.

Francine set her jaw. "Since Grace isn't lying dead under the dirt of her own back yard, she has to be somewhere else. Slim's right that it's weird that there's no personal paperwork, no photos, no notes on calendars, no checkbooks or receipts and the like. However, the police didn't look at the playbills or dress tags as clues because they didn't view them as personal. Men don't think about things the way women do."

"And it wasn't a super detective team doing the looking, like on TV," Toria said.

"If it had been they would have someone like me to point it out to them," Francine said. "I'm convinced Grace and Barry were who they claimed to be, only they were hiding something. To learn where Grace might have gone, we have to follow the clues we have.

The tickets and playbills are at the police station but I remember the names of shows they attended. And her clothing was from fine stores I patronize."

"So you're really thinking of going to New York to poke around see who might have known Grace?" Toria said.

"Well, there is a problem," Francine admitted. "I remembered I once overheard Barry make a remark about Grace's dead husband. Her married name wouldn't have been Mather."

"Maybe she took back her maiden name," Toria said.

Francine looked thoughtful. "When they moved in and I went over to welcome them, I'm pretty sure Barry gave his name and simply introduced Grace as his sister. Her last name never came into it. Slim said he couldn't find a driver's license, but he couldn't have found it if he searched under the wrong name."

"If Grace never had one, they couldn't have found it anyway. How about tracing backwards? Grace and Barry had to live somewhere before coming here. Did they mention things about their past?"

Francine sighed. "It wasn't like we had long conversations. I gave the police the impression I knew them better than I actually did," she admitted. "If I hadn't overheard an argument between Barry and Grace in the market I wouldn't have even known she'd been married."

"The parents lived here," Toria said. "Were their funerals held here? If so, there would be a record."

"They weren't here when they died. The father had a fall and the mother said they would stay with relatives while he recuperated. She'd called me over to her back yard to tell me they were leaving. That was the last I ever saw of them. I don't know where they went, but it still wouldn't prove anything to Slim. A nice old couple, but they kept to themselves as much as Grace and Barry."

"Forget about Slim and his they-were-squatters idea," Toria said. "That gets us nowhere. Grace and Barry moved back here after their parents were dead. How long ago was that?"

"Ummm...maybe twelve years ago."

"I thought they'd been here longer, like forever," Toria said. "If I ever saw them, I don't remember. I wouldn't have known who they were anyway."

"Probably nobody in town really knew them. Living in a house on a dead end road, never mingling with anybody." Francine shook her head. "It's funny how invisible people can make themselves."

"What about their car?" Toria asked. "You said they were always driving somewhere. The car must have disappeared at the same time as Grace. The police had to have checked that."

"I suppose. It was a green car, that's all I recall. If the police checked it out, they must not have come up with anything helpful. Besides, the mystery is with Grace, not Barry. They know where *he* is, even if they say they can't prove that it's really him, still lying unclaimed in the county morgue. Slim said his cremated remains will be interred at county expense as an indigent." She snorted in disapproval. "Besides, it's not a situation police term high priority. If Barry had been murdered, there would be more of an investigation."

"The mystery may be Grace," Toria said, "but if her unknown married name keeps us from finding more about her, let's look at Barry. He must have had a driver's license. And the car had a license, too."

"That's right!" Francine straightened, her blocky body fitting neatly against the back of her chair. "And I just thought of something else. Barry took his car to Bob's for tune-ups and repairs. I know it's been awhile, but Bob's a pack rat. He might have kept related paperwork."

Excited, Francine hauled herself to her feet. "He's still at the garage. I'm calling him right now to ask."

CHAPTER 33

The next day after Toria returned home from work, she and Francine headed over to Bob's Auto Repair and Towing because Bob had promised to look up Barry's old car records. The summer air remained clear but the stalled tropical storm remained in the news. Uncertainty about the weather made people uneasy, especially Francine, who resented the fact that she could not control the weather.

Expression set, she and Toria bypassed the bays where vehicles sat in various stages of repair and entered through the door where customers came in. Bob, who had been leaning on the counter talking with a distressed looking man, stepped off to the side to talk with them.

"Sorry," he said to Francine. "I didn't get around to it."

"What?" she snapped. "I told you why it was important."

Bob, a medium height man in his late sixties with a clean-shaven face and crew-cut blond hair going gray, was accustomed to his wife's volatile manner. Calmly, he explained there had been a smash-up on the highway with vehicles to tow and cars to repair. I also have upset drivers and insurance to deal with. My time's not been my own."

"Oh." Francine turned down her burner. "Then I'll find it myself."

When they were first married she'd been the bookkeeper and secretary to the business. Bob now had people to do all that, but she remained confident of her abilities with the paperwork.

"Look in the filing cabinet under Mather," Bob said. "If the folder is there, take it, it's no use to me. I've thought of something that might be even better. Nero Gibeau knew Barry pretty well. Barry would stand around while Nero worked and they'd shoot the breeze the whole time."

"That lush?" Francine said. "Barry was gone and dead by the time Nero got out of the service."

"This was before he went in. He was just out of high school, saving for college, only he went into the service instead. He hit it off with Barry. Even though he was young, he's the guy Barry always wanted to check out that Dodge of his. Nero might have come back damaged, but he's always been a first rate mechanic."

"So what are we supposed to do, now?" Francine demanded, clearly not convinced.

"Buzz his cell. The number's over my desk. He came in today and I was glad for his help. He's got issues, but at least he stopped drinking. He's grabbing dinner then is coming back to help with this mess I've got. Call him."

Still doubtful, Francine consulted the number and made the call. Nero told her he would be there as soon as he finished eating.

"Might as well fetch those records," Francine said with a sniff. "They're a better bet." She found the Mather folder without trouble and shoved it toward Toria. "You're the researcher, besides you've got that big straw purse to put things in."

Standing over the desk surface, a curious Toria slid papers from the folder, finding estimates, invoices, copies of canceled checks and vehicle notes. Some notes were handwritten on the back of various business cards, all clipped together. She unclipped them. Several were for medical appointments, one a reminder for a dental appointment. Toria paused at that card, feeling a chill when remembering it was though dental records that the body was identified as the person who called himself Barry Mather. The back of the card read: *oil change, new wiper blade, rotate tires.* Clearly Barry's reminders for the mechanic.

The front of the next card showed an artistic wolf in the background

and imprinted over it in a bold print was, *Acer Wolfgang, Investments.*
She turned the card over. On the back were Barry's jottings about his
car, but also a message in a different hand: Signed *AW*, it said, *"Have you
come to a decision about the property?"* The next card was newer looking
and had only needed car repairs noted on the back. The front had
the imprint, *Acer Wolfgang*, this time with the profession: *Engineering,
Planning & Land Development.*

Toria's eyes opened wide. "Francine! Remember that talk about
a new development?" Earlier she hadn't wanted to say anything that
might stir up the rumor again, but the cards gave her second thoughts.
"Do you suppose there's truth to it?"

Francine frowned. "You know as well as I do how it got started.
Mary McConnell explained it. The damage to the lilacs made her think
that work was being done along that dead end road and then that
loud-mouth husband of hers got others thinking in the same wrong
direction. What brought this up?"

"This." Toria showed Francine the business card with the question
about the property and the front of the other card with Wolfgang being
a land developer. "Somebody was interested."

"It had to have been more than four years ago when Barry was
still hale and hearty," Francine answered with annoyance. "People are
always speculating about land. It has nothing to do with the recent
rumor nonsense."

At that point, Nero stepped in, an outstandingly good looking man
with bold, sculpted features. He greeted Francine and was introduced
to Toria. Towering over the two women, he ran a tanned hand through
his dark, curly hair. "You said on the phone you wanted to ask about
Barry Mather?"

Francine charged right in. "Grace Mather was my neighbor and
Toria and I are trying to find out where she's gone. If we knew where
she and Barry came from, that might help."

Nero frowned. "You're thinking she went back there? Leaving her
brother dead in the house?"

"That doesn't make sense to me either," Francine said, "but
knowing where she and Barry came from still might help."

Nero kept his frown. "Barry was a nice guy. I felt sorry when I heard he was dead and from what I saw of the two of them, she wouldn't have run out on him. Unless—" He touched his own head. "Sometimes things happen that mess people up. Then they might not react in their usual way."

Toria said, "You and he talked. Can you remember things you talked about? Anything?"

"It was like a lifetime ago. I was a kid who had never been anywhere. He'd tell me about New York City and Broadway, plays he and Grace had seen, fancy eating places and big concert halls. The only times I'd ever been out of town was for baseball games in Philadelphia with the Scouts. Barry told me about a different world."

Francine flashed Toria a triumphant look at the New York City confirmation. She said to Nero, "Was that where they were from? New York?"

"Could be, I don't know. They had a relative in North Jersey, an aunt, I think, that they visited."

"Her name was Elizabeth, right?" Francine demanded. "An old lady?"

"I don't know." Nero smiled, his perfect teeth flashing against his tan. "He referred to her as a screwball, but in a nice way. He gave examples of strange things she did. I don't remember what, except that they were funny."

"She was senile even then?"

His smile faded. "That's not what I meant. She wasn't senile. I guess you could call her eccentric. She had her own way of doing things, impulsive things that often didn't work out."

Toria asked, "Did he ever say anything to identify where she was? She's supposed to be in a nursing home, but the corporation that owns the Mather property won't give out information."

"I remember Barry talking about the place they visited, a big house. I guess it could have been a nursing home."

Francine huffed scornfully. "Some people don't know what to do with big houses. Convert them, chop them up into apartments." Her superior tone conveyed the conviction that unlike 'some people,' she understood the gracious living that could be achieved by maintaining a larger home, which she really didn't have, but it was bigger than her sister Peggy's.

Nero gave her a sidewise glance without comment, then said, "Barry talked about the view of Manhattan from the third floor and across a river, the Hudson River. How the city looked at night with the lights." He frowned thoughtfully. "It was in a town with a funny name. Barry would bring the car in before they went there. He said he broke down once on the Jersey Turnpike and it was a nightmare. He didn't want it to ever happen again." He shook his head. "Look, I should go. Bob has jobs I need to help with."

"So you can't remember anything else?"

Francine's discontented tone seemed to amuse him. "Like I said, it's like a lifetime ago. Tell you what. I'll look at a North Jersey map and see if I find place names that sound familiar, but don't hold your breath."

After he left, Toria said, "He actually told us quite a lot. He confirmed the New York trips, the plays and the relative in a big house that could have been a nursing home. Slim and Holly both agree that a woman connected with the corporation is in a nursing home. It has to be the same person, Elizabeth Mather. If we go there and ask for Elizabeth, it should lead us to somebody who remembers Barry and Grace visiting."

Francine screwed up her face. "So where is this place located?"

"Nero said he'd look at a map. "

"And that will tell us how to find this home? In what was a private house?"

"The name of the town will give us a place to start."

"Ha! And he also told us not to hold our breath."

They both glanced out to where Nero, tall, dark and handsome, stood talking to Bob about a wrecked silver BMW, one side squashed almost flat. Blinking, Toria studied the scene, and then she said, "What did Mar-see-ah say to Iris? *A tall, dark-haired young man will come to the rescue.* "I'm not saying I believe in everything Mar-see-ah says, and it wasn't a message to either of us, but still, let's give Nero a chance before we count him out."

130

CHAPTER 34

While Toria was hoping Nero would provide further information, Jessi Spellman was hoping Arnie would stop dragging his heels. What was the hold up?

Annoyed with his inaction concerning the wrecked old land he'd discovered that was adjacent to the upcoming development, Jessi had visited the realtor they'd intended to use for the deal. She discovered Arnie had second thoughts about the old barn and gas station property because a gas station meant underground tanks. It cost to have them removed and if they'd leaked, it would take a king's ransom to satisfy the Department of Environmental Protection. Also, the title was murky and taxes hadn't been kept up. Jessi fumed. Why hadn't Arnie shared his doubts? Did he think he was protecting her? This was their chance to make the biggest flip ever when the adjacent development got going. (She refused to believe it was only rumor.) Didn't Arnie know she could find solutions to any problems that confronted them? She'd never been so insulted!

And now Arnie was off for a culinary event in New York State so she couldn't even read him the riot act. She had a good mind to go there and embarrass him in front of all the other attendees, except that she had previously accompanied him to a similar dull event and it had nearly put her in a coma. The subject had been nothing but food. Cooking was a serious hobby with Arnie and she supposed she did benefit. After all, he did the cooking although she occasionally had an impulse to bake. Except that once she got started she would remember how tedious it was. All that mind-numbing measuring and mixing. So she would throw everything together, give it a stir and into the oven it went. The outcome was marvelous of course. Arnie was always so proud of her, like he thought the results should be bronzed.

None of which had anything to do with them getting their hands on that property.

She nibbled on a fingernail, planning how to overcome the difficulties that had sent scaredy-cat Arnie running.

CHAPTER 35

The tropical storm had taken an erratic path, crossing the Florida Keys and into the Gulf of Mexico then sweeping up through Louisiana and leaping across to the Atlantic where it careened up the East Coast. Held off from JumpRope until midnight on Friday, it then hit with a sassy grudge. With a starless sky that was as black as a Cajun recipe, the tempest carried on the remainder of the night like an evil Mardi Gras. Lightning and torrents of hard-driving wind and rain blew off shingles, twisted awning frames and scuttled anything loose through the streets like drunken revelers.

Around four in the morning the storm finished its amazingly brief but wild parade, packed up its beads and sequined stick masks and rolled out of town. Dawn arrived as perfect as a newborn. Residents rejoiced despite the debris and flooding that the sunshine revealed.

Emergency crews, including Holly and other men from the county, had started working in the night with medical emergencies and then by daylight switched to helping police rescue homeowners stranded when the Hitchmile stream flooded Mile Estates—a row of log cabins built in the late 1800s as homes for workers at a local circus that provided summer entertainment. When the circus tents folded permanently the cabins were later converted for year round use. Flood water from the stream ran around the high ground and left the cabins on an island. This would have been fine if a falling tree hadn't splintered the canoes that cabin owners had for just such an emergency.

Toria and Francine were as stalled as the storm had once been in their quest to learn the location of Elizabeth Mather's nursing home. Nero Gibeau, now working at Bob's to tow weather damaged vehicles, was too busy to come up with the name of the town where Elizabeth might be found. If he even bothered to think about it. (That thought from Francine.)

"With the bad weather over, we might as well enjoy the weekend," Francine said on the phone to Toria that Saturday. "Iris and I are going to visit shops this morning to ask for donations for next month's Auxiliary Banquet and Penny Auction. We already have some nice things, but we need more. Are you busy later on?" She explained that she and Bob were going over to her sister Peggy's house for a barbecue and then added in her crusty way, "There'll be a neighborhood crowd, so a tag-along won't be noticed."

"You're inviting me?"

"Isn't that what I said?"

Toria gulped and then squeaked, "Okay."

As soon as she had agreed, Toria was filled with second thoughts and uneasy questions.

This barbecue was at the home of Holly's parents—would he be there?

What should she wear?

What would her friend Kay tell her to do?

What difference did it make? Who would pay attention to her anyway?

Like a pendulum, she swung between anticipation and despair.

The barbecue had been planned for the Kingstons' back yard, but after Holland Sr. and Peggy spent a good part of the morning clearing away storm-broken branches, torn-off leaves and other storm debris they realized the lawn was still too soggy for a gathering. With the exception of a deck for the grill and a few chairs, the party was held inside their neat bungalow. With the windows open to fresh and cooling breezes, the party couldn't have been more enjoyable. By the time Toria had been there for a half hour, she relaxed and started enjoying herself. She had lived in town all her life and knew any number of people and while she knew Peggy, she had never seen her together with Francine. It fascinated her to see how much the sisters resembled one another yet still seemed so different. Peggy was so much softer and easier going.

Holland Sr. was manning the grill on the deck in the company of other men, the brim of a white sailor's hat pulled down hard over his eyes. Toria didn't feel she knew Holland Sr. in a personal way although she was familiar with him because he'd been mayor for so many of her younger years. On the deck, the topic was geocaching, a current hobby in town, which she knew about because people had been coming to the library for books on the topic. It was an outdoor treasure-hunting other players had cached the "treasure" usually inexpensive trinkets and a log book to sign to prove you've made a find. The fun was in the finding, not what was actually found. The "treasure" is then re-hidden for other players to locate.

When the "food's ready" call came, Toria accepted a platter of cheese burgers and hot dogs to pass around to the crowd and exchanged a few shy words with Holland Sr. She decided Holly didn't look much like his dad. From a collection of old family photos she'd noticed on the living room mantel, she decided Holly favored his late mother. She found it exciting to discover these things about him—as if she had gained forbidden knowledge. She knew she was being silly, yet she couldn't help feeling a thrill.

Holly hadn't arrived home yet from the storm clean-up work—he had called to let his dad and stepmother know that he would be late. Toria had overheard Peggy mentioning it to one of the other guests. She had mixed feelings. As long as he was away she could be comfortable, but when he joined the party...well she just didn't know. Anticipating the unknown unnerved her. Best not think about it. No matter what happened, she at least felt she looked good, feeling almost bold in her blue and white nautical top, white slacks and courage-inspiring red high heels. She had also tied a red bandana around the handle of her straw purse. The jolt of colors gave her a lift. Why had she hidden herself in browns and greys for so long?

The house, with no entry hall, had a front door that opened directly to the stairway with the living room off to the right. A beverage table had been set alongside the partial wall of the open staircase and Toria had been about to pour a refill glass of iced tea for Francine when the front door opened.

She turned toward the door as Holly stepped inside. He saw her straight-away and his eyes lit up. "Hi," he said. "I didn't know you'd be here."

Toria, feeling as if her breath had been snatched like a bird from its nest, heard a voice in her head admonish: Remember ... stay in charge! She recaptured her breath and managed to stammer, "Francine—she— she invited me," and in that awkward moment she knew her boldest color was the blushing red of her face.

Peggy, coming from the crowd in the living room, approached Holly. "Oh—dear, you look exhausted!"

It was true. As he stepped further inside the house and closed the door, Toria saw that his face was drawn and his clothes, a long-sleeved work shirt and matching trousers with a county insignia on the shirt pocket, an outfit she had never seen him wear before, was soiled and rumpled.

He took a bottle of water from a cooler on the beverage table, drank and then, wiping his mouth on a napkin, said to his stepmom, "The people at Mile Estates are safe, but there were cats trapped in a mud and brush outcropping in the flooded Hitchmile."

He included Toria and several others who had stepped up to greet him as he spoke. "There were newborn, two of them." He shook his head, looking sad. "We rescued the mother and one kitten, but it was too late for the other one."

Peggy murmured words of sympathy and then said, "As busy as you've been, you're going to end up aching all over. Let me draw you a bath."

Francine, who had come up in time to overhear, scolded, "Don't baby him!"

Holly gave Francine a vague smile of acknowledgement, then said to Peggy, "I'll grab a shower and clothes I keep in the spare room and be right back down. I'm starving." Giving a general wave to the crowd, he moved to the steps.

"Coddling people," Francine harrumphed disapprovingly as Peggy followed Holly up the staircase.

He was near the top when he looked back over his shoulder and found Toria, who stood where he'd left her as if fixed in place. "Don't go away," he called with a grin and then was gone on up the steps.

Feeling Holly's words could have drawn attention to her, Toria, blushing hotly, quickly turned back to the beverage table to finish the interrupted job of pouring Francine's iced tea. Taking it to her, she then returned to people she'd been with earlier and tried not to glance toward the staircase and Holly's expected return. When forty minutes went by and there was no sign of him, Peggy went upstairs again. When she came back, she went to the group that included Toria, who was trying to keep her mind on the conversation about a new town volunteer who had everyone impressed with her energy.

Wearing a motherly smile, Peggy said, "Holly took a shower and got dressed, but he's exhausted. He must have planned to just rest a moment on the bed in the spare room before coming downstairs. Instead, he's fallen asleep."

Toria felt a mixture of disappointment and relief. Maybe it was better to imagine his "don't go away" comment meant something special rather than finding out it had just been an offhand friendly remark. Only then, Peggy moved closer and said to her quietly, "When Holly and I first went upstairs he mentioned that he was glad to see you here. If he sleeps away the rest of the day, I have a feeling he might be calling you later to apologize for disappearing."

Toria wasn't sure about that, but the words warmed her anyway.

CHAPTER 36

Jessi Spellman, feeling hot and vengeful, decided that with Arnie AWOL she would seal the deal on the property before he returned home. If there were problems, she'd solve them. She wasn't sure how, but that had never stopped her before. The only thing she knew was that she was finding a new realtor. Their usual guy must have been a panty-waist like Arnie not to have pushed the deal. And for sure she would steer clear of Arnie's most frequent deed search client, Pastor. He wasn't the right realtor for this dynamite project. Pastor had no conscience. His capped teeth would gleam in a wide God-loves-you-my-child smile while at the same time he was playing games with the deal for his own advantage. Jessi had no patience with that kind of person.

Earlier in the day she'd gone to the property site and snooped around. Under weeds and trash heaped along the foundation of the old barn she had found a weathered realtor sign. (She was just so lucky she sometimes couldn't stand it.) She didn't know the realtor, but a phone call told her that he knew about the property although it was no longer listed.

He was willing to meet her to tell her what he knew so off she streaked to his tawdry office, which was in equally tawdry Rancine. The realtor turned out to be a middle-aged man with dyed hair and a too-fussy mustache. His male vanity signaled easy pickings to Jessi. Tilting her little face to an enticing angle, she had already decided she wouldn't use her real last name. The name, Spellman, would show a broker a history of property buys and sells, so she gave the last name of a neighbor whose only real estate purchase of record was the house they lived in. Smart thinking, and besides, it was so much fun to lie.

With her voice all bright and chirpy and her tilted green eyes as wide and guileless as she could make them, she explained to the realtor, "My husband and I thought it might make a nice location for a little plant and garden center. It's probably cheap enough and we weren't figuring to put much into it—we could use that old gas station to fix up as a little show room and those old buildings could serve as storage. But we don't know how to go about buying it. I couldn't find it online."

When she'd first come in she had edged her chair far enough away from the desk so the realtor could have a view of her curvy legs and her tiny feet in their strappy sandals, and now she crossed her legs. "Could you please help us?"

The realtor gazed at Jessi, who sat relaxed, yet prim—except for her fetchingly crossed legs and hiked up skirt.

Clearing his throat, he said, "As you say, that property has been languishing. I've done some research since you called. The former broker couldn't find a buyer. A surprise, because as you say, it's a nice location and the owner had the gas station tanks removed back when it wasn't so expensive, but still, no interest. The owner has since retired to a warmer climate for his health."

"Oh, the poor man," Jessi said with phony sympathy, concealing her delight. With the act she was putting on, she wouldn't be sharp enough to know that having the buried oil tanks removed was a bonus. Tone soulful, she said, "It might be a help to the poor man to sell now and have something coming in for his golden years."

The realtor gave her the price it had been listed for, and then said in a sad voice, "But here's the unfortunate thing. Bad timing for you and your husband. Only a week ago someone else expressed interest."

"What!" She was suddenly ramrod straight, both feet on the floor. "Has there been an offer?"

"Nothing completed. The owner lives on the Florida Keys.

Apparently there's been some back and forth conversation, but nothing was settled. The hurricane that hit us slammed into them several days ago and cut them off from communication."

"Who's the other interested person? Could you find out for me?"

"Oh, no!" He seemed shocked that she'd asked, and then as if realizing she was too innocent to be aware that her question was out of line, he added, gently, "I'm sorry, but it just wouldn't be ethical."

"I see." She looked down as if wounded, but it was to hide her fury. Another interested person! How could it be? She'd believed that she and Arnie were way ahead of the curve, but clearly, things were moving faster than they had anticipated. Or maybe, she thought with sudden hope, it was a fluke. Someone who had simply become curious and asked about the property, with no real action intended.

She had to find out. And there was only one person to ask.

Pastor, she thought, grimacing and gritting her pearly whites.

CHAPTER 37

Jessi parked her car in the strip mall in Melton where Pastor had his office. She hoped he was still there on a Saturday afternoon. She hated to tip her hand, but Pastor, a dependable stranger to principled behavior, could find the answer she needed.

With the storm over, the weekend was gorgeous, a crowd jostling around the mall and skipping over rain puddles as they patronized stylish food shops. Jessi approached Pastor's office, passing by a shop where young men were still clearing away windblown shingles and other storm debris.

She noticed that the short steps and broad landing to Pastor's office were swept clean, but the wind had twisted the aluminum awning over the entry, breaking the weld where the support had attached to the railings.

The railing felt shaky under her hand.

The door was unlocked. She shoved it open and entered an empty reception area and called Pastor's name. He emerged from an inner office.

"Jessi, my dear!"

He was dressed in khakis and a casual shirt, but still with a clerical collar. The faker. Stooped and scrawny, except for a pot belly, his large eyes and a short neck gave him a curiously frog-like appearance.

Pressing his hands together as if he felt a prayer coming on, he intoned, "To what do I owe this honor?"

"Stuff it," she said, sweeping past him to the inner office and taking a seat.

He followed and took his own seat behind his desk.

Without further niceties she told him about the property and her desire to know who else was interested.

"Wait a second," he said. "What are your plans? I'd hate to see you and Arnie get in over your heads."

She didn't like him asking questions, but since she wanted cooperation, what the hey? Deciding against the guff she'd handed the other realtor, she went with the truth. "As soon as that development we've been hearing about starts we'll flip it."

"I thought you might be planning a restaurant. I've done some research. In a growing area, it would be a good investment."

She shrugged. "Too much work. Arnie might think a restaurant sounds good on account of he loves to cook, but flipping property is easy and doesn't take big bucks."

"I thought you might want to take advantage of the liquor license," Her surprised look revealed she hadn't known.

He nodded. "Years back, half of the gas station was a package store, selling mostly beer and wine. In addition to that license, the owner held a consumption license that's still on the books." A cunning look came into his eyes. "If young people were interested and could gather the extra capital—from say, a partner who had the finances, but not the time nor the energy—that land offers unique possibilities."

"Partner?" she said suspiciously.

"Just a thought," he said. "Now, please continue with what you wanted to know."

"I told you. Someone showed interest in the property. I want you to find out who."

He made no reply, but sat with his hands now comfortably folded across his stomach, his smile as smug as if he had a belly full of flies.

Puzzled, she said, "It shouldn't be much trouble for you—" She saw his smug expression and suspicion narrowed her eyes. "You knew about the liquor license! You've been snooping around, haven't you? Damnit! *You're* the other interested person!"

He chuckled. "Dear child, you and Arnie know how we work together. He will tell you how pleased I am when he notices what interests other researchers and passes on a tip. He's not the only one in my employ. Someone noticed that Arnie had become interested in a certain property. Arnie even made a pencil mark on a county map. Naughty-naughty." He wagged a finger. "I've been discounting rumors about a new housing development in JumpRope, but should there be one, this site would be a prime business location. Even without it, the site is excellent for a new restaurant, which appeals to me greatly."

Jessi swallowed her rage. "How much are you willing to offer to the owner?"

"It doesn't matter because you wouldn't be able to top my competitive bid. Presumably you wanted to know who else was interested in order to deal with them. Arnie and I have had a good working relationship. And, I've seen how you've fixed up houses you've flipped. You could do wonders designing a restaurant. A partnership is an idea to consider. I would be the controlling partner, of course. Something to discuss, and since you're here…"

"You can hold your breath until hell freezes over!" she raged. When she and Arnie worked a deal, the profit was all theirs. They weren't going to hook up with anybody.

"Then I guess our discussion has come to a close."

She clenched her fists. "You stole our information. That's not fair!"

"Always one of your prime concerns, I know."

And then he laughed.

The laugh was the final straw. Fuming, Jessi leaped to her feet and stormed from his office and out through the reception area. She threw open the exit door with such force it slammed back against the wall. She was already flinging herself outside when the broken awning framing caught her eye,

To observers shopping at the strip mall, it happened in a flash.

To Jessi, it seemed in slow motion.

She lunged forcefully, faking a stumble and grabbed the wobbly railing she'd touched coming in, feeling it give way under her hand as she deliberately pitched forward, bending her knees and tucking her body so that when she fell the short distance to the concrete she would roll.

She hit harder than anticipated. And she didn't roll.

Stunned, she lay sprawled on her back, the breath knocked out of her. Even before she felt the pain she saw the blood on her left hand where it had scraped the rough metal of the broken railing. She squawked in genuine alarm. Then she heard voices and the footsteps of people running toward her. She recognized the dramatic effect of blood. A fling of her hand sent red droplets flying onto her face and the front of her blouse.

"Get an ambulance!" screamed someone as a crowd gathered around the pretty little woman lying like a broken bird.

"My back," she groaned.

"It's okay, take it easy," soothed someone.

"We called for an ambulance," said another.

She looked up past the sympathetic faces clustered around her to see Pastor standing on his threshold, his bulging eyes huge and his wide mouth agape with shock.

Ought to paint the old froggy lawsuit green, she thought to herself in triumph.

She piteously groaned one more time, "Oooooh, my back," then she fluttered her eyes shut in a theatrical swoon.

CHAPTER 38

On Tuesday morning Holly arrived at town hall braced for unwanted attention. The inner spread of the morning *Monitor* featured a roundup of the Hitchmile stream flooding over the years, including photos, the most recent from the previous weekend. It showed him, looking half-drowned but smiling as he waded out of deep water with the surviving kitten in his hands.

Iris made the biggest fuss, embracing him to her sweetly fragrant pillowy bosom, crying, "Hon, that's just the dearest picture I've ever seen." A voice mail from Slim said, "Good job, but I've seen you looking better." His step-mother telephoned. "Your dad and I saw your picture, we're so proud of you. Shirley DeGarmo saw it too. She called to say she's proud of you and Ruth Wilson is, too."

Back from vacation, the town clerk, Susanna, met him before he reached his office. Holly figured she'd have something to say about the picture too, but what she said was:

"A word to the wise—Darlene's on the warpath. After her visit with her daughter and the new baby she came back yesterday to find herself in hot water with the woman who bought Jessi Spellman's house. Oh, and have you heard that Jessi went to the hospital on Saturday? She had a fall of some kind in Melton."

He nodded. "Our ambulance squad brought her home yesterday to recuperate. She's supposed to be seriously hurt."

Susanna wrinkled her nose. Exotic and dark-skinned, with a cloud of ink-black curls, she shook her head, her enormous earrings swaying. "That may be what she's claiming, but I have my doubts."

Agreeing inwardly, Holly only shrugged as they parted. To his consternation, he felt a bit disappointed that Susanna hadn't mentioned the photo. He chuckled to himself. He was more self-centered than he'd thought.

Having been warned about Darlene, he was prepared when she tore into his office.

"Didn't I say that the inspector from Rancine was a jerk?" she raged. "While I was away he was called for an inspection because Jessi Spellman was selling that house. Bet she knew I was gone. That Rancine idiot gave her a Certificate of Occupancy. He ought to be shot!"

"Whoa!" said Holly, putting his hands up as if he were the one facing a firing squad. "What happened?"

"He didn't do his job! Jessi bought the place with a Conditional Certificate of Occupancy, the condition being to repair a hole in the bedroom ceiling caused by a raccoon falling through from the attic. It had probably climbed up a drainpipe and crawled through an open window. Filthy creature—ought to be in a circus. Anyway, I told you about it."

Holly hid a smile. "Right, if she didn't fix it, she couldn't rent it, or of course, sell it. She didn't like you telling her what to do so she started that bogus china repair nonsense to make you waste your time on nonsense. Don't tell me the Rancine inspector missed seeing a huge hole in the ceiling."

Darlene uttered a sound of disgust. "He never looked. I'm sure Jessi was all charming and flirty and he didn't see much except her. The water, electricity and heat worked and there were smoke alarms and a carbon monoxide detector so he handed over the CO."

"He should have done a walk through, but what's done is done. The buyer should have gotten a home inspection before she took ownership. How could she miss a hole in the ceiling?"

Darlene folded her arms. "Jessi disguised it. She draped the ceiling with a printed fabric—she swagged it from the central chandelier and told the buyer it was the bedroom of a beloved daughter who was sick with a horrible illness. She said she was selling the house at a loss and moving to the west coast where there was a doctor who could cure her child.”

“And Jessi being childless, as we know. But at a loss? Doesn't sound right.”

“Ha! She sold it for $30,000 more than she'd paid. The point is, she said the child had loved her bedroom and, while of course, the buyer could do as she wished, Jessi had promised the child that she wouldn't take down the ceiling canopy.”

“I get it. So when the woman took it down—“

“No, she found Jessi's story so touching she had decided to leave it. What disclosed Jessi's lie was the hurricane. It tore shingles off the roof and dumped water into the attic and down through the hole in the ceiling and on the brand new guest room bed the new owner had just placed in the room.”

Holly kept his face straight. Although he felt sorry for the buyer, the story had a comic side. Not that Darlene could see it at the moment—if ever. “There's something in New Jersey law about full disclosure from a seller,” he said. “The buyer should talk to a lawyer.”

“Exactly what I told her.” Darlene tossed her head and smoothed her long hair. “The buyer came in here wanting to sue the town, but after we talked, I think she'll go after the real culprit.”

Holly nodded. “You handled the situation perfectly.” He saw that Darlene liked the lawsuit idea against Jessi and was calming down. Still, he was unable to keep from adding, “You've got to admit that Jessi has a lot of imagination.”

Darlene, leaving the room, called back, “Ha! If she would only use it for good.”

Holly lifted his voice. “Sounds like an epitaph.”

Already in the hall, Darlene yelled back, “If anybody wants to arrange for Jessi to get a headstone, call me. I'm the woman for the job.”

Chuckling, Holly was thinking that the session with Darlene hadn't been as bad as he'd been prepared for.

Donny the cop, who had come to Holly's door with papers in his hand, had politely stepped back to allow Darlene to go by. By that time, Holly had forgotten about the photo and the Hitchmile article and everybody else had too. The Hitchmile was always flooding— nothing to be done about it.

"Reports from the Chief for tomorrow night's committee meeting," Donny announced smartly, virtually clicking his heels.

"Thanks, Donny. Set them here on my desk."

After doing so, Donny said, "The Housing Inspector seemed upset with Mrs. Spellman."

"It's all blown over."

"She used harsh words."

"Empty talk, Donny."

"Dangerous talk often precedes dangerous action," Donny said.

Holly wondered which seminar that had come from.

CHAPTER 39

On Wednesday evening, Francine burst into the library to see Toria on her regular volunteer night. "Nero called," she said. "He said he remembered the name of the town."

Toria led her into the office where they could talk.

"He told me that the New Jersey town that Barry talked about visiting was named Weehawken," Francine said. "I asked if he was certain. He told me he got a Jersey map and traced up the turnpike toward Manhattan and looked for a familiar name and found it." Francine made a face, her initial excitement fading. "But maybe it's nothing. A distinctive name, yes, only with Nero's pickled brain?"

Toria was exasperated to hear Francine be so judgmental. Even if Nero did have a problem, he had been more than willing to help. Besides, if Francine hadn't taken his information seriously, she wouldn't have rushed to the library. She said, "Did Nero have any more thoughts about the nursing home?"

"No, that's why I'm here, for help with a computer. We can see what nursing homes are in that area."

Toria set Francine up on the computer and returned to library duties. After an hour she went back to where Francine was stationed.

"I can't find any place in Weehawken like Nero described," Francine said. "There are facilities in nearby towns and more across the river in New York, but nothing like what he remembered from Barry. I looked on all the likely websites. We have to go there and look for ourselves. Are you working at the county tomorrow?"

"On Thursday? Yes."

"Take a sick day."

"I couldn't do that!" Toria was shocked at the suggestion. She thought a moment. "I do have time coming. I could see if I could arrange something for Friday. But why don't we wait until the weekend?"

"Because I have things to do on the weekend for the Auxiliary banquet and auction. Nero said he had items for the auction." Francine's laugh was derisive. "Things he said he'd found. Iris is going with me on Saturday to look them over. Still, can you imagine? A drunk wandering the road."

"I don't think so." Toria was done with Francine's negative attitude toward Nero. "Your husband thinks he's good enough to hire him. And last Saturday at the barbecue I heard Holland Sr. and some others discussing geocaching. They mentioned Nero being with the group and if you don't know what geocaching is—"

"I know what it is," Francine snapped. "My sister's in with it. A childish hobby. Instead of traipsing all over the countryside with empty foolishness, she should spend a little more time spiffing up her house. She needs pride, that's what. After all, her husband is a former mayor."

Knowing of the friction between the sisters, at least from Francine's side, Toria left the subject and said, "I'll see what I can do about getting free on Friday."

Friday morning Toria and Francine set off for Weehawken, wearing sensible shoes because there might be a lot of walking on city pavements.

"Our first stop will be their main post office," Toria said, having already looked up the address. Francine was usually the leader, but this time, Toria was in that role. She wasn't sure if she liked it or not, but Francine, unsure of how to proceed, was uncharacteristically quiet.

In Weehawken, there was unfortunately no one at the post office who was either able or willing to help them identify a nursing facility in an old private home with a view of New York City.

"Customer friendly, not," Francine huffed. When it came to finding fault with people, she was back on sure ground.

"They probably just didn't know," Toria said. "We need to speak with a mail carrier."

Because Nero had told them of windows that looked across the river to Manhattan, Toria drove to the area where big homes had water views. They saw a parked mail truck almost immediately. They cruised on hoping to find the mail carrier on foot. They lucked out, finding a postal employee making his rounds and willing to help as well.

"Some kind of an old people's place?" he said after Francine, being in charge once again, told him what they were trying to find.

"It was a private home. With a view of Manhattan," Francine said. "The person we're trying to find is named Elizabeth Mather."

Toria thought he blinked as if the name was familiar, but what he said was, "You don't have the address?"

Francine launched into their agreed upon story, part truth and part fabrication—she was a neighbor of one of Elizabeth's relatives who had died and she wanted to tell Elizabeth about his final days.

The mail carrier scratched his head. "I can't say anything for sure but there's a place nearby that might be the one you want. Art stuff going on there. Big old house with a view." He gave them the address.

"That doesn't sound right," Francine complained when they returned to the car and started moving.

"We don't know that Elizabeth wasn't an artist," Toria said

Francine brightened. "Artists, like the wacko who cut off his ear? Nero said the old woman was a screwball, didn't he?"

Toria ignored the questions.

The address led them to a massive and elegant three-story brick Georgian house. There was no identifying name in front, but from their position across the street she saw a third story balcony that would give a view across the Hudson River to the city.

"Let's check it out." She pulled the car into a small on-site parking area.

Their ring of the doorbell was answered by a young woman in street clothes.

"Doesn't look much like a nurse," Francine whispered into Toria's ear. "I think this is the wrong place, but since we're here, I guess we might as well go ahead." She focused on the girl and launched into their story, concluding with, "So we really need to see Elizabeth."

"I'd better have you talk to someone else," the girl said, stepping back to allow them inside.

Francine settled her well-padded form in an overstuffed chair with yellow velvet upholstery and glanced around. Eyes wide, she said, "The fabric of those draperies looks like Fortuny."

Toria knew Fortuny fabric was expensive, but she wouldn't have recognized it and her mind was on other matters. She glanced around, seeing a bookshelf that contained albums of some kind. Maybe photo albums?

"Elizabeth must be here," she said. "The girl would have told us if this was the wrong place."

"I suppose you're right," Francine admitted begrudgingly.

They waited in silence for what seemed a long time and then an older, but still youthful, woman, also in street clothes, came from a hallway that led to the rear of the house. She introduced herself as Jade and said, "I understand you wish to see Miss Mather?"

Francine flashed Toria a triumphant glance as if she'd been the one who'd insisted this was the right house all along. She turned back to the woman and launched into the story for the third time. She finished it by asking, "Has she been told about Barry's death?"

"She'd been told, but we don't know what she processed," Jade said. "Back when Barry and his sister, Grace, visited, she was less withdrawn than she is now. Visits from family meant a lot until she started to fail." After a thoughtful silence, she said, "You may see her, but I'm afraid you won't derive much satisfaction from your visit. Please, follow me."

"See," hissed Francine to Toria. "Grace and Barry were relations and had a right to be in that house."

Toria hoped Francine hadn't said it loud enough for Jade to hear and realize they didn't know the family as well as they pretended. Lagging behind, she moved to take a quick look at the top album on the bookshelf, then caught up with Francine as Jade led them up the stairs. Moving along, Francine treated Toria to a running commentary of the decor: "Bokhara," she said of the design of the red stair runner, "antique Venetian," she said of the wall mirror, and at the turn of the stairs and past a big window overlooking the street, she touched a silk taffeta panel of the window treatments, and murmured, "Scalamandre or maybe…" She rattled off other names, impressing only herself, because Toria was thinking that the words "old lady in a nursing home" conjured up an entirely different picture than the richness that was presently surrounding them.

They were conducted all the way up to the third floor where a generous landing led in through double doors to a high ceilinged, light filled space.

"The therapy room," Jade said, stepping back to allow them to enter. She followed behind them,

"Elizabeth? You have company," Jade announced with a gesture toward the only occupant of the space, a heavy woman sitting in a wheelchair, a paint brush in her hand and her attention fixed on a large canvas before her. An array of oil paints and related supplies were on a table within reach of her chair. Wearing an old-fashioned flowered muumuu, her sparse gray hair was skinned back from her head and pulled into a knot at her nape. She gave no sign of being aware she was no longer alone.

"You may speak to her all you want," Jade said quietly to Toria and Francine, "but don't be disappointed if she fails to respond." She then seated herself on a bench along the wall near the door.

Frozen with uncertainty Toria and Francine stood with their shoulders almost touching. Francine recovered enough to whisper to Toria, "She looks like an older version of Grace. Her hair is gray instead of black but that's how Grace wore hers and she has the same thick glasses. I wonder how they're related."

"Shhh," cautioned Toria. "We're supposed to know. Nero thought she was an aunt."

She edged forward to see what the woman was painting, expecting to see random lines. Instead, she saw a well-executed panorama of Manhattan as seen from the window overlooking the balcony. That's when Toria noticed that leaning against the walls around the room were numerous paintings of the same city scene only at different times of day. The night scenes were especially spectacular.

"Elizabeth—" Toria impulsively spoke to the woman as if she weren't a stranger. "Your work is wonderful." When she received no response, she turned to their guide. "Is the city all she paints?"

"She'd obsessed by it," Jade replied. "We have no idea why. Sometimes we move her out to the balcony, but today the air seemed breezy. When the air tries to dry the paint too fast, she doesn't like it."

"You can tell?" asked Francine bluntly.

"We can tell," the woman answered with a quiet smile.

"Well, I'm going to tell her what I came to say." Francine approached the side of the wheelchair and started talking. She told Elizabeth everything about how she had believed Barry and Grace had only gone away on a trip. But then she saw the house was boarded up. She continued on to the discovery of Barry's body and finally, the realization that no one knew where Grace was.

She concluded. "We thought you could help us find out where Grace is now."

There was no sign that anything Francine had said penetrated. Through all of Francine's monologue Elizabeth had continued painting, pausing only to select other brushes, other colors.

Toria thought there might have been a bit of reaction when Francine talked about Barry's body being found. Maybe no more than Elizabeth's hand tightening on her brush, but the impression was so fleeting she couldn't be sure.

Frustrated by Elizabeth's lack of response, Francine stuck her head forward like a turtle and turned to demand of Jade, "What is this place, anyway? Who brings the paint supplies? Who takes care of things?"

Jade stood and moved toward the door, her gesture making it clear she had determined that it was time for them to leave. "An individual with artistic interests established this as a home for indigent female artists. Elizabeth is currently one of three in residence. All needs, including artistic supplies, are provided."

Toria said, "You heard us ask about Grace. One of the things we hoped to find out from Elizabeth is how we can find her. Could you give us any help?"

Jade shook her head. "I met Grace and her brother when I first came here almost five years ago, but I never spoke with them except in regard to concerns for Elizabeth's needs. There's no way I can help you."

She ushered them downstairs and then outside and closed the door behind them.

Francine and Toria descended the steps and faced one another on the sidewalk.

"This has turned out to be a fine kettle of fish," Francine spat, glowering.

"I discovered something," Toria said. "There are stamp albums in the downstairs bookcase. I took a quick peek at the top album when Jade was heading up the stairs. The name Ibbi was written inside the cover. Just as we thought, Grace was saving stamps for a collector. Ibbi must be one of the other residents. Grace probably brought the stamps for her when she and Barry visited Elizabeth."

Toria was pleased for solving that part of the mystery, but Francine would have none of it. "Water over the dam. A wasted trip."

Toria stood for a moment, glancing back up at the stately brick home and thinking of its fine interior furnishing, attentive staff and superb view. And up on the tippy-top floor was a gifted artist who had shut herself off from the world except for an obsession with one of the world's greatest cities.

"At least there's one thing we've proved for certain, Toria said as she turned toward the car. "Something you'll enjoy telling Slim."

"What's that?"

"Two things, actually. You already remarked about one of them— this trip proved that Barry and Grace were part of the Mather family and *not* squatters. And, when that corporation lawyer said he'd never heard of Barry and Grace, it had to be a lie."

CHAPTER 40

Toria arrived home in JumpRope around three in the afternoon. After dropping off Francine and going to her own place, she called Holly at his office over at the county, not giving herself time for second thoughts.

When she had him on the line but before she could say anything, he said to her:

"This is so good. I was going to call you."

For a second she was speechless and then before she could start tripping all over herself, she rushed into her story.

"I wanted you to know that Francine and I did some detective work. Remember that old lady who is one of the Mather Corporation principals—Elizabeth Mather, the one in the nursing home? Francine and I discovered she's in Weehawken. We went up there today and saw her."

He laughed. "You're going too fast for me, I need to hear more. I missed having dinner with you at the barbecue on Saturday. How about dinner tonight? That's what I was going to call you about. If the answer is yes, where would you like to go?"

Talk about going too fast. Her thoughts went like they were wearing the red shoes. "I'll meet you at the Giraffe's Neck." It was out of town and driving over would give her time to really be sure she had herself in hand. When they met she would be suave and serene, making up for the dunce she was always making of herself with him, but then he said:

"I'll pick you up. You must be tired. Francine hates driving long distances, so you were behind the wheel, right?"

"Yes, but—"

"Great. I've got work to finish up so I'll be here late. Get some rest and I'll pick you up at seven." He paused and then added with sudden uncertainty. "That is, if you don't mind riding in a pickup truck."

There was a dizzy moment before she could think of how to respond, but then after taking a breath, she managed, "That's fine. Perfect." Not having her own car wasn't what she had planned, but this was more exciting. He was picking her up. Like it was a date!

"Okay," he said. "See you at seven"

Toria hung up the phone and stood staring out the window. What had happened to the butterflies that had been swirling in her stomach? Now they were dancing outside her window, golden wings fluttering like a scene from a Disney cartoon.

When Holly arrived at her door he was dressed the way she figured he had been at work. His necktie was a Monet *Field of Poppies* print, mostly a soft red-orange that went well with his tan summer sports jacket and brown trousers. She had changed to the outfit she'd worn to the barbecue—he'd never gotten much of a chance to see her in it.

He escorted her to the passenger side of his blue pickup and held the door, his hand lightly on her arm. She was taller, yes, but he didn't seem to mind. With her long legs and high heels, she had no trouble stepping up and inside.

"Thanks," she said. By the time he was around to the driver's side she had her seat belt buckled. "So what was it that kept you working late on a Friday?" she asked. *Ask the questions...stay in control.*

He told her about his day. He'd been out early on county business with a crew, still clearing up after the storm and then, after a late lunch, he'd cleaned up and dressed for the rest of the day in town hall finishing up work there. With a warm glance in her direction, he said, "Save your adventures with Francine for when we've relaxed over something refreshing. I want to give you my full attention."

He smiled. She smiled back. He returned his gaze to the road.

Toria realized he appeared content for the two of them to simply be together in silence as they rode along, but she kept wondering what he was thinking. In his mind, was this a date? Immediately, she scolded herself. Of course he didn't think that. They were simply two people who casually knew one another because they lived in the same town and suddenly had an interest in common. So she should just sit there and keep her mouth shut. Which is what she often did regardless of what she was really thinking. Only this time, it was torture. She felt she should say something, do something. Only what?

The silence stretched. A swift glance at Holly's profile—his good looking profile—showed he was driving along with none of the thoughts that tormented her.

Of course not.

But the silence was driving her crazy.

Without giving it much brain time—which again wasn't typical of her—she shoved a hand into her purse and came up with the business card with the wolf imprint and burst out with:

"Did you ever hear of somebody named Acer Wolfgang?"

Startled, Holly glanced her way. "I did. He wanted to have a meeting with me and some county people but it was canceled." He frowned and looked back at the road. "It was a proposal for a solar farm. The plan would have had to go a lot further before public works was involved. I never understood why I would have been included at that stage of the game." His glance returned to Toria. "Where did you hear of him?"

"I have his business cards. Old ones."

She explained how she and Francine had found the cards in auto repair records for Barry's car and that Barry used the reverse side of cards to make note of wanted repairs. She said, "There are two Wolfgang cards. One has it that he's into investments. The other one is about engineering, planning and land development. That's the important one. It has a note to Barry, signed *AW,* that reads, 'Have you come to a decision about the property?'

She saw that Holly was again looking at the road but his frown remained.

She added, "I could only think he was asking Barry about the old farm property surrounding the Mather house. Francine says it doesn't mean anything because it was written when Barry was still alive. The farmland has all grown up into woodland. It doesn't seem like the best location."

"I agree," Holly said. "Not for a solar farm or a housing tract. Developers prefer open land. The county has many parcels that would be far better suited for either use than the Mather property."

Seeing he was still frowning, Toria ducked her head contritely. "I shouldn't have brought it up. Francine was right. It was several years ago and means nothing now."

"Except that this Wolfgang character is still around."

"Except he canceled," Toria said.

"Except I said I didn't know why I was included in the first place."

"Yes, there was that," Toria said. "It's a puzzle."

Holly grinned. "We'll have to hang in there until we get some more of the pieces."

Toria nodded. *We'll have to hang in,* she mentally echoed, thinking she shouldn't make too much of it. But all the same, she couldn't hold back a smile.

Chapter 41

At the Giraffe's Neck, where Holly had made reservations, he and Toria were led to a small, first floor table that was far from the bar and the clamor from the start-of-the-weekend crowd. A decorative lantern on the table added enough extra light to clearly see the menu in the otherwise candlelit atmosphere.

They ordered drinks, beer for him, iced tea for her (she wanted to keep a clear head) and their meals. They each chose the crab cakes special so they wouldn't be interrupted with menu selections later.

"So," he said with a grin when their orders were taken care of, "suppose you tell me about your day."

Determined not to stammer, she began with how she and Francine thought it out. Since they couldn't trace Grace, they would trace Barry though his car. That led them to Nero and his memories of his conversations with Barry. That took them to the next step, which was actually finding Elizabeth.

"And you decided just like that?" he asked. "You took off for Weehawken, even if you weren't sure where to go?"

His tone held admiration and it rattled her. Quickly, ignoring the tell-tale blotching that she knew had colored her throat and cheeks, she said, "It wasn't just me. It was Francine and me," she explained, trying to take the focus off herself. She hurried on, outlining the events and telling him how they'd finally found a helpful mail carrier. "That's how we learned the right place to go."

At that point, their food arrived.

When the waitress left Toria began describing to Holly the unexpected luxury of the house. "And then, on the third floor, there was an art studio." She gestured as she spoke. "The guide, or caretaker, Jade, her name was, conducted us in. I felt I had walked onto a movie set. There was this heavy old woman in a wheelchair paying no attention to the interruption of two strangers. She acted as if the canvas in front of her was the entire universe. Her work, a cityscape, was spectacular. Jade told us that Elizabeth was obsessed with that one subject. All around the room were other scenes of Manhattan, all done from the view outside Elizabeth's window."

As she spoke, Toria suddenly realized that with both of them seated the advantage of her long legs was gone and she and Holly were eye to eye. Momentarily flustered, she babbled, "Her cityscape painting was spectacular." Realizing she was repeating herself, she hurried on to say something new. "If they were printed on silk they could make one of your wonderful ties."

"Oh?" He glanced down at his necktie and when he looked up, his expression seemed a bit strained and she thought she saw, even in the soft light around their table, a darkening flush along his jaw. Abashed now herself, she realized that for some reason her comment had disconcerted him, which made no sense. He couldn't possibly imagine no one noticed his neckties. What had she said to cause such a reaction?

Hastily, she did what she always hoped people would do when some comment had knocked her all out of shape—she kept talking as if she hadn't noticed anything. "I was tempted to ask Jade if the paintings were available for sale, but it didn't seem appropriate. Jade made another comment that made it sound as if Elizabeth could become unmanageable. Still, I wish you could have been there to see the room where she painted." She bit her tongue to keep from repeating that it was spectacular.

"The entire third floor?" he asked.

"Almost." She could see that Holly seemed to have steadied himself. "There was a hall outside and the opening for the staircase." There had been something else she had wanted to say about the Mathers, but it had flown from her head. "The space was all open with huge windows on three walls."

Holly gave a faint smile. "I live in a single family house converted into apartments. I'm on the second floor and the apartment next to mine is in the part of the house with a stairway to the attic. That tenant is leaving and my landlord knows I'd like to move there."

"For the attic. So you'll have more room?"

"Yes, but not exactly that."

Trying to put it all together, attic, painting, his ties, she tilted her head inquiringly. "A third floor room...something like Elizabeth's?"

"Maybe." His attention was suddenly all on his almost finished plate.

She bit her lip and then ventured, "You think it might be fun to paint?"

He looked at her, and then in a tone slightly different than any she'd heard from him before, he said, as if he expected an argument, "Yes, I do."

"But that's wonderful," she said, meaning it. "It's so totally different from either of your jobs. Of course, I know mostly about your job as mayor. You're so good at it, so many things to keep track of, but still, it must be nerve-wracking to always be dealing with people who mostly don't show up unless they're upset. But if you had space all to yourself for when you wanted to get away from it all and relax ... well, it just sounds great."

His eyes brightened at the enthusiasm in her tone, then he blinked and shook his head. His attention back on his plate again as he gathered the last morsels, he said, "My father always thought I'd be an accountant like him. He couldn't imagine anything else,"

"But it wasn't your thing?"

He shook his head again. "To be honest, I had no true vocation in accounting, my chosen field when dad sent me to college. I'd hoped I'd find inspiration, but I didn't so I decided it was time for a break. I took an outdoor job with the county and that's when Dad quit being mayor and I found myself in his place, wetter behind the ears than those poor animals caught in the flood. But somehow I managed and I soon switched to night school and finished my education with a degree in municipal management and in finance. I also kept my county job and worked my way up to the supervisor position I hold now. One thing though—" He grinned. "The financial education Dad wanted me to have now means I'm a wiz come municipal budget time."

"But you would have rather studied art?"

"I don't know. I took art electives in high school, but I never explored art as a career. I was in the drama club in high school for the fun of painting sets. Fooling around with photography was great, too." With another chuckle, he interjected, "Not that the cell phone pictures of the Mather property I showed you were any kind of an example. But as far as actually studying art—" He looked down at his tie again. "You nailed it—this is my only expression."

"Until you get your garret. I'll buy you some paints and canvas to celebrate."

He stared at her.

She felt he was stunned at all he had revealed. And she had a feeling, no, she *knew*, that he'd said things to her that he'd never said to anyone else, at least not all at once, not like he'd just done with her.

The way they were sitting at the small table, his hand was inches from hers. She had the impulse to reach out and touch him, but she squelched it and instead said,

"We should have dessert."

He blinked as if she had caught him by surprise.

She realized that her words had made the idea of dessert sound like a celebration. She felt silly, but then, with their eyes on level exactly, they each broke into laughter at exactly the same time.

Toria was like a kid on Christmas morning. She had never felt so happy in her life.

CHAPTER 42

On Saturday morning, Francine, accompanied by Iris, arrived at Nero's grandmother's farmhouse to see the found items he had called about. He hauled things from a bag that he'd put on the porch, a smile tickling the corners of his well-shaped lips at the sight of Francine's long-suffering expression. Back in high school she had been the math teacher for general math and business. She had also been his teacher for his first year of algebra. He always had a sneaking suspicion that she didn't much like teaching algebra and that she would have liked him better if his high test scores had been the result of her excellent teaching rather than the simple fact that he was good with numbers and logic.

She had amused him then and she amused him now.

"These were just lying along the road," he said, showing packages of socks and men's underwear, and a woman's scarf, still in the original plastic packages. "I don't know why anyone would throw these away when they're all brand new," he said.

His grandmother, who was currently plucking a chicken that would be Sunday evening's dinner, couldn't bear to see good things go to waste. It was she who had told him to make the call to Francine.

He had warned her that the Auxiliary event wasn't the place for found items, but she had insisted. Grand-mère was a strong-willed woman and he almost always went along. No rule said he couldn't see the fun side in presenting them to Francine.

He lifted a plastic bag and unfastened its plastic tie.

"Somebody must have cleaned out their car and tossed it into a ditch," he said. "Despite the rain, the bag kept it dry. There's a trowel in here, gloves, a hanging planter with the plant still in it and a rug…"

Taking his time, aware of Francine standing silently, stiff with indignation, he pulled out a heavy rug, shook off bits of potting soil that had fallen from the plant pot, folded the rug and set it aside. He pulled out other items, including a comical-looking ceramic ornament and finally, the plant.

"Geraniums are tough," he said in an admiring tone. "Still has flowers and new growth is starting. If you don't want it for your auction, I'll hang it up on our porch for my grandmother to enjoy."

"You're welcome to it along with the other items," Francine said, holding her head high. "Those things might do for a Ladies Group yard sale, but the Auxiliary auction features brand new items. And, although the scarf and socks are new, they aren't our type of thing."

Nero shrugged at her uppity tone and bit his lip, holding back a teasing smile. "Then you don't want to even look at this cosmetics set. The box is nice, but somebody may have started using the makeup."

Francine rolled her eyes.

"Guess none of it fits your bill." He placed the remainder of the items on the table and straightened to his full height. "I'll save them for the Ladies Group yard sale." His gray eyes with their fabulous black lashes twinkled. "Their second sale in October sounds like a super event. Not something everyone's bored with. Something really special."

Before Francine could react to his preposterous praise of the rival group, Iris gripped her arm.

"Look!" Her attention was fixed on the ceramic ornament, a garden elf. "I know what these things are! I typed up a list for a report."

Her eyes big, Iris gazed at Nero. "Hon, You've found some of what was stolen from those houses in Peach Acres!"

CHAPTER 43

Over beers at Sean's Pub. Slim said to Holly "Gotta love it, bud. Gotta love it when things come together."

"So Nero actually found the items that we thought were stolen by kids?"

"Sure did." Slim was in a celebratory mood. "Found it doing his geocaching routine. Iris recognized them. She and Francine came to the police station toting a plastic garbage bag of the stash. Inside the bag was the type of trash from the inside of a car, empty food and drink containers a copy of a charge slip for a video game. We figured we could try to trace that, but then we found the prize, a JRope High School hall pass with a name." (Melton Regional High School was just over the JumpRope town line and the town kids always called it JRope High even though they were only one of several sending districts.)

"One of our kids?"

"Yep. His parents were fit to be tied. He's one sorry young man. He gave up his two pals like that." Slim snapped his fingers. "The items were all from the houses of girls they knew. They did it because of some party, who did or didn't get invited, who knows with kids? After that guy got stabbed, they laid low for a while. When they got up their nerve for the last three tricks, they only took outside stuff....too scared to take anything from inside the houses."

"So what's going to happen to them, police-wise?" Holly knew it was illogical, but when something went wrong in his town, he felt personally responsible.

"Nobody's pressing charges, so we're out of it, thank God. Nice enough kids, but kids, you know? I think they've learned their lessons." Slim drained his beer. "That's not the best part. We've got a lead on the real robbery where the guy was killed."

"Just today?"

"Yep. A Peach Acres resident who lives across the street from the house where the thief got stabbed, was leaving that evening on a trip out west. He noticed a dark car with a New York plate pulling into the driveway of the house across the street. He said he wouldn't have paid attention except there was enough light to see the plate had a number sequence the same as his Jersey plate. He hadn't heard about the crimes because when he's away he doesn't keep in touch with local news. He arrived home last night, heard about the robbery and stabbing and called us this morning."

"So you've got enough to locate the car?"

"We hope. The neighbor says it was a four door black Chevy and we've got New York state plate numbers in sequence. Come Monday, let's hope some work at the county will lead to an address and the killer."

"And if this was the same vehicle that was spotted behind the Mather house, we can hope for progress there as well," Holly said.

"You've got it, bud. It's slow, but it's coming together." Slim raised his hand in a signal to the bartender. "This calls for another round."

CHAPTER 44

The following Monday afternoon Jessi Spellman's doorbell rang. A postal truck was parked outside. She wasn't expecting a package and she wondered why the driver hadn't simply dropped the mail in the box set into the fieldstone pillar along the street. The stone was the same kind that trimmed the front of their house, making their place, she was convinced, the most attractive one on their block. Remembering her pretense of horrific injuries, she paused to slip her scraped arm into a sling before she opened the door.

"Yes?" She made her voice sound weak and wan.

The postman offered a certified letter from an unknown lawyer.

She signed for it without hesitation—she was right handed—it was the left arm in the sling. Why should she be inconvenienced? She was thinking that the lawyer-letter meant a distant relative had died and left her a bundle. It happened to other people, why not her?

Sitting at her kitchen table she pushed away the unwashed plate and cup from her lunch and opened the letter with anticipation.

She squealed in outraged disbelief. She was being sued! The fish who bought her Apple Corners property had found a lawyer to bring suit for some real estate infraction—failure to disclose or some such nonsense about that big hole in the plaster ceiling. That was the trouble with America these days. All rules and regulations that did nothing but hamper and harass legitimate business people.

She narrowed her eyes. She knew who was behind it. Darlene Gage, that Botoxed witch in the JumpRope housing office. It was obvious. The guppy who'd taken the bait for the property would never have had the guts on her own.

There could be no doubt of the plot against her—she was being set up. She could win it, no question, she was too smart to be beaten, but it still made her furious. Somebody sues you, guilty or innocent, you have to pay a lawyer. She wasn't spending her own money. She had cast bread on the water and it was time for her and Arnie to eat cake—or however the saying went.

She grabbed her cell and called Arnie, who was doing deed searches over at the county. "Arnie, you've got to come home as soon as you can."

When she'd fallen off Pastor's office steps and was rushed to the hospital, Arnie had met her there. When he learned there was no oil tank issue and that Pastor was interested in the same property as they were and wanted to go into partnership with them for a restaurant, he'd gone out of his mind with delight.

"You know the property is a super deal if Pastor's on to it," he'd said. "With your smart tumble on his property we won't have to touch our bank account. We can sue Pastor's insurance company and the payoff will finance our end of the restaurant partnership. The rest will be on him. He has the bucks and I know from past conversations he's talked of someday owning a restaurant. He knows I've had restaurant experience. He just never thought of putting it all together until now."

"You're out of your tree," Jessi had spat. "Instead of the insurance windfall being all ours, we're supposed to share with that old goat? I'm the one who got hurt. I'm the one who decides where the money goes." A restaurant might have been Arnie's dream but it had sounded like nothing but work to her. Besides, she hated to share.

But then Arnie started talking about classy celebrity eating places and how he could make the food a terrific attraction and how she could make the place look totally unique. With the right publicity—she could figure out how to do that—they could start luring in important people. With her all gussied up to greet her guests, she would soon be playing patty-cake with all the big names. Gradually, she found herself convinced. A snazzy watering hole would be her ticket to schmoozing with important people and having her true worth shine. She had previously been content to keep Pastor sweating about her slip-and-fall lawsuit, but now, with somebody trying to sue her, it was time to make the move.

When Arnie arrived home, she told him how that rotten inspector, Darlene Gage, must be in cahoots with the Apple Corners bottom-feeder to make trouble. "With somebody after us with a frivolous lawsuit, it's time to visit Pastor and fill our coffers."

They got into the car, her wearing a skirt that showed the big ugly bruise on one leg. She wore her arm sling and cervical collar. She'd decided that back trouble was too incapacitating so she had relocated the injury to her neck. The collar had come from the hospital and she had a chiropractor lined up who would work with her lawyer in her lawsuit against Pastor.

"As soon as he discovered you were looking at property that he thought was interesting too, he should have come to us," Jessi said as they rode along. "He should have been open and above board with his idea of a partnership. If he had, I might have gone for it. But nooooo, not him. It was only luck that I went to him for information and found him out. The old sneak." She adjusted the sling so she could fold her arms comfortably. "I can't tell you how much I despise deceptive people."

They were soon in Melton and approaching Pastor's real estate office. Noting that the broken awning had been repaired and the railing made secure—too late, darling—Jessi entered the reception area.

Laddy, Pastor's thuggish twenty-year-old son sat behind the desk. Pastor's only child and the son of his fourth wife, Laddy did chores for his dad, mowing lawns and handyman work for properties that were getting ready to be sold. He'd probably been the one who'd finally fixed the railing. His shaved head displayed a tattooed purple dragon flapping across his crown. Would that ink nightmare fly off with the top of his skull? Would a brain be revealed? Stay tuned. Like his father,

Laddy had a short neck, but overdeveloped muscles from working with weights made it appear even shorter.

"Your dad around?" she demanded.

He gestured toward the office. "He's busy making phone calls."

"Well he can take a call in person from me," she snapped and sailed on by.

"Hey!" Laddy bellowed, but she kept going, dragging Arnie along as she shoved the office door open and moved inside.

The real estate broker was on the phone, but he hung up when he saw his visitors.

"Well," he said.

"Well indeed." Jessi plopped herself down in a chair. Arnie, not certain of his role, remained standing. She said, "I've come to make a deal."

Pastor's eyebrows rose. "I thought you would have had me served papers by now. Such a horrible accident. I came out just in time to see your performance. I would have applauded but it might have been misunderstood."

"Misunderstood by at least ten witnesses. It's no accident that the word 'injury' has the word 'jury' in it. You don't stand a chance."

Doing his best to look smug and unconcerned, he clasped his hands across his puffy stomach. A frog on his lily pad. "Thus, your offer to deal?"

Her laugh was mean. "Thus my offer." She launched into the scheme in which his insurance company payoff would be their financial contribution to the proposed restaurant deal and everything else would be on Pastor's dime.

"Hold on," he objected. "You're not getting away with that. You told me that you and Arnie had planned to acquire the property and flip it when the housing development got under way. I keep tabs on real estate you've recently sold. You can afford to pay for your own share."

Jessi grinned. "Forget about that, boyo. Our money is off the table. You want Arnie's ability as chef and my ability to turn those old buildings into a showplace. That's our contribution to this equal partnership. If you can't go along with it, I'll sue you for enough to put you out of business."

She stood and gestured for Arnie to get moving. "Make up your mind by Sunday, Pastor. That even gives you time to pray about it. Considering that I suffered a ghastly injury, I'm being more than fair."

With Arnie in tow, she breezed from his office and into the reception room where Laddy stood glowering.

"You threatened my Dad," he accused, bunching his shoulders as if ready to take a swing.

Not answering, Jessi swept on past and through the outer door and down the steps.

Feeling a sudden and uneasy chill, she spun about when she reached the pavement. Laddy stood on the landing outside the door, his shaven tattooed head inclined toward her as if he imagined himself an avenger in a video game, shooting dragon flames.

She sneered and eye-tossed a flame back at him and then continued to the car. Realizing she was forgetting to limp, she corrected the situation, and made a display of needing Arnie's help to go the rest of the distance.

Waiting for Arnie to come around to the driver's side, she thought of how generous she had been. Pastor could have been socked with a lawsuit for millions. Instead, she had made settlement offer of a far more reasonable sum. Now she could turn her mind to getting even with Darlene Gage. That woman had stood in her way too many times. Jessi hadn't figured out yet how she'd do it, but she knew vengeance would be sweet.

Arnie, always awestruck with desire when he saw her in full-force action, would have been happy to be bedroom bound to celebrate the gauntlet she'd flung down before Pastor, but she wanted to hold off and enjoy the anticipation. Arnie might not have looked like much to other people, but she knew what a man he could be. She decided they should go a club in Trenton that she knew would be lively even on a Monday night. No one there would know them, no one would know how banged up she was supposed to be. They could drink and dance and imagine the grand moment when Pastor gave in to them, and then, they could finish the splendid evening with a grand finale at home.

CHAPTER 45

It was after a wonderful night at the Trenton club when the Spellmans neared their house. Jessi reached a mischievous hand across to Arnie that had him whimpering in anticipation.

"Kitten, Kitten ...." he gasped as he slowed, preparing to turn to the left into their driveway up ahead.

There was a sudden sound of a furiously accelerating motor off to their right. Jessi turned just as a car darted out from a side street and roared in their direction.

Jessi screamed. Arnie instinctively yanked the wheel, swerving away from the roadway. The other vehicle, still speeding, just missed sideswiping the Spellman passenger side door. With tires screeching, the other car careened on down the road.

With no time to recalculate, Arnie was helpless to prevent their vehicle from jumping the curb and smashing into their fieldstone mailbox pillar, throwing both him and Jessi forward and exploding their airbags.

"What in the hell was that?" he cried when the airbags sagged away from his face. His eyes stung and his nose was bleeding.

"It was Laddy!" Jessi cried in a strangled voice. She'd seen his stupid, empty bullet head in the flashing second as he zoomed his vehicle away. He must have been lying in wait for them for hours, the idiot. Because of how she'd been sitting close to Arnie, she'd not only gotten socked on her scraped arm when she was thrown against him, she'd gotten smacked on her good arm by the airbag. Her head got a knock too. Her ears rang.

"Call 911," she ordered, gasping for breath. Her arms felt too numb to grab her cell out of her purse. "Don't say anything except that there's been an accident. Don't give any names except ours!"

Waiting for the police gave Jessi time to think.

How could she use what happened to best advantage?

She had no doubt that Laddy had been acting on his own. This kind of a scare attack was not Pastor's style. Could she use it to put more pressure on him?

O fficers Donny DeGarmo and a rookie came rolling up in the JumpRope Township police vehicle in answer to the call.

Jessi, still inside the Spellman vehicle, sat sideways in the passenger seat, her feet on the road. Her one ear still felt funny. She was angry about that. Angry about the whole stupid attack. Who did Laddy think he was, going after her? She'd like to carve him a new tattoo—"Loser" in scraggly letter across his moronic forehead.

Arnie had helped her return her arm to the sling. And he'd carefully fitted on her cervical collar. She was all set and charged to go, sobbing theatrically into her hands when the uniformed policemen came up.

"Sir," said Donny, to Arnie. "The ambulance is on the way."

"I'm all right." Arnie held a handkerchief to his bleeding nose. "It's my wife."

Donny bent down to Jessi. "Ma'am, take it easy now. Emergency care will be here in a minute." The lights from the police car were turning, slashing red lights across Donny's face. Lights were on in several nearby houses and neighbors were peeking out, drawn by the commotion. The rookie had moved to circle the vehicle, inspecting for damage. From a distance came the sound of an emergency siren.

"Thank you, Officer." Jessi gasped between sobs. "It was so horrible.

I've recently suffered a bad accident, and now this! The car…it came at us out of nowhere! It almost smashed into us on my side. It was deliberate. I could have been killed."

"Sir?" Donny directed his attention to Arnie. "Are you aware of the identity of the perpetrator?"

Whatever Arnie might have said, Jessi gave him no opportunity.

"Oh, course he didn't," she interrupted with a sharp wail. "It didn't happen on his side of the car! I saw the driver and there's no mistake. The person who tried to run us down and kill me was the town housing inspector, Darlene Gage."

CHAPTER 46

It was past 8 o'clock the next morning. Slim sat in a comfortable slump in his office settled with a cup of extra sweet coffee. He was reading the report on the Spellman accident that Donny had turned in before going off duty. As reported, shortly after one in the morning, a legally sober Arnie Spellman crashed his Honda Accord into his own fieldstone mailbox. Jessi, who accompanied him, claimed Darlene Gage had deliberately run them off the road. There were no witnesses. Donny went to Darlene's, found her car engine slightly warm and knocked on her door. Wearing robe and slippers, she said she had come home after a late meeting and had been nowhere near the Spellman home.

No way did Slim believe Jessi's accusation but he cracked a smile as he imagined Darlene's foul mood at being accused and questioned. A knock on the frame of his open office door made him glance up. Ed Lakewood, an officer Slim always felt able to depend upon, stood looking troubled as he announced, "Mrs. Spellman's here and Donny's with her."

"What?" Slim dropped the report. "Donny should be home asleep."

"Mrs. Spellman called him to meet her here," Ed said. "She's filing charges, accusing Mrs. Gage of attempted murder. She says Donny is her witness."

Slim was on his feet. He didn't know what nonsense this was but he sure in hell was finding out. He stormed out to the police window in the corridor.

He found Jessi and Donny standing together on the outside of the window. The police clerk had handed a citizen complaint form to Jessi. She stood with a pen in one little hand and a sweet little smile that might have worked had Slim not caught the malicious glint in her eyes when she saw him. Donny saw Slim as well and gave rise to a flush that risked turning the roots of his orange-red hair to tinder.

"Officer!" Slim barked. "In my office!"

H olly was in his own office in town hall. He had papers to read and sign and then he was off to the county, but what he'd been doing instead was thinking about his dinner with Toria. Things she said, things he said. She seemed shy, but in other ways, she seemed confident. He couldn't figure her out. What he did figure was that he was falling for her. Where that would go, he had no idea. So much of life was figuring things out. He couldn't remember it ever being so interesting.

He looked up as Slim burst in. Throwing himself into Holly's visitor's chair, Slim growled, "Someday I'm going to tear Donny DeGarmo's head straight off his shoulders."

Holly said, "This about the Spellmans' smashed car?"

Slim narrowed his eyes. "What do you know about it?"

"Francine called me. She said that Bob towed the car. The Spellmans claimed that Darlene had wrecked it trying to murder Jessi. Jessi's latest stunt, of course. Francine called my office to see how Darlene was doing because she didn't answer her work phone. I said she had an early morning inspection and hadn't come in yet."

Holly smoothed his tie. "Oh, and Iris went on an errand that took her to your end of the building. She said it looked as if Donny was in hot water with you."

"Damn right," Slim said. "That lamebrain must have gotten his hair color from being slugged with a copper pot when he was a baby. What a numskull."

"He was the officer at Jessi's accident?"

"Yeah." Slim reached for one of the candies Holly kept in a bowl on his desk. "At the scene, Jessi told Donny that Darlene was out to get her. Instead of turning a deaf ear, the moron sympathized and told her stuff. She showed up this morning to file charges against Darlene for making terroristic threats. She expects Donny to testify on her behalf."

Holly looked appalled. "What did Donny say to her?"

"He told Jessi he heard Darlene say she wanted to wrap her hands around Jessi's neck and throttle her, probably a direct quote if I know Donny. He also told her that Darlene said she wished she could arrange for Jessi's headstone. Donny told me you were present on both occasions. Fortunately he didn't blab that to Jessi or she'd call you as a second witness."

Holly shook his head in disbelief. "Darlene was blowing off steam. Donny heard it and remarked something about dangerous words leading to dangerous actions, but why would he say anything to Jessi? Doesn't he think?"

"Donny? Hell no, he's got no judgment. Grew up in town, passed all the academy requirements…I can't bounce him, but times like this, I'd like to." Slim made a sound of disgust. "Maybe rig up a job for him in Rancine."

"They'd probably promote him to chief."

Finally relaxing, Slim laughed. "That might work. He's good with record keeping and it would keep him off the streets. Anyway, speaking of Rancine, if Jessi persists and the charges make it to court it will probably be heard before the Rancine judge. Darlene's a town employee and works with our judge—it would be conflict of interest for him to hear the case."

"Can't Darlene prove she didn't do it?"

"She can prove she was at a late committee meeting but not that she wasn't near Jessi's street afterwards. By the same token, Jessi can't prove she actually saw Darlene. The Rancine judge is an okay guy. Best scenario, he'll see it as two women scrapping and send it to mediation."

"Still not good," Holly said. "It would be ruled that the two of them have to stay away from one another for a specified period. Darlene won't be permitted to inspect Jessi's rentals if she has a change of tenant or she wants to flip a property, which she's always doing. The Rancine inspector, who Darlene already despises, will have to come over. With us paying for his services."

Slim took another candy. "Time for some good news. Before this mess with Donny, I received word from the county. The New York State tag belonged to a stolen car that links to the Peach Acres robbery and the stabbing death of the New York criminal. It also ties in with the car with the New York plates a witness saw near the Mather house the night Barry's body was discovered."

"Discovered because somebody broke in to steal stuff," Holly said.

"Right. Plus, the Brooklyn police recovered pawnshop items that match the descriptions of what was taken from Peach Acres the night of the stabbing, plus the silver Francine listed as missing from the Mather house."

"Making it the same thieves," Holly said. "Is there a lead to the criminals?"

"Here's where it gets hinky," Slim said. "When a pawn shop accepts stolen goods and it's confiscated, they're out the money given the thief in exchange. In this case, Brooklyn learned that in addition to the standard stolen goods update, the shop owner had received a private alert—it was in his records, although he claimed he'd never seen it. A mystery guy put out the word that if silver of a certain description was pawned, he was to be notified. Brooklyn thinks that when the goods came in, the shop owner notified this private contact as well as them. They suspect the shop owner knew he'd be reimbursed when he accepted the items, but he's playing dumb because it's illegal. He claims he never saw the thieves before and his security video was recorded over. That leaves no lead to the thieves or the killer."

Holly frowned. "This mystery guy wanted the stolen items recovered, but didn't want the thieves caught?"

"It seems so, and here's what I'm thinking," Slim said. "Remember the theory that somebody else was involved back when Barry Mather died and Grace Mather went missing?"

"Sure," Holly said. "That after Barry's death and if Grace didn't drive, she might have either gone with or been taken by a third person."

"I think we're finally getting a line on him," Slim said.

"I can guess who." Holly said. He told Slim about what Nero had remembered and about Francine and Toria going to Weehawken. "They learned that Barry and Grace were connected to Elizabeth Mather and the family—they *weren't* squatters." He said the last part with a smile.

"Yeah, so I was wrong," Slim said, breezing it off.

"So the corporation lawyer was also wrong when he claimed no knowledge of Barry and Grace. I can't figure out the motive, but could the lawyer be the third person we've speculated about?"

"Logical," Slim said, "but here's a new direction. The Brooklyn P\p olice have suspicions about a businessman in connection with the thefts. Brooklyn doesn't have enough facts yet, but they've got a name—Acer Wolfgang."

CHAPTER 47

Home from a two-day conference where he represented an advocacy group for endangered children—he was the chairman of the board—Acer Wolfgang was having a rare easy morning at his Chelsea penthouse. Before him was a brunch he had prepared himself from his seldom used kitchen: link sausages and pancakes dripping with butter and maple syrup. He thought of how his family would have enjoyed such a treat when he'd been a child. He did not often allow such thoughts. There was nothing one could do to change the past—he was too pragmatic to imagine one could do anything with the past except learn from it.

Beginning to eat, he wished, not for the first time, that he had someone with whom to share such private moments, someone who he could relax with and enjoy what wealth had to offer. A reflective smile brightened his eyes. He had long ago decided he would live to be one hundred, and now, at age fifty, he tended to cross off the years like a vacationer with a return ticket date looming: forty-nine years left to enjoy this glorious world before stepping off into the great unknown. It amused him, this illusion that one could make plans and play dice with fate.

His smile faded. It was this present world that had a problem for him to deal with. Specifically, adorable old Auntie. Acer had been traveling that summer and had only recently caught up with the latest on the JumpRope disasters in the *Melton Monitor*. They had Auntie's guaranteed-to-go-wrong stamp all over them. He didn't understand what she had done or why—she had never discussed any of it with him. However, Acer was sure of her involvement when he learned that the police were on the lookout for sterling flatware possibly stolen from the Mather house, a distinctive Reed & Barton fruit design.

His sources had also informed him there was suspicion that the thieves' vehicle bore a New York State plate. In addition, the stabbed thief at the scene of the Peach Acres break-in was also from New York State as was the vehicle that had been sighted on that property. It seemed too much of a coincidence that different sets of criminals from New York State were suddenly interested in JumpRope.

While Acer didn't understand the purpose, he couldn't shake the suspicion of Auntie's involvement. He therefore sent out queries, answered when a cooperative pawn shop owner informed him that a pair of low-level thieves had appeared with Reed & Barton sterling flatware and an old coin collection that matched a description of that stolen from the Peach Acres break-in. In addition, the pawn shop owner overheard the thieves' reference to one old house they'd robbed—a place where the only guard was a dried-up stiff on the stairs.

Acer had recoiled from the callous description of what could only have been the late Barry Mather, but it convinced him that Auntie had gotten herself into a serious situation. She was dear to him—the woman who had rescued him as a youngster from the street. He was interested in her JumpRope property, yes, but she herself was far more important. He wished that young Vivian, who was like a niece to him although they were not related by blood, had been at home. As smart as she was beautiful, Vivian would have been helpful in speaking to Auntie. However, her job had once again taken her on a worldwide jaunt.

Even though he was in the dark about motive Acer took matters into his capable hands. Speedily, he had made a beneficial arrangement with the shop owner that would result in protecting Auntie—if she would cooperate. Acer was convinced that everything she had done in connection with the JumpRope debacle, as misguided as it might have been, was to protect a loved one.

There was only one person that could be.

Acer took heart from it.

Auntie must be protecting Barry's beloved sister, Grace.

On the way to his county job, Holly thought more about Acer Wolfgang. How he'd almost met the man and that Toria had found his business cards with Barry Mather's car repair records at Bob's garage. Cards from four years ago, but, yes, the man was still in the picture. That is, if the Brooklyn police were right, and they probably were. Holly had work that would take him out of the office, but he thought of asking his secretary to do a quick run on Wolfgang's name on the Internet but then she needed to leave early to run errands with her elderly father, so he let the matter be. Slim and the Brooklyn police would do a better job of finding information anyway.

At the end of the day he was back in his county office and getting ready to leave when his secretary surprised him by showing up again.

"Glad I caught you," she said with a giggle. "I couldn't resist returning to give you the latest issue of the *JumpRope Jive*. One of the places I took my dad had fresh copies—they just came out today."

She dropped a copy on his desk and fled with yet another giggle.

Bemused by his usually staid secretary's manner, Holly picked up the newsletter. So, he thought, after a hiatus of nearly six months, the four pages of Pilar Fanshawe's publication had popped up like a long-awaited jack-in-the-box.

He figured most of the *Jive* was written ahead of time, yet wasn't complete until Pilar had enough hot gossip for her Madam Jive's *News and Noose* section. Then it was off to the instant copy center and word to her loyal minions who distributed copies everywhere that JumpRope residents gathered, including the churches.

Holly was willing to bet that when he and Toria had seen Pilar and her son at Teddy's restaurant they were preparing the final pages of the issue he now held in his hands.

The front page contained decorating tips from Pilar and inside was another tedious scene from a work in progress by her son, Alexander, a would-be playwright. The title was "Windows of Paris" or *Fenêtres La Ville Lumière,* an overblown tale of a young man finding himself in the City of Light in the 1920s. Idly wondering if the insufferable Alexander had ever graduated from his university, Holly's gaze moved down the page to a rehash of the Mather house mystery, starting with the fallen tree and the desecrated lilacs and moving to the house being broken into and the gruesome discovery of Barry's remains. The article was followed by questions:

> **Who were the thieves and where are the stolen items?**
> **Under what circumstances did Barry shuffle off this mortal coil? Is Barry's missing sister dead or alive? Either way, where is Grace Mather? And what is the JumpRope Police Department doing to answer these questions?**

Usual *Jive* fare, Holly thought, and not seriously harmful, although it would annoy Slim. He imagined that the reading public would next poke their eagerly twitching noses into the *News and Noose.* Holly found Pilar's editorial obligation to social happenings submitted since the last issue: Eastertide events, June weddings and vacations tidbits. He imagined readers, except those whose names were printed, would skip on to Madam Jive's captivating morsels on the back page, because that's exactly what he was doing. There, he found:

> **Everything's not so peachy in Peach Acres.**
> **What dashing curly-haired hero with a French heritage surname single-handedly solved the mystery of the Peach**

Acres thefts? Madam Jive is so proud to be a Francophile. And what JRope football star and his buddies are currently cooling their heels after their light-fingered pranks were uncovered?

The French heritage mention seemed to confirm gossip he'd heard about Pilar and Nero Gibeau. Every once in a while, Pilar, who had been widowed young when her husband drowned, would take romantic interest in some man who was in difficulty because of some tragedy or sorrow. A form of mutual comfort, although in this case, Nero was only a few years older than Pilar's son, Alexander. Maybe JumpRope was too small for a million stories, Holly thought with a tolerant smile, but it had at least one story for every resident.

He then read:

Then there's the Peach Acres stabbing. Far more serious indeed. What are the police doing about that?

Holly didn't care for the reminder about the stabbing and more implied police criticism. His gaze dropped to the next to last item and he gasped aloud.

Charges have been filed by a certain green-eyed spitfire against a certain town official. Guess who will be her star witness? None other than a certain redheaded officer of the law.

Holly shook his head, dismayed. The incident with Jessi and Donny—how had Pilar found out so fast? Then he remembered that Pilar and Jessi sometimes put their heads together to no good purpose. He bet Jessi couldn't wait to tell Pilar what she'd cooked up against Darlene. At least there was no mention of terroristic threats.

Holly moved to the last item and it jangled his nerves like an electric buzzer.

Madam Jive recently paused for a repast at TBear's Bar and Grill where she was inspired to pen the following ditty—
> **The Mayor and the Librarian up in a tree**
> **K—I—S—S—I—N—G**
> **Were they really?**
> **No, but it looked as if they might like to.**

Stunned, Holly sat back in his chair. Pilar had written about him and Toria! There it was in black and white, but he read it the second time just to make sure. Had Toria already seen it? He glanced at the clock and figured she was already home. Yes, she'd had time to see it. So had everyone in town. Lord! As shy as Toria was, he could only imagine how embarrassed she must feel. Should he call her? Or would that be making too much of it?

The only thing Pilar had seen was the two of them having dinner. Had it looked to her as if he had wanted more?

That was the real trouble—he had!

His reaction to the *News and Noose* jibe assured him of just how hard he had fallen for quiet Toria Dahlgaard. He remembered his first lukewarm impression—nothing much to see and easy to forget. How that had changed! Changed for him, but probably not for her. The first time they had gone out to eat together, he'd learned she seemed overly impressed because he was mayor. Voting for him was just habit for a lot of residents, he thought, first his dad, now him. Not that he didn't make every effort to deserve the public trust. Which was why the rumors about him playing sneaky property games nagged like a sore tooth whenever he thought about it. It had died down except for the times when Reds Burke would give him a jab about it. The older Reds became, the wider his streak of nastiness. Holly hoped he'd never get like that. Then he remembered how he'd gibbered non-stop about the art stuff to Toria. What had possessed him? He wouldn't get nasty, he decided. He'd become doddering, like one of the Old Geezers, a self-named club of old men who hung on the bench in front of Krupple's Diner, remembering times gone by. Now that Toria had gotten to know him better, the initial shine she'd seen on him was no doubt wearing thin.

He grabbed his truck keys. Enough empty wondering what she thought about what was printed in the *Jive*. A phone call wouldn't tell him how she really felt. They needed to be face to face. He would go to her house and find out.

CHAPTER 49

Toria was looking forward to seeing Holly again. She'd been at work that day when she remembered what it was she wanted to tell him, which was the odd thing about Elizabeth Mather's setup. She'd also made a discovery during her lunchtime at the computer. It went through her mind to call him, but she decided to wait until after she got home.

In the late afternoon when she reached her tiny house on a street of similar houses constructed way back in the 1950s, and found a rolled copy of the *JumpRope Jive* stuck in her door handle. Courtesy of one of the runners who got such a kick out of distributing the gossip sheet.

Inside, she saw the blinking light on the portable phone on the kitchen counter. Putting down her purse and the copy of the *Jive* she pressed the buttons to retrieve her messages. There were two of them, both from friends asking her if she'd read the item on the back page of the *Noose* section. Leaning against the counter she flipped the publication and saw what they'd been talking about. Her mouth dropped open.

Pilar had written about her and Holly!

She tried to calm down. It was silly, but that was Pilar. A ridiculous rhyme, making a big deal out of nothing.

She and Holly had simply been having dinner. Pilar must have been desperate for copy to have dreamed that one up.

She wondered if Holly had seen it yet. Probably not. She was sure he would have called her if he had. The *Jive* was only distributed in JumpRope. Nobody saw it over at the county buildings until somebody brought it in the next day. But wouldn't somebody have called him over at the county to tell him he was in the news? People had sure called **her** fast enough.

So why hadn't he called? It seemed only right that he would.

She started feeling upset. Her conclusion was that he had known about it but it had struck him differently than it had her. Being the mayor and all, he must have been offended. Toria's first impulse was to blame herself. There had been something in her manner to inspire Pilar's comment. Those red shoes, maybe acting flirty. Had she?

She told herself she hadn't done anything wrong and she wasn't going to think that she had. And if Holly thought differently, the heck with him. And then, right on top of it, without giving herself another moment to think, she followed through on the impulse to call his cell.

She heard his voice, and said, "I have something to tell you."

He heard her voice, and said, "I'm leaving for your house."

"Yes. Do you know where I—" She shook her head. "Of course, you know where I live," she said. "After all, you *are* the mayor."

A bit of sharpness in her tone puzzled him and it showed when he answered in confusion, "Right."

She noticed that he had sounded different. Ha, she thought. Big shot mayor *had* been offended. Well, his problem, not hers. When he arrived, she wouldn't even mention the *Jive*. She would be cool about it. What she had to say to him had nothing to do with stupid gossip. All she had to say was that she'd come up with more thoughts after her visit to Weehawken. And that was all she had to say to Mr. Bighead, the mayor.

But when he arrived at her front door, what she burst out with was, "I thought we would laugh about it."

Inside now, he stared at her blankly. "What?"

"About that stupid thing Pilar wrote about us in the *Jive*. Don't say you didn't see it."

"I did, but—"

"I thought so." *But had he called her? Oh, no. Not him!* She crossed her arms. "What she wrote was so ridiculous. I thought you would call me and we could laugh about it."

She could feel the blotches on her face getting worse and worse, like she had giant hives and her hair was like the Bride of Frankenstein's. Why hadn't she at least tried to fix it? The way she looked, the way she always looked.

No wonder he hadn't called.

"But why should you call me?" she said aloud, her voice rising. "I get it. It just hadn't meant anything. And why should it? All we were doing was having dinner. And then some stupid person writes some stupid thing...." She spread her arms. "Why should anybody... anybody pay any attention? I get it. It was so stupid, so stupid...."

She was going to cry and she didn't even know why.

But then somehow his arms had slipped inside her open arms and around her back and he was pressing her close up against him. And she was hugging him, and crying, her hot, red face buried into the crook of his neck.

And he was murmuring, "There...it's okay, it's okay," and he was thinking how adorable she was, and how he'd had her all wrong, and what a jerk he'd been not to call. No wonder she'd been upset.

She felt him shift and before she knew what was going on, one of his arms was under her knees and he was picking her up as if she weighed nothing and then he was seated in the big overstuffed easy chair by the door and she was nestled on his lap, her head against his chest and he was still murmuring things like, "There, there...it's okay...."

She took a gulping breath and put a hand to her nose, which was running, but then his hand was there with his handkerchief, like he was a magician or something.

With a strangled, gulping laugh, his handkerchief clutched in her hand, she said, "You really know how to sweep a girl off her feet."

Darling girl, was what he was thinking, but what he said, was, "A man of many talents."

"I didn't know you were so strong."

"I'm deceptive."

"In a nice way, I think."

"I've had you fooled."

Leaning against his chest she could feel as well as hear his soft chuckle.

She was thinking that once she was sure she had taken proper care of her nose, if she should lift her face a little, then his face would be right there....

And he was thinking that if he gave a little nudge under her chin and she lifted her face a little it would be no task at all to find her lips with his....

CHAPTER 50

It was after a great many kisses that Toria whispered, "If Pilar could see us now, I wonder what she would say?"

"That she was right all along?"

Toria gave Holly a look. "Did I hear a question in your voice?"

He caught her smile and saw that she was teasing. "Let me run that by you again," he said softly. "If Pilar could see us now she would know for sure she'd been right all along about the mayor and the librarian ... K-I-S-S ..." His punctuation of each letter with a kiss got lost in the middle with a really long kiss.

Toria finally drew back and said really fast, "I-N-G," and gave Holly three more quick kisses. They laughed and then rested in each other's arms for a long and lovely time.

It was later and they were seated at her little kitchen table, both pleased, yet both somehow a little shy in a way that was exciting and fun, as if they had just discovered one another and were starting out all over again, which was just about the truth. She made tea and served it and then sitting down again she said, "There's several things I wanted to tell you, but one is about my visit with Francine to Weehawken and a thought that escaped me until earlier today."

"Escaped you, huh," said Holly with a smile, reaching to smooth her fly-away hair, the texture like gossamer, fairy-princess hair.

"You're not paying attention," she chided. Taking his hand, she put it on the table, but kept a hold on it. She could feel his strength—she felt a thrill just touching his hand.

"Now listen," she said firmly, the admonishment as much as for herself as to him. "The whole set up with Elizabeth being in a retirement home for destitute artists doesn't make sense. I thought back to the property here in town. A bank pays the taxes on the Mather house and on all the property that was once the family farmland. Plus, a lawyer speaks on behalf of the principals for the Mather Corporation, which is Elizabeth and that Vivian person. So how can Elizabeth be destitute?"

Holly forced himself to pay attention to something other than Toria. "Maybe it has to do with medical needs. The costs can be horrendous. If she's demented and unable to care for herself, funds might have been shifted out of her name because of that."

"Logical, only they weren't shifted. Elizabeth's name is on the corporation papers, right? I'm wondering about something. Do you remember how Grace looked?"

"I saw her with Barry...saw her enough to recognize her."

"Describe her," she said.

Puzzled, he complied. "She had black hair pulled back tight in a knot. And she was big, no, actually, she was fat."

"That's the same as Elizabeth," Toria said. "Only her hair isn't black, it's gray and thin. Francine said she saw a resemblance to Grace. Elizabeth wears glasses. Did Grace?"

"Yes, big thick ones." Holly's face went still. "Are you thinking that the person you saw might really be Grace?"

"I think I am. Francine said Grace and Barry were about her age. So now she would be early sixties?"

"Early to mid, I guess."

"Elizabeth looks older," Toria said, "but sickness ages a person and maybe changed her hair. Suppose Grace went bonkers and killed her brother? The family—I guess that's Elizabeth and Vivian—may be hiding her. They claim it's Elizabeth in the nursing home when it's really Grace, an unhinged murderer."

Thoughtfully, Holly said, "That may tie in with something I learned from Slim earlier today."

He told Toria about the pawnbroker. "The New York mystery man who was on the lookout for the stolen Mather silver was the developer whose cards you found—Acer Wolfgang."

Toria's eyes lit up. "That's another thing I wanted to tell you. I looked him up on the Internet."

"Ahead of me, huh?"

"Yes, so watch it." She bit back a giggle. "If you're after his past, he's a mystery man all right, but not in recent years."

"Slim said he's a wealthy society guy."

"That and more. He has several companies and serves on various boards. His photos show up in classy magazines—*Vogue, Architectural Digest, Vanity Fair*—mostly when he's attending charity functions. Then, he's with an opera singer in Rome, another with him on his corporation's private island, and several at various soirées—"

"Soirées? Francine, eat your heart out."

Toria laughed. "Stop! This is important. There were photos of him with a gorgeous young brunette and her name is Vivian Mather."

"Whoa! Then in addition to having an interest in the Mather land, he's in with the family."

"Exactly. And if Elizabeth is actually Grace, I bet he knows all about it. And if you saw her, you'd know for sure yourself."

"Like seeing her in Weehawken?" Holly said. "I'm free on Saturday." And if he hadn't been, he'd find a way to arrange it.

Toria nodded, feeling excited. *Off on an adventure,* like Mar-see-ah said. "A bunch of us will help Francine Saturday morning with her Auxiliary banquet and auction preparations and then I'll be ready to go."

"A deal," he said. He'd be Watson to her Sherlock. A little squiggle of male vanity wormed through. Shouldn't it be the other way around? Then he grinned to himself. It made no difference—what mattered was they were in it together.

CHAPTER 51

On Saturday morning, with August finally beginning, Toria helped with preparations for the auxiliary events, Holly went along to lend a hand. In the glow of their new-found relationship, he didn't want to have her out of his sight. The evening before, after having made their decisions about Weehawken, they had ordered pizza and then had just talked. He couldn't remember all the things they had said to one another and he hadn't wanted the evening to end. Toria, however, wasn't a girl to ask him to stay the night so soon—but that was okay with him. Everything about Toria was okay with him.

The spacious banquet hall at Teddy's was a busy place. The Auxiliary Banquet and Penny Auction was a week away. Since Teddy had nothing scheduled for the banquet space beforehand, he'd told the ladies they could start decorating. Members of the Civic Club worked with the Auxiliary members. Even though the groups tried to best one another, they cooperated on big events. The rivalry was mostly for fun—even Francine would agree to that. (Mostly she would.)

Toria recalled that at the previous year's banquet and auction Holly had been accompanied by a little blonde with spectacular curves displayed in a low-cut silvery dress. Toria wondered if he was already fixed up with someone this year. What had happened between them was so sudden—he would already have a commitment. Not wanting to think about it, she moved to where people were either bringing in items for the auction, or declaring items they would bring on auction day so that the women running the tables would know what to expect.

Holly greeted Daisy from Daisy's Doughnuts and Cakes and said to Toria, "If Daisy's auctioning her éclairs, I might make a bid ahead of time."

"No bidding until the big night," Toria said. "Daisy's donations are gift certificates for pastries throughout the year. Your stepmother, who isn't in either woman's group, will do something similar."

"Peggy's chocolate cake will top everything else. It's wonderful," Holly said.

Toria smiled at his affection for his stepmother. Then she said, "There's Nero and his grandmother. She bakes, too. Guess she had to do the driving." (Nero's god-only-knew-how-old-she-was-grandmother was the chauffeur since Nero had gotten nabbed for driving under the influence.) "And there's Shirley DeGarmo and Ruth Wilson. If they do what they've done in the past, they'll each contribute baskets of homemade goodies, one of candy and one of cookies. They'll bring them in on the day of the event so the items will be fresh."

Drawing near, Shirley said, "Mr. Mayor?" Every gray curl on her head was arrayed and sprayed into perfect, yet unmovable, sausage shapes. She gave an apologetic glance to Toria. "If I may speak privately to the mayor for a moment?"

Ruth, who apparently knew Shirley's plan, was already hanging back and chatting with Nero's grandmother.

"Go right ahead," Toria said, moving over to assist Iris Roundtree in the removal of crepe-paper streamers from their store packaging. The banquet's theme that year was a luau and the colors were pink, yellow and green. There would be leis for each guest and strings of silk tropical flowers running down the middle of each table. Still talking together, Ruth and Nero's grandmother joined Toria and Iris, Ruth's brown eyes penetrating as she carefully removed staples from the flower packages. Iris carried unwrapped streamers and blossom strings over to where Nero and Holly and several other men, under Francine's strident directions, were getting stepladders ready to drape the streamers from hangers installed for that purpose. Colonel McDuff trailed Iris everywhere, looking splendid and important, but doing nothing much. Francine issued the orders to everyone, far more the military presence.

After a light lunch at Teddy's News/Booze room, Toria and Holly took off in his truck for Weehawken. If anyone had noticed that they were a couple (of course it was noticed—this was a small town for heaven's sake!) nobody said anything, at least not within their hearing.

Toria, to her surprise, found she didn't care. Let them talk! After dreaming of Holly for so long, but almost afraid to admit it even to herself, they were at last together. Smiling at nothing and everything, she gazed out the truck window. It was a beautiful day, the air hot, but not muggy, wonderfully clear for August. The trees lining the highway were richly full and green and real, a pleasant change from the paper palm trees she'd been dealing with that morning.

They were on the Jersey Turnpike when she said, "I overheard Ruth telling Nero's grandmother that she's worried about Shirley's high blood pressure, but it's Ruth who looks like the fragile one."

"Yes, she's so thin that people wonder if she ever samples any of her own candy. She and Shirley bring in their treats to town hall. There's a rumor that the candy is enchanted. You can eat all you want without calories. Don't know who started it, but everybody's happy to fall for it."

Toria said, "Shirley had quite a chat with you."

"She wanted to apologize in case her son, Donny, offended anyone."

Toria winced. "Officer Letter of the Law, or whatever Pilar called him in the *Noose*. I can't believe he intends to be a witness for Jessi in her case against Darlene."

"I hope it won't go as far as court," Holly said, reaching for Toria's hand and looking fondly over at her as the turnpike traffic slowed and came to a stop. "Not to change the subject or anything, but are you hooked up for next Saturday?"

"For the banquet?" She hoped she knew where this conversation was headed. A flush began hot at her throat, but she kept her tone cool. "The Ladies Group always reserves a table for members."

"Could you break tradition and be with me?"

She could feel the increasing heat and knew her skin was blotchy. "You...you mean like...like your date?" she stammered

"Exactly like."

If Holly could disregard her splotchy complexion, she could too. She pretended to consider. "Who was your date last year?" Said as if she hadn't noticed or cared.

The traffic problem eased and they could move ahead again. Reluctantly, Holly released Toria's hand as he said, "She was the daughter of a friend of Francine's."

What he didn't say was that the girl had been a miniature fit-under-his-arm thing, who Francine considered his perfect match. Holly had no trouble finding companionship, even though none of them had ever been exactly right, but Francine always wanted to fix him up with somebody she thought looked good with him size-wise. The banquet was the Auxiliary's big event and Francine wanted to arrange everything about it, including him. He'd gone along for the sake of keeping peace.

He grinned approvingly over at Toria. His perfect banquet date. What a difference a year makes.

CHAPTER 52

At the Weehawken house, Holly's cell rang as they left his truck. "Hold on a second," he said. "I need to see this message."

He read the text on the screen. Looking satisfied, he returned the phone to his pocket. "Sorry, something I asked someone at work to follow up on."

Toria flashed him a glance—he looked awfully pleased for it to have something to do with work. She was about to ask if the message was connected with the Mather business, but then he took her arm and they were at the front door of the impressive house.

As before, they were met by a young woman at the door who had them sit while she went and fetched Jade. Introductions were made. Jade said there would be a short wait while she made sure Elizabeth was ready for company.

After Jade left them alone, Toria said to Holly, "This seems strange. The woman identified as Elizabeth was totally unresponsive to Francine and me, and now I'm back again with a public official and there's no questions?"

Holly started to reply but then the door greeter returned, so they waited quietly until Jade made a reappearance to conduct them to Elizabeth—or, as Toria thought, *Grace*, if her theory was correct.

When they reached the third floor, their guide opened the double doors to the so-called Therapy Room. As before, there sat the heavy woman in a wheelchair before her easel, busily painting. The only thing different that Toria saw was a different colored muumuu.

"You have visitors," Jade announced. "Toria Dahlgaard has returned, this time with someone new. Instead of her friend, Francine Smithers, who was a neighbor of your niece, Grace, she has brought along the mayor of the town of JumpRope. His name is Holland Kingston."

Toria didn't remember receiving such an elaborate introduction before, but she dutifully stepped forward and said hello to the silent woman.

Holly followed suit and somewhat at a loss, added, "Most people call me Holly."

Through it all the woman kept painting, focused on nothing else.

As before, Jade explained that although they could speak to Elizabeth, they shouldn't be disappointed if she failed to respond.

Nodding at this comment, Holly studied the half-finished canvas on the easel then he crossed the room to take in the view out the big window. He then he directed his attention to the same city-themed paintings along the wall.

He returned to the figure in the wheelchair. While pretending to be only watching her at work, he was also studying the woman herself. The room was warm and she had kicked off one of her slippers, revealing gnarled toes. Her heavy legs were veined. His gaze lifted to her face.

When he'd been in high school he had taken an elective art course. The instructor, who was also a respected portrait painter, sometimes spoke about his work. He had once given a lesson about the changes in the aging human face, changes in skin, fat deposits, muscle tone and so on. Holly had not forgotten.

He returned to Toria and spoke in a low tone the caretaker couldn't hear. "If Grace is the same age as Francine," he said, "this woman can't be her. She's much older. I think this is Elizabeth, exactly as we've been told, and if there's a resemblance, it's because they're family."

"But wouldn't sickness hasten the aging process?"

"To some extent but not that much. Elizabeth has physical problems, but is she truly ill? There are things I would like to say to her, but I don't want to do anything harmful."

"You won't get help from Jade," Toria whispered back. "She's totally loyal to her charge."

"Agreed, and I don't want to get myself thrown out." He thought, then, "I have an idea."

Moving to the caretaker he said, "This facility is in charge of Elizabeth's physical wellbeing, yes? Her physical health, her nutrition?"

Jade straightened. "Certainly. The best of everything."

"I can't help noticing that she appears overweight."

"Eating and painting are her only pleasures," Jade said, clearly offended.

"So what about high blood pressure, diabetes, or—"

Jade cut him off, "Elizabeth suffers the natural effects of age but she is one of those fortunate people of whom one can say, she's never been sick a day in her life. Her problems are not physical, they are problems of cognition. The doctor has no explanation. For whatever reason, her entire life has narrowed down to nothing but her interest in painting. Her hearing is functional, but she responds to nothing said to her because her only life is paint on canvas and food." Jade rose to her feet. "Perhaps you have visited long enough. I—"

This time it was Holly who interrupted.

"No, please," he said. "I wasn't intending to question her care. I can see that her condition indicates a mental disturbance. However, since you said we might speak to her I wanted to be assured that if I said something that did get though, it wouldn't cause a physical problem, as it might with a person who had, say, dangerous high blood pressure. You've reassured me. Since nothing will get through anyway. I can speak simply for my own satisfaction and it will do her no harm."

He turned back toward the woman in the wheelchair.

Jade, who now looked as if she didn't want him to speak to Elizabeth after all, had robbed herself of a reason to stop him.

Toria wasn't sure what Holly was attempting, but she was impressed by his handling of Jade. And what he did next totally floored her.

Speaking to the woman in the wheelchair, he began to relate

201

everything that was known about the Mather house mystery including the fact that the gang that had stolen silver from the house had previously robbed a Peach Acres home, a crime that had ended with one of the gang being murdered. He revealed that the pawned items had been recovered by the police and then went on to exaggerate how close the robbers were to being captured.

He then said, "The police are also aware of a connection between the thieves and a man named Acer Wolfgang. He is somebody who knew Barry years back and now he's shown up again. Although Wolfgang tried to stay behind the scenes, he has attracted the attention of the local police as well as those in Brooklyn."

All through this monologue the woman in the wheelchair kept painting, giving no sign that she wasn't totally alone.

Holly continued, "What we have here are thieves and a murderer, but we suspect the mystery goes back to the time when Grace left the Mather house—without Barry. The police found nothing to prove foul play in Barry's death and they don't think Grace is directly involved with wrong-doing, however, they do believe she has valuable information. When the police find the men who committed the crimes the truth will come out. By keeping hidden and stalling the investigation, Grace makes herself look bad. It's best if she comes forward."

He paused for a long moment in which he watched Elizabeth paint. Then he said, "If Grace doesn't come forward on her own, the police will be here with questions. I'm leaving my card—" He placed it on her work table. "If you have thoughts about where Grace might be, then sometime, when you're not too busy painting, give me a call."

Turning, he flashed Toria a wink and then faced Jade.

"Thank you very much," he told her. "We're done here."

For a moment it seemed as if Jade was frozen in place. Then, tone expressionless, she said, "Follow me." She turned and swiftly led them into the hall and down the three flights of steps. When they were outside, she closed the door behind them more forcefully than necessary, a gesture that said "good riddance" more clearly than words.

Toria held her tongue until they were in the truck and away from the house, but she was thinking with admiration that Holly had been like a trial lawyer with Jade. He set her up without triggering the protective lies she would have expected, and found a way to say his piece to Elizabeth without being stopped.

She said, "So if that's Elizabeth, do you truly think she knows where Grace is?"

"She knows something" He looked pleased with himself. "Her mental disturbance is an act."

Toria gasped. She didn't doubt him, but she had to know. "Can you be sure?"

"While I spoke, I saw she was becoming uncomfortable. She kept her face immobile, but she started doing things with her paints that I didn't see in any of her other work. She started handling colors in a vastly different way."

"So that's why you suspected her of faking?"

"Yes. If what Jade said about Elizabeth was true, then nothing I said would have had enough meaning to make her uncomfortable, but I could tell she had stopped paying attention to her canvas. Not only was she selecting colors at random, she started loading her brush thickly and scrubbing the color in. Her painting technique is light with almost feathery brush strokes. It's how she achieves her effects. She doesn't scrub like that, but she did when I was talking because what I was saying upset her. Despite what Jade claimed, Elizabeth hears and understands people very well. Fortunately with oils she'll be able to lift off the mess and no harm done, but it convinced me she's keeping secrets. From the start, I wondered if having it proclaimed that she's unable to communicate has been a scheme to head us off. Elizabeth never dreamed anyone would go to the trouble of locating her. When you and Francine showed up, she and Jade devised this big act."

Toria cocked her head. "I remember we had to wait before Jade took us to the third floor. From what you've said, they probably kept us waiting while they scrambled to select only city pictures, matching the story of Elizabeth being so single-minded."

"Makes sense," he agreed. "And with that view, no artist could resist doing at least a series of skyline paintings."

"You left your card. What do you expect to happen now? The caretaker, or whatever Jade really is, refers to Grace as Elizabeth's niece. If Elizabeth is keeping Grace in hiding, she could be there in the house."

"She possibly is," Holly said. "There are criminals involved in this Mather business. And it appears that Grace is the key. I was high flying on some of the things I said to Elizabeth. Maybe the police aren't so close to catching the men who stole the silver and maybe Grace isn't quite as innocent as I made out, but I thought it was worth it to spur some answers. Slim is out of town for the weekend, but on Monday, I'll tell him what we did today. He can take it over to the county and they can decide the next step."

"He's going to think you were brilliant." Toria said. "I sure do."

Holly looked sheepish. "I've got to confess something. When we went into the house I had more information about Elizabeth than I let on."

Toria remembered the business with the phone call. "That text message just as we arrived?"

"Yes, clever girl. The caller was Kurt, from our tax office. I had asked him to research property owners in Weehawken."

"For the house we just left?"

"Bingo. Prime real estate assessed at five point six million dollars. You and Francine were told nothing but lies from the get-go. It's a private home, not a nursing facility owned by an art-loving benefactor who has kindly taken Elizabeth in as a charity case. Together with Grace and Vivian Mather, Elizabeth Mather owns the place."

CHAPTER 53

Around the time that Holly and Toria were on the way home from Weehawken, deciding where to have dinner and where they would go afterwards (any way to prolong their time together), a figure approached the door at the Spellman home.

Jessi looked out her window. "It's Pastor!" She hooted in jubilation. "I knew he would knuckle under." She waved to Arnie, who had been watching a game on TV. "Let him in. I have to get dressed."

Jeans and a T-shirt weren't what she wanted for her triumphant conversation with the old reprobate. She'd given him until Sunday, but here he was, a day early. *Victory!* She paused at the landing to hug herself. *It was just so sweet!*

Light-of-heart, she skipped on up to the master bedroom to choose her outfit. The more she had thought about owning her own rave restaurant, the more enthusiastic she had become. It wouldn't be long before posh celebrities from all over the East Coast would be dropping her name. "Let's give Jessi a call and make our reservations," and, "Let's meet at Jessi's for our picture deal," and "If we want to throw the best kind of party, it's got to be at Jessi's." She might buy slick magazine ads at first, but word of mouth would soon pack them in. She imagined

Pastor had been thinking the same thing. He might not like it that she and Arnie weren't dumping in their nest egg, but using the insurance windfall as their share wouldn't take anything from him. That's what insurance was for, wasn't it? Besides, older people like him had a responsibility to help younger people like her. It was the American way.

Downstairs, Arnie invited Pastor to take a seat and asked if he wanted something to drink. Pastor was a man who had provided him with a lot of work, plus opportunities for lucrative real estate deals. He didn't see the point in getting on his bad side. Jessi might take a different attitude, but he was more comfortable playing the good guy. Good guy, bad guy—that's what made them a successful team.

When Jessi flounced downstairs she wore a snow-white dress with white embroidery around the hem. Her sling and cervical collar were white as well. Arnie gazed at her in open admiration. All in white—his kitten angel. What was the word Pilar had used? *Spitfire.* His spitfire kitten angel. How did he ever get so lucky?

With a swing of her skirt, Jessi took a seat on a hassock beside Arnie's chair and tucked her feet under like a demure and dutiful little wife. "What brings you here, Pastor?" she asked, her expression managing the trick of being snide and innocent at the same time.

He sighed like an old man with a heavy load and hunkered down so that his short neck disappeared entirely. "I was thinking of our future business arrangement and how it will work to the advantage of us all." He began talking—rambling, actually—describing the possible renovation of the building. "You have such talent and imagination," he said to Jessi. "And Arnie, I've feasted on your cooking and checked out the restaurant you ran a few years ago—you're exactly what I need."

Sure, sure, Jessi thought, not that she and Arnie didn't deserve praise, especially her, but Pastor was wasting time. She wanted to get down to the business of signing papers that clearly stated an equal partnership—with Pastor and his insurance company footing the finances and she and Arnie only contributing their considerable and valuable talents, imagination and skills.

Pastor continued rambling, but his gaze cut to Jessi. "I walked around your most recent sale at Apple Corners and was filled with admiration. The way you decorated the porch was charming. Your landscaping design was genius, the way it so cleverly concealed cracks in the foundation."

Jessi preened at this praise, but then, Pastor continued, "Later I was able to get a peek at the charges that disappointed buyer filed against you. All your marvelous artistry to conceal a damaged ceiling—too bad the storm revealed it."

Jessi's curvy little body had gone rigid. "That property's no business of yours."

"Oh, but it is. Everything about you is of interest to me. At my office, I said I'd kept tabs on the funds you'd been accumulating to buy the restaurant property, money I expected you to kick in on our deal. Then you wanted your share to be your injury claim from the fall at my office. But I've since learned you're being sued yourself. Are you planning to use insurance money from the incident on my property to pay for your housing defense?"

"What?" Although she'd been found out, Jessi's tone was highly insulted. "My attorney says it will be settled out of court with me agreeing to make the repairs." At least that's what she hoped and Pastor's money would pay for the lawyer. Continuing with bold confidence, she lied and said, "You will receive every penny I get from your insurance money to seal our restaurant deal."

Arnie jumped in, all eager, his eyes as bright as a squirrel's. "And it's a great deal! JumpRope is located to draw from a wide area. Teddy's Bar and Grill will be our only real competitor. It's a dream come true."

Jessi was done with the talk. "You've heard my offer, Pastor. And, as Arnie pointed out, your investment will pay back a thousand fold."

Pastor shook his head. "It can take years to settle a medical claim."

"Not if you don't fight it."

"Come, my dear. Since when did a prosperous businessman roll over for a lawsuit? The company would smell something fishy. I'm willing to pay your medical expenses. My railing was at fault, although I do feel you might have been a bit careless." He held up a palm to forestall any argument. "But no more than that, and I'll tell you why."

He pulled a paper from his pocket and unfolded the *Noose* page from the *JumpRope Jive*. "Even in Melton, we get our hands on this fine publication. I read the entry about you and learned you are pressing charges against the town housing inspector for running you off the road. However, the driver was actually my son, Laddy. He is eager to swear in court that you looked him directly in the face as he went by. You held his gaze. That means the charges you swore out against Darlene Gage were knowingly false."

"I held Laddy's gaze?" Jessi screeched in disbelief. "What a load of horse pucky! Laddy was gunning for me because I'd threatened you earlier. That lunkhead was too busy trying to avoid crashing himself to look in our direction as he zoomed by."

Pastor's reply was calm. "That's not how Laddy will tell it. He'll also swear that Arnie, who was speeding and driving recklessly, rammed his own mailbox trying to avoid running into Laddy. Tomorrow, we will all go to the police station and repair this confusion. Otherwise, once the housing inspector learns of your little game, and I'll make sure she does, you'll have a new lawsuit on your hands."

Expression sympathetic and looking even more froglike than usual, he touched his heart. "I understand you don't want to put your money into the restaurant project, but you had planned to use it for the purchase when you intended to flip the property, didn't you? Isn't this better? Arnie sees the possibilities. I'll put in a lion's share in exchange for your youth, energy and talent, but you either agree to kick in the nest egg or I walk out of the deal. Plus, Laddy and I will be in town hall in the morning, telling how you falsely accused the town housing inspector."

Jessi gave him a look that would have gigged a lesser man. "You think you're so smart—let's see how smart you are when I drag my injury case against you through court."

He forestalled any further comment she might have made by pulling a tape recorder from his pocket. "A lovely gadget," he said, fiddling with it. "Listen how clear it is—"

Jessi's recorded voice rang out. "Laddy was gunning for me because I'd threatened you earlier. That lunkhead was too busy trying to avoid crashing himself to look in our direction as he zoomed by."

He snapped the recorder into silence. "There's quite a bit more, including how you plan to blackmail me and defraud the insurance company for your own gain, but we've heard enough."

"That's invasion of privacy!" She was on her feet now. "If you think you were in trouble before, that was nothing. You know what you've done?" Her mind cast around for terms from TV news, big time charges against big time people. Her voice rang clear and authoritative, her tone putting words in capitals. "You have violated FEDERAL WIRE TAPPING LAWS! The FBI will be on your tail. I'll take you all the way to the SUPREME COURT." She whipped her head around. "Arnie, snatch that recorder away from him."

"Now, Kitten… " He made no move.

Unperturbed, Pastor said, "The point is, dear, you swore out false charges against the housing inspector. False charges that Laddy and I, with this recording, prove. Think of the rentals you and Arnie still have in this town and think of how many delays and stumbling blocks that will be found in regard to those properties when your chief enemy is the official in charge of housing. Your properties are so run down your tenants will have to be relocated and put up in motels at your expense. You'll be lucky if you ever see a rent check again."

Pastor stood, his smile beneficent. "My partnership offer is generous and sincere. You two think it over. I'll phone you Monday morning."

CHAPTER 54

Acer Wolfgang entered the spacious upper drawing room of the three story Weehawken home overlooking the Hudson River and Manhattan, the city skyline gilded by the sun sinking in the August sky.

He had been summoned by a frantic telephone call.

Taking a seat and adjusting the crease of his well-tailored summer-weight slacks, he said, "So, the mayor of that strangely-named little town actually came here and told you all that?"

The heavy woman in the wheelchair nodded. "Yes. He has me more than worried. The police are close to catching the men who robbed the farmhouse."

"One of whom, in another break-in, unfortunately stabbed and killed one of their number?"

"That was never supposed to happen. Never!"

"Of course not, Auntie. Unfortunately, your schemes rarely allow for contingencies. I don't know what you originally planned. I do know that you should have consulted with me."

"I depend on you too much."

He sighed. Although Acer called her "Auntie" there was no blood relationship. He had become friends with Grace and Barry and the much younger Vivian, after their Aunt Elizabeth had taken him under her wing. She was a wealthy woman involved in various charity efforts among the disadvantaged. He didn't know what she had seen in him. Although he had been determined to find his way out of the streets he hadn't known how to gain the formal education he wanted. But there she had been with her helping hand. He felt he owed her everything good that he had become. He was on his own for the not-so-good.

His name for her, "Auntie," had come from a youthful time when he'd been treated to a musical called *Mame*. He'd immediately recognized a kinship between the personality of Elizabeth Mather and madcap central character, Auntie Mame. From then on, "Auntie" was what he called her, although he hadn't realized at the time that her impulsive inclinations, with their comically disastrous results, could become as serious as they were now.

"Depend on me too much?" he echoed, lifting his dark eyebrows. "You didn't even inform me of Grace's tragedy until I had returned from the Far East."

Elizabeth, who had been sitting stoop shouldered and defeated in her plus-size blue and red flowered muumuu, abruptly looked up, a snap returning to the faded brown of her eyes.

"Exactly. You were in the Far East and Vivian was off somewhere. Grace was a mess and I took care of her as best as I could. Barry and I worked together. We did a good job."

"I agree. I visited them in JumpRope and saw for myself. Yet then, four years ago…"

"Again, you were off somewhere. And so was Vivian. She's the most restless young woman. I have no idea where she is…lickety-split from one foreign county to another with that job of hers. So, there was no one except me. Thank goodness I wasn't as crippled-up then as I am now. I was able to make Grace feel safe."

He remembered what she told him then—that Barry and Grace had left the Mather house, which she had boarded up—that the two of them were in seclusion at an address they insisted on keeping private. He had known that was a lie when the body found in the house turned out to be Barry, but Auntie had still not reached out to him and he had been busy abroad. Building his empire he supposed it would be called and yet, what did it all matter if he stranded the people he loved?

"You knew," he said. "You knew all the time that Barry was dead in the house."

She tore herself away from his gaze and for a long moment was silent, looking at nothing. And then she turned back to him. "Yes, I knew. And you should know why."

She began to speak, laying out a shocking array of facts. For his ears only, he realized, but also, if he knew Auntie, the whole story would eventually come out.

There was another long silence between them when she finished and sagged in her chair, exhausted. Acer, having come to terms with what he had learned, signaled to Jade, who had remained out of earshot, but had kept visible at the far end of an adjoining room.

Knowing what to do without further instructions, Jade, a treasure, Acer thought, soon returned with a sweet sherry for Elizabeth and a small Scotch and water for him.

After Jade withdrew, Acer sighed and said, "When you learned that the property was attracting attention and you knew it must never be investigated, you should have contacted me, no matter where I was."

Elizabeth fidgeted in her chair. She could walk, even climb stairs if necessary, but it took a lot out of her. "I never dreamed it could turn out so horribly. I thought I had succeeded in keeping the ownership of the farmhouse hidden and clearly failed for how else could that mayor have known to come here? He frightened me."

"Was he aware of your charade?"

"Jade said he couldn't be. The whole time I kept painting. Jade kept a close watch and she said I never looked at anything but the canvas. She said I never trembled or gave any sign. But he wouldn't have said what he did when he left his card if he wasn't suspicious."

"You believe his sole purpose is to find Grace?"

"That seemed clear." Her troubled eyes met Acer's. "I don't understand what difference it makes to him. If the matter is in the hands of the police, why does he care?"

Acer looked thoughtful. "Did you know I once planned to meet with him?"

"Before there was trouble? Why?"

"If you think carefully, you'll know. I want to develop the Mather land that's in his town. Since you wouldn't help me, I thought I would go behind your back. I assumed the little mayor was corruptible. I thought I could find a way to persuade him to put pressure on you."

She chuckled. "You rapscallion. And now you tell me about it? What did you plan?"

He waved a hand. "There are always irregularities that can be found if you have a politician on your side. Fines for this and that, endangered creatures no one ever heard of before that would render the land so useless you would have nothing worthwhile to leave behind."

"You would do that to me?"

He drew up sharply. "Of course not! I said it was to put pressure on you. It's your land yes, but there it sits. I want to develop it. I know you have a sentimental attachment that makes it worth more than anything I could pay. But you're getting on and what then? You can trust me to make sure that Vivian and Grace receive their rightful share. As for the old family home, I would take pleasure in restoring it."

"Where did you get this desire to develop land?" She studied him as she spoke. Acer was a handsome man, assured and compelling in manner, his eyes an unusual blue-green, his dark hair going attractively gray at the temples, his height allowing him to carry well the few extra pounds that came with a healthy appetite. "Land development is a fairly new interest," she said.

"True." He had an especially charming smile, lifting a bit more at one corner than the other. He showed his smile now, the slight irregularity playing up the perfection of the whole. "I've had various interests over the years, bridges, dams, highways, and also housing."

"They've all been big government or private corporation jobs," Elizabeth corrected. "A private housing development in a little community seems too small-time."

He shrugged. "I've reached the point in my life when I can do as I please. A housing development, if designed properly, can be a beneficial thing. It would be leaving my good mark, I suppose. Comfortable, well-made homes for families, for the children to grow up in."

"Things you never had."

"Yes, although you did your best to make up for it. This project would give me satisfaction."

"That I can understand. But I still don't see why that little mayor would come here. Explain what difference it makes to him."

Acer thought back to a recent issue of the *Melton Monitor*. It showed the JumpRope mayor rescuing a kitten when what was called the Hitchmile stream had flooded. "My guess," Acer said, "is that it's his town and he cares about it. All the aspects. There's a mystery about Barry and Grace and the disorder you've created. I think he's the type of person who wants disturbing questions settled."

"That simple?"

"Not really so simple, thanks to you, but then maybe nothing is simple in a small town."

He remembered the article that told the history of the creek's flooding, which worsened after a housing development was built on reclaimed marshland. Acer had sent a copy of the article to his development team to work up a report. When he was ready to present his housing plans to the powers that be in JumpRope, he wanted to be prepared to show that his engineering and construction firm could create an asset without inadvertently creating a problem.

Elizabeth, who had confessed everything to Acer, not even holding back when he winced over things she had done, said, "Once the police find the thieves, there's no way for me to be kept out of it."

"Except, this time, you have called me. I'll take care of it."

She looked at him with hope. "Do that and if I can ever get Vivian and Grace together I'll see that they will agree that you should develop the land as long as their interests aren't harmed."

"I would do my best for them, regardless." He shook his head. "You and your hard-to-find family members. Our footloose Vivian could be anywhere in the world. As for you—" Rising, he bent to kiss Elizabeth's aged but still plump cheek. "Don't worry," he said softly, but with assurance. "I'll see that you're kept safe."

CHAPTER 55

The pawnbroker knew more than he had told the police. Without much trouble, Acer found the pair who had committed the two JumpRope robberies.

Their place was in a run-down apartment house. To fit in better with the neighborhood, Acer had dispensed with his customary business attire.

Gaining entrance by saying he came with a message from the lady who had hired them for the Mather job, he was soon seated on a chair of uncertain stability in their small and tidy living-eating space that contained a miniature kitchen behind a sagging curtain. He had a sense that there were more people in the place than he could see, women, yes, and children. *There.* A little boy peered out from a doorway and then disappeared so quickly he must have been pulled away.

Acer wondered how they could stand it, all crowded in like that, while at the same time he remembered the nights when he would have been grateful for any shelter. He also saw what a benefit their rude circumstances would be to his plan.

The men he had come to see, one pony-tailed, all lard and muscle with huge, misshapen hands, the other all skin and bones, with a cap of raggedy brown hair that half hid his eyes, looked simple, but not totally simple-minded. A relief to him, that.

They listened in stunned silence as Acer explained how close the police were to finding them.

"How could anybody see the car? There was nobody around," argued the brown haired man, whose name was Twin.

"The New York plates stood out enough to be noticed, that's all I can tell you," Acer said. "And then there was the pawnshop. Police have an aversion to stolen goods. You should have known better."

"We didn't start to steal anything important, only little stuff," protested the man with the misshapen hands, who was called Mittens.

"I'm sure the police will be impressed by the argument. How about the murder?"

"Oh, Gawd!" Twin broke into tears. "That never should have happened."

"I didn't have anything to do with that," Mittens defended quickly. "I was the driver."

"Is that true?" Acer asked the other man.

The dark-haired man snuffled and said, "Me and my brother went inside the house in what was called Peach Acres. The lady told us what to do—just pick any house in the development, break in, make it obvious, but take nothing like, you know, valuable. Then wait a day or so and then do what she wanted done at the old farm house and don't steal anything there. We'd promised and I'd intended to stick to it. Only the first Peach Acres house that looked empty had an unlocked back door. It was like it was calling me in, so I went. The coins and jeweled cufflinks were in plain sight. I couldn't resist. When I came out, Twin was so mad."

"I thought you were named Twin."

"I am. We both were. We were Twins. Twin One and Two, I was One 'cause I was the oldest."

The man blew his nose on a handkerchief that looked surprisingly clean. "We got into a stupid fight about the stuff I swiped. He showed the knife and I tried to snatch it. We went around, you know. I don't know how it happened but he ended up dead."

A big-eyed boy, little more than a toddler, appeared and dashed against Twin's knees, calling him "Da." Another child, a girl a bit older, followed, running to Mittens.

Still snuffling, Twin picked up the boy. "Ben here belonged to my brother. We looked alike, being twins and all. I don't know if this little guy knows the difference." Clutching the child like a stuffed comfort toy, his sobs renewed.

Mittens, the girl now on his knee, glanced from Twin One to Acer and made a see-what-I-have-to-put-up-with gesture with his huge hands.

"All right," Acer said, directing his words to Mittens "You were not part of the knifing, but were part of stealing items of value at Peach Acres and the Mather house." He shifted his head. "And while you, Twin, did not mean for your brother to die—that was an accident— you also robbed both houses. Your lawyer will help you obtain the best arrangements for your respective charges."

"Lawyer!" Mittens jumped to his feet, the little girl in his arms. "We've got no money for a lawyer. Cripes, man, we're not even caught yet!"

"But you will be. And what of your families? You can't run with them and you can't leave them behind."

There was more discussion as Acer revealed his plan.

Two hours later, he telephoned Elizabeth.

"It's settled," he said. "The lawyer I arranged for is with them now."

He explained the plan that would keep her out of it. Accompanied by the lawyer, the pair would turn themselves in. The lawyer would present what would be purported to be the thieves' copy of the *Melton Monitor* with its article about a series of robberies in Peach Acres. The criminals' story was that the article gave Twin One the idea that the development was so poorly guarded it could be easily robbed. While in the area, he heard about an abandoned house that might contain valuable items. He and Mittens broke in. The shock of finding a dead man on the steps didn't discourage them from gathering valuable silver and they successfully escaped when they heard the siren of an approaching police car.

The instructions from Acer were clear: being in JumpRope and entering the Mather house was Twin One's idea and the sole purpose was robbery. With this settled, not only would the lawyer do his best by them, Acer would see that the two men's families were provided for during the time they were in the hands of the law—for however long that might be. And, when they were free men once again, Acer would continue to see that things went well for them and their families.

As he later explained to Elizabeth, Twin One, who was already riddled with guilt, agreed to this plan almost at once. With Mittens, it took longer, but as the lawyer had explained to him, they would be caught anyway and since Mittens had no serious convictions in his past, the law would not go too hard on him. It would be better all-around to turn themselves in when accompanied by an attorney.

Elizabeth thanked him, her voice shaky. "I can see how much I risked, the trouble I would have been in if a connection was made between me and the crimes." Fighting tears, she thanked him again. "If only that old tree had never blown down! And those stupid lilacs! What a mess I made of everything. If I'd been arrested, who would have been here to help Grace?"

"You're safe now, that worry's behind us," Acer said.

"But Grace is still a worry." She caught Acer's expression and said quickly, "I've learned my lesson. I'm not trying to think of doing anything more."

"Excellent," Acer said, fervently hoping Auntie's promise meant she was done with harebrained schemes.

CHAPTER 56

On Sunday, Holly accompanied Toria to services at the Presbyterian Church where she was a member. Holly was raised a Methodist, but his habit was to visit each worship house in turn, enjoying mingling with people in the community when town hall wasn't the purpose. Afterward, he and Toria visited with the friends from Rutgers he vacationed with. They all met at the home of one of them for pre-dinner drinks and snacks and then went to a restaurant near New Brunswick. The conversation was about movies and experiences and getting-to-know-you talk.

His friends had told Toria they hoped she would join Holly next summer at their vacation house. She hadn't said no, but what had she really thought? The shore house didn't have enough bedrooms so she wouldn't have her own room if that's what she would want. His friends' children slept in bunks in the low-ceilinged attic of the house.

If Slim knew, Holly thought ruefully, he could almost hear him quip, "She'd rather sleep with the kids instead of with you, right bud?"

"Did you tell Slim?" Toria said.

"What?" Holly said, startled.

"About yesterday's visit to Weehawken. He should know Elizabeth is faking, and not an old lady stuck in a nursing home. She owns the place! Slim should know all that."

"I'll tell him," Holly said, amused because just for a second he'd thought Toria could read his mind. Then again, who better?

CHAPTER 57

Monday morning, Slim went looking for Darlene, who was inspecting a resale property.

He always thought the Pullen Farm houses looked nothing like what should be found in New Jersey. Nose wrinkled, he cruised along the wide, flat boulevard of huge white stucco homes with red clay barrel roof tiles. All it needed was palm trees. The area always made him feel as if he'd slipped sideways off the map and fallen into California. He saw the former police car the town used as a municipal vehicle with the magnetic signs reading "JumpRope Code Enforcement" that Darlene always slapped on the doors before she took off. Not noticing Slim's approaching vehicle, she stepped briskly from a house, her long ash blonde hair and name tag swinging, her clipboard under her arm. She wore black slacks and a sporty looking black jacket over some kind of knit top, her attitude making the outfit look like a uniform even though it wasn't.

Parking, Slim got out and hailed her. She came to a stop on the irregularly cut paving stones that made up the walkway, her look challenging, although the once permanent frown grooves that used to cut between her eyes had miraculously disappeared. Now Darlene's smoothed out forehead matched her personality—starched and ironed twenty-four hours a day.

"Got good news for you," he said, cutting across the green turf to reach her.

She clicked the ballpoint pen she held in one hand. "Good news to me would be a realtor who remembers to call for inspection before a sale goes through and not until a summons is issued." She clicked the pen again. "Why are you here?"

She looked good, Slim thought, but even though he liked long hair on a woman, and he liked blondes, she was too skinny and had too many angles for his taste. He liked soft, rounded curves. Lots of them.

He said, "Jessi withdrew the charges against you."

Darlene's eyes went wide and her mouth fell open. She got her face reassembled. "You've got to be kidding."

"Nope. She came in with that smarmy realtor who calls himself Pastor and his kid, leather jacket, skull tattoo and all." He waved a hand. "The kid says it was him that almost sideswiped Jessi's car. The old 'swerved for animal in the road' excuse, like I believe it. At midnight? He was probably flying on something. Regardless, he swore to it and Jessi's complaint has been withdrawn and she pretended she didn't even remember about the threats you supposedly made against her. She didn't seem so happy about it. I think that Pastor character has some hold on her, but you're off the hook."

Darlene sneered. "Now I've got to wonder what trick she'll try next."

"Would be true to form." Some imp made Slim add, "At least with Pastor you've got a realtor who did something good."

"Ha!" She clicked the pen so rapidly it sounded like a tiny machine gun. "Thanks for letting me know."

"Always a pleasure," he said, not entirely meaning it. Did that woman ever smile? As he drove away he saw in his rear view mirror that she stood in the same place on the walkway, probably still considering the possibilities of Jessi's next dirty move.

CHAPTER 58

The week sped through to Friday. Toria and Holly had each been especially busy. They hadn't been able to keep to their schedule of taking turns driving to their county offices. They told each other it was all about carpooling and saving the planet, but the truth was, any reason they could find to be together was a gift. Neither would have ever imagined they could find so much to talk about to another human being. They thought that by that evening they should finally have time to be together.

Around one o'clock that day, Slim called Holly at his office over in Melton. "Got two pieces of good news to share," he said. "Had lunch yet?"

"No, I'm having food brought in. Want to add your order?"

Slim said he did. He'd been busy all week, too. Holly figured that lunch together would give him a chance to reveal what he and Toria had learned in Weehawken. In addition, Holly welcomed the distraction of the visit. That morning he'd stopped in at Krupple's for coffee. There had come a moment at the checkout counter when he'd overheard men in a nearby booth discussing an application coming up before the Land Use Board. The properties in question were lots where two huge homes had been torn down years ago. The new owner wanted to join the two lots and build five houses. Holly had seen the plans. The proposed houses were attractive and in keeping with the neighborhood and the properties were wide enough so that when joined, it would take minor variances for the five new houses to comply with existing zoning. Holly had felt good about it until he overheard one of the men behind him say, "Since nothing's happening out on that dead end road, maybe this is the development the mayor's involved with."

Holly had cringed then and cringed now, remembering. Would that rumor keep dogging him? There was no sense stewing about it because there was nothing he could do, but it hurt that folks doubted he was as straightforward as he always tried to be.

Slim entered Holly's office in the County Public Works garage. Although the office might be part of a garage, it was clearly the setup of a managerial professional. Taking a seat and thanking Holly for the food, Slim unwrapped it, took a bite, and said around a mouthful, "First good thing, Jessi dropped her charges against Darlene."

"She get religion?"

"She did come in with a man of the cloth."

"What?"

Slim laughed. "It was that Melton realtor who calls himself Pastor. With him was his kid, dressed like a convict wannabe although he's never been picked up for anything." Slim filled him in on the details, plus Darlene's reaction, and then said, "My second piece of good news comes from the county prosecutor's office. I was just there. They've got the two creeps who pulled the robberies."

"Whoa! I hoped the Brooklyn police were getting close, but I didn't expect it this fast."

"They turned themselves in." Slim took a hefty swig of the chocolate milkshake that he had ordered along with a double burger, double fries and two apple turnovers. "Run-of-the-mill lowlifes, one of them wailing up a storm. He turned himself in because he got a guilty conscience. He's the one who did the stabbing. The dead guy was his twin brother and his lawyer is claiming it was an accident. I guess the weeping is supposed to convince us. The other guy was involved in both thefts, Peach Acres and the Mather place. He doesn't have much of a sheet. Probably get off light."

"The robberies coming to trial in town?"

"They've got a fancy attorney who's pressing to argue manslaughter for the one guy, and then the robberies for both altogether, going for best plea he can get. All part of the capital case for the county. Save us court expenses. I won't argue."

Holly, eating his similar, but smaller, lunch, said, "How did Brooklyn thieves come to JumpRope?"

"That thing in the *Monitor* about the little thefts in Peach Acres, the ones our kids did, got them thinking."

"That almost invisible article?"

"Must have gotten picked up by the news wire."

"Even so, it's weird to think it would catch their notice. And how did lowlifes get a so-called fancy lawyer?"

"Where've you been, bud?' Slim waved his straw and quickly sipped the end when he saw it was about to drip. "Don't you watch TV, see the legal ads?" He mimicked, "*Are you a falsely accused lowlife? I'm the man to spring you.* Besides," he said in his normal voice, "it was the Brooklyn cops who were impressed by the lawyer and once I heard the guys were caught, I asked no questions. There's enough going on around here for me. I spent three hours in the emergency room this morning with Donny."

"What happened?"

His main meal gone, Slim turned to his apple pies. "Kiki Vera got a flat tire in the food market parking lot. Donny rode to the rescue and tore a rotator cuff using a lug wrench. I finished with the tire and took our local hero to the emergency room. Place was a zoo." He hoisted his nearly finished milkshake. "Then I got the call from the county, so at least I was in this neck of the woods to stop in and find out that they'd caught the guys."

He rolled up his lunch papers and napkins, finished the milkshake and wiped his milk mustache off with the back of a hand. "So—don't bother me about details from Brooklyn. It's now the county's headache."

"But we still don't know how Barry Mather's body got left in that empty house," Holly said. "Or what happened to his sister, Grace."

Slim screwed up his face and further mussed his streaky blond hair. "One doesn't seem to have anything to do with the other. For me it was about robbed houses and a fatal knifing. That's taken care of and I'm too pleased about it right now to be chasing mysteries."

CHAPTER 59

Holly and Toria met that evening as planned. It would be an early dinner as Toria wanted to go back to Teddy's to help Francine with touch-ups for the banquet. Holly said he would help.

The restaurant they chose was within easy driving distance, but on the far side of Melton. "Pilar will never find us," Toria said with a light laugh as they started off.

Holly said, "You mean she won't find us kissing?" They had stopped for a traffic light and he leaned across the console to demonstrate. She cooperated to such an enthusiastic extent that horns from behind blew because the light had changed and they hadn't noticed.

"We can do better at the next light," he said.

She bit back a giggle and said, "Practice makes perfect."

Neither of them could remember being so delighted to see red lights.

They were still in a wonderful mood when they reached their destination, a Viennese bistro tucked into a strip mall. On their way in they greeted a man from town coming out and proceeded on inside. The restaurant was tiny with a narrow bar along one side, wood paneling and simple chairs and tables just perfect for two, which was exactly what they wanted. Once they were seated, Toria noticed a difference in Holly.

"What's wrong?"

He started to say it was nothing and then he shook his head. If he could tell anyone, it would be Toria. He told her that the man they'd just greeted had been in Krupple's that morning. He explained about the man's disturbing comments.

"That had to be upsetting," Toria said. "Do you know the people wanting to build five houses?"

"No, I only know what's on their application."

"Do you have a financial investment in the land?"

He gave her a funny look. "No, how could I?"

"Are you receiving kickbacks from builders or suppliers?"

"Of course not!" He was annoyed until he saw the sparkle in her eyes. "You're saying that it's gossip and there's nothing I can do except what I've already decided—ride it out."

"Exactly." She smiled. "The rumor started about a specific large property and even when nothing happened some people won't let it go. It could be five houses or a chicken coop, they're determined to find a connection. After a while they're going to start hearing themselves and shut up."

He laughed. "Even a chicken coop, huh?" He remembered the feeling he'd had not so long ago about life passing him by. Now he felt that he was in the middle of life and it was good. Just being with Toria made everything seem better. What had he ever done without her?

As they ate, she said, "I never heard what Slim thought about Weehawken and Elizabeth Mather."

"I thought I'd have a chance today, the first time we'd had time to talk all week," Holly said. "But then, he was so pleased over other things that I let it slide." Holly explained about Jessi withdrawing charges against Darlene and about the police in Brooklyn arresting the men who had robbed the two houses in JumpRope, one of who had killed the other man during the Peach Acres break-in.

Toria smiled. "He likes solved crimes a lot better than mysteries."

"That's the truth," Holly said. "I mentioned we still didn't know what happened to Grace Mather, but he didn't want to hear about it.

I figured I'll bring it up another time. Knowing him, the unanswered questions will stick in his craw."

"Good, because it's still a mystery. The whole Weehawken visit was so strange. I was wrong about Elizabeth being Grace, but that stage-playing has a reason. It means that Grace is still there.

"Slim will go back to it, don't worry," Holly said, "but that leaves the other problem. What happened in the Mather house four years ago that made Grace need to hide?"

They stayed longer at dinner then they had planned and by the time they finally reached Teddy's there really wasn't much more to do. Over in one corner Francine, Darlene and Iris were accepting auction donations or taking care of selling banquet tickets. (No tickets were sold at the door.)

Toria nudged Holly's arm. "There's Jessi and Arnie Spellman. Watch out for fireworks. Jessi's heading toward Darlene to buy tickets. And look at Darlene's expression. You said Jessi withdrew those phony charges, but I bet she will say something nasty."

"No bet, not with those two. Darlene would bristle if Jessi only said the ticket Darlene sold her would win a good prize."

"Well, she'll have a nice assortment to choose from." Toria gestured toward a double long table already loaded with door prizes. The penny auction items were on separate tables, with a jar beside each item. Participants would buy auction coupons to stuff into the jars beside the items they liked and hope their number would be selected.

Holly's phone buzzed. It was Donny, back on light duty after his injury, working the police desk. It was where Slim liked him—kept him out of trouble. After disconnecting, Holly said, "Donny says a woman's come in looking for me...she wouldn't give her name. I'd better go. You want to stay here and catch a ride home with somebody if I don't get back soon?"

"You're dumping me for some mystery woman?"

He grinned. "I guess that means you're coming?"

"Sure, I'm curious. Who would come in that Donny wouldn't know?"

"You're just a tag along," Holly said, taking her hand.

"Don't you forget it," she said.

Reaching town hall, Holly saw a car he didn't recognize outside the police department end of the building. Inside, he and Toria rounded the corner to see a large figure taking up considerable real estate on the visitor's bench. When they saw who it was they stopped at if they'd hit an invisible wall.

CHAPTER 60

Dressed in a voluminous purple top and matching slacks, Elizabeth Mather peered at them with bleary eyes, light glinting off the thick lenses of her glasses. In answer to their obvious but unspoken question, she spoke with sly and weary humor.

"I imagine you're surprised, but let's simply say that the doctor changed my medicine. It worked wonders."

The twinkle in Holly's warm blue eyes was the only hint that he wasn't as surprised as she might think. "Did you come to tell us about Grace?"

"I came to collect Barry's ashes."

"You drove here alone?"

"Yes, and if you're wondering about my wheelchair, I can manage without it, but I don't like to." She gestured with a puffy looking hand to a four pronged walking cane by her side. "I'm staying for a few days. I saw a cafe with a sign for rooms to rent. It didn't look fancy, but anything first floor will do."

"Not the best place for you," Holly said. Juan Buenaventura had obviously put his sign up again despite yet another fine for improper procedures. Darlene was always after him.

"How about asking Francine?" Toria said to Holly. They both knew how she liked to be on the inside of things. "She'd never forgive us if we didn't at least give her a chance."

Elizabeth's face brightened. "That's the woman who was Grace's neighbor, the one who came with you to my house? Would she have me?"

"I think she would be delighted," Holly said.

"She's probably home from Teddy's by now," Toria said to Holly. "We should drive over. Except, your truck has a high step—"

"Use my car," Elizabeth said. "And since you know the way, you drive. I'm sick of driving anyway. I made this trip on impulse."

None of them spoke during the short ride to the Smithers' house. Holly and Elizabeth waited while Toria got out and knocked on the well-lighted front door.

Toria had never told Francine about going with Holly to Weehawken and ending up suspecting Elizabeth of faking. There had been no way to prove it and Francine so often pooh-poohed other people's ideas. Having Elizabeth show up this way would be a surprise, but knowing how impressed Francine was with wealthy people and stylish homes, Toria thought she had a way of bringing her around.

Francine, who had just returned home from Teddy's, came to the door.

Toria said, "Elizabeth Mather is waiting outside in her car. It turns out that she's in much improved health. That mansion we visited in Weehawken is actually her private home."

Francine's mouth dropped. "That gorgeous house belongs to her? And she's here?"

"Yes, parked in your driveway. She's a fabulously wealthy woman and she's come seeking your help. She needs a place to stay for the night."

"Oh, my goodness! Bring her in, No wait, I'll go out."

Pushing past Toria and seeing Elizabeth in the car, Francine ran out to throw open the passenger door. "Oh, here, dear," she said, "I'm delighted to have you as my guest. Please, let me help you inside."

Assisted by Toria and Holly, Francine steered purple-clad Elizabeth out of the car and up the low step of the porch.

Inside at last and sagging like a sack of grapes on the living room couch, Elizabeth sighed. "Ah, this is lovely." She arrowed a glance at Holly. "I imagine you don't have visitors overstaying their welcome on that hard police station bench."

Running roughshod over whatever Holly might have answered, Francine said, "Toria said you were improved. This is more than that. What miracle happened to you? You're normal!"

Elizabeth smiled. "Let's say the doctor changed my medicine."

Francine goggled. "And fixed everything? Your head…your legs?"

Elizabeth waved a hand. "Don't be gullible, Francine. I still spend time in a wheelchair, but the rest was pretense, for my own reasons and my own business."

"You tricked us?" Francine drew back, tucking in her chin. "That business in Weehawken was an act? You, posing as a brain-damaged artist and playing deaf and dumb while Toria and I stood there making fools of ourselves?"

"Oh, my," Elizabeth said, her expression dismayed. "I never intended to make anyone feel foolish. That wasn't what it was about at all."

"Then what was it about?" Francine challenged. "And why are you here now?"

"This is turning out all wrong, and the fault is mine," Elizabeth said. "All too often I charge ahead without thinking things through."

Francine leaned forward about to speak again, but Toria, always the peace-maker, who, along with Holly, had been dumbfounded by the conflict, recovered and spoke.

"Francine! Look at her—" Toria gestured toward Elizabeth, who had wilted like a large flower. "She's apologized, she's driven miles to reach us and she's exhausted."

Drawing on what she hoped was a winning card, Toria said, "You know that Elizabeth Mather is a person of means and fine reputation." (She didn't know about the fine reputation, but she figured it would work with Francine.) "Elizabeth wouldn't have deliberately tried to embarrass us—she said she had her own reasons and you're right to question her, but let's relax a bit first." Knowing Francine's pride in being an excellent hostess, Toria added, "And perhaps we could have refreshments?"

Still unappreciative of having been fooled, Francine was about to snap back, but then bit her tongue. If Elizabeth had eccentric ways, maybe they simply went along with privilege. Explanations were due, yes, but first, she must remember her own position.

Struggling for a more moderate tone, she said, "Elizabeth, would you like a nice cup of hot tea?"

Elizabeth blinked. "Thank you, but if you please, sherry would be better."

"Certainly!" Francine left the room with a pressurized walk toward the kitchen storage area, pleased for an opportunity to use her oh-so dainty crystal glasses, decanter and tray with the nautical scenes that Peggy and Holland had sent back from one of their trips. Such good taste. It had surprised her.

While she was gone, Francine's husband, Bob, still dressed in his garage coveralls, came in from the back door and to the wide archway with its view of the living room.

"Hullo," he said looking from one face to the other. Tired from his day and having slipped past Francine, he said as he escaped, "I'll hear about it in the morning."

Francine returned with the sherry. Setting the tray on a low table she poured a glass which she handed to Elizabeth and then, as the gracious hostess and holding the decanter at the ready, she looked around brightly. "Anyone else?"

Toria reached to accept, and Holly followed suit. He was not a large man, but he was strong and the sherry glass looked fragile in his hand. He studied the pale cream beverage, not his drink at all, and momentarily envied Bob his escape.

Resuming her seat, Francine, still adjusting to having been fooled, looked at her guest, "Elizabeth, you say you've done things for your own purposes, nevertheless, an explanation is due."

"You're right, of course," Elizabeth said. "As I told your mayor, I came on impulse to do what I should have done earlier, and that is to make arrangements for Barry's ashes."

"Very proper and about time," Francine said with a sniff, back to being her bossy self. "Only that's not good enough. The town has been in an uproar about the Mather house. Think what we've been through—the discovery of Barry's dead body, Grace's disappearance, secrets about the property and your own charade in Weehawken. And now you say you've come for Barry's ashes as if that explains everything? It explains nothing."

Francine's voice gained force as she continued, "I have a psychic friend, Mar-see-ah, who stopped off earlier at the auction we're planning. She told me, 'You're going to hear a story, but it won't be the whole story and it won't be the whole truth.' I don't normally believe predictions, but that one surely fits this situation." Leaning back, Francine crossed her arms.

"You tricked me once, Elizabeth, but never again. It's time for you to tell the entire truth about everything."

CHAPTER 61

Elizabeth let her head sag in a gesture of defeat.

There was a long silence.

Holly and Toria, seated on a rolled-arm couch made for two, clenched hands tightly. Neither of them would have spoken to Elizabeth as Francine had, but they couldn't deny that she had voiced their thoughts.

Elizabeth drained her sherry as if in farewell to the silence of the past. "The truth is owed to all of you," she said, setting down the empty glass, her gaze moving over the three of them, seated around her as if at the foot of a teller of old tales, which indeed she was about to be. The thickness of her glasses magnified her eyes, making them look owl-like and wise.

Francine leaned forward, her lips parted eagerly. Holly's arm was now about Toria's waist and one of her hands gripped one of his. It was as if they were at the movies and the part they'd been waiting for had finally begun.

"Allow me to tell this in my own way," Elizabeth said. She spread her hands, palms up, as if releasing a long-held burden.

"I swore I would never tell this because telling it was unacceptable, but too much has happened to hold it any longer. It is a story with three parts, one from long ago when Grace was a young woman, the other two parts, more recent. The last of which, I messed up royally. I'll speak of the parts in turn.

"First, Mather Family background. The couple who were my great-grandparents established an impressive family farm in JumpRope. They had four children, who then had children of their own. One branch moved to northern New Jersey and built the Weehawken house. Wealth was accumulated—not from here—farming was a livelihood and land always held value, but not the tremendous worth it can hold today. The bulk of the wealth came from industry, railroads and investments. Barry's and Grace's grandparents continued life in JumpRope, but with age, they abandoned farming. One of the sons, my older brother, continued to live in the house with his family, his wife and two children, Barry and Grace. The once large Mather family has dwindled over the years. Finally, there was only myself and Barry, Grace and Vivian, the late-born orphaned daughter of my much younger brother. Although Vivian constantly travels, she still calls Weehawken her home. And, of course, as you all know, not too many years ago, Grace and Barry came back here to the farmhouse in JumpRope to live."

Elizabeth sipped more sherry, then said, "As a girl, Grace was always tender-hearted and more fragile than I thought was good for her, but at age twenty-five she made a perfect match with a surgeon in Connecticut where she had worked after college. They married and lived happily in New England for a number of years. Without warning, just after he stepped inside the home they shared, he collapsed from a massive heart attack and died. He had patients to see the next day and when the hospital couldn't reach him, the police were called. They broke in and found Grace in a catatonic state, still lying beside her dead husband's body. I went to her, of course. This was years ago and I was far more fit at that time. When she could be moved from the sanatorium where she'd been taken, I brought her back to Weehawken but it seemed she would never recover. She only wanted to stay in her room and cry and sleep.

Gradually, Barry and I understood that she couldn't bear the slightest reminder of the life she had shared with her late husband. To even step across a carpet in my house that she remembered walking across with him gave her immeasurable pain. Barry, who had his own money from his genius in electronics, developed health issues and had retired. It was he who suggested a solution. The old farmhouse in JumpRope was empty after their parents had left it to return to Weehawken in their final months. Barry and Grace went to their old home to live—a place where her late husband had never set foot.

"Blessedly, this seemed the solution. They kept to themselves, lived quietly and Grace healed. They had money to do anything they wanted and they began to use it, traveling frequently to visit with me and to go on into New York City to attend theaters and concerts. They were Grace's youthful enjoyments and never with her late husband, although by that time she seemed healed from painful memories."

Breaking off, Elizabeth made a motion toward her empty glass, which Francine jumped to refill. With a nod of thanks, Elizabeth sipped and then continued.

"Now we move up to more recent years. A new tragedy came to Grace. She and Barry had their little tiffs and spats. I see you nodding, Francine, so you must have had some knowledge. Each would say hurtful things and make threats to one another, but it always blew over. Their most ridiculous threats often had to do with money, such as, 'I'll sink your boat in the middle of the Atlantic and I'll get all your money,' or 'I'll shove you in a hole so deep you'll never get out and I'll have all your money.' Childish, inventive jibes, as if they were youngsters again, trying to outdo one another, sparring just for the sake of it."

After another sip of sherry, Elizabeth said, "Then came the time when Grace followed through on a threat to go to Atlantic City on her own. As usual, her final sally to Barry had something to do with surviving him and getting her hands on his money. Off she went with a long-expired driver's license in her married name. I think she felt quite smug when she returned late at night after being away and quietly crept into her bed, thinking how surprised Barry would be to see her home again in the morning.

"What she found in the morning was him dead in bed."

CHAPTER 62

"In bed?" said Francine. "But I thought the police said…"

"Please," Elizabeth said. "This is hard enough without being interrupted."

"I'm so sorry." Francine looked embarrassed—as she rarely was. "Go on, please."

Elizabeth nodded. "For Grace it was as if the horror with her husband was being repeated, but instead of becoming withdrawn and unresponsive, she refused to believe Barry was gone. She saw herself at fault for being away and thus, she was the one who had to fix things. Determined to get him to a doctor she managed to roll him from the bed to blanket-covered pillows and then used the blanket to pull him from his room. When she reached the stairs, she realized she couldn't get him down the steps without causing further injury. Still refusing to accept his death, she thought to call for an ambulance, but as she turned to go to the phone, her foot tangled in the blanket. She tripped and fell on Barry. She's built like me and her weight slid them both halfway down the steps. Dazed, as she lay on his cold body, the truth finally impressed itself upon her: Barry was dead.

"Filled with self-blame, she fled to me. She made little sense and there was no arguing with her. She was positive she would be accused of murder because in her heart that's how she saw it. All those foolish childish threats came back to haunt her. She was his heir and believed she would be accused of killing him for financial gain.

"Perhaps she unhinged me as well. Once she fell into an exhausted sleep, I drove alone to the farmhouse and removed every scrap of paper that tied Grace and Barry to it. I then ordered the house boarded up and made sure no workmen went inside where Barry's body still lay on the stairway. You might think me horrible and my actions a crime, but my aim was to protect the living. I never doubted that Barry would have agreed to protect his sister."

"I don't recall seeing all this," Francine said, sounding miffed.

Elizabeth found a smile. "It was on that dead end street and you were the only neighbor with a view. Workman didn't move around the back until your car was gone."

"Well, you certainly hid things well," Francine said, sounding reluctantly admiring.

Another smile, then Elizabeth continued. "Grace saw the personal documents I had removed and knew the house was secure, but she still wasn't calmed. I had our lawyer remove her name and Barry's name from the papers connected with the Mather house. The corporation papers were only in the bank's name, but even that didn't fully satisfy her. She wanted to stay hidden and I agreed. And, in case authorities tried to question me, my lawyer was to report I had lost the power to communicate. In the ensuing months, Grace regained her stability. She said she needed to be on her own. What could I do except give her my blessing?

"And now," Elizabeth said, "we come up to the most recent events. Grace saw on the Internet that a storm was causing people to poke around the house."

"A tree blew down in the yard," said Holly.

"Yes, that old oak in the back and the lilac hedge damaged as well, all planted by my great-grandfather. Grace's feelings of guilt—that her absence had caused Barry's death, came again to the forefront. Terrified that people would end up entering the house and finding Barry's body, she was convinced she'd be charged with his murder."

"That wouldn't have happened," Holly said. "Once the police

determined his death had been natural, it ceased to be an active investigation."

"We couldn't have foreseen that. Seeing Grace was going backward, I took action."

For a moment Elizabeth bowed her head, her clasped hands to her lips as if she could somehow hold back what she had done. "Foolish, impulsive action, I can see that now. But at the time—" She straightened. "I didn't know how much attention authorities in the town paid to abandoned houses. Jade helped me find the website, *JumpRope Jive*, it was called, that Grace had looked at. In it were comments about the lilacs, and also robberies in another part of the community, a development, Peach Acres. I found a pair of brothers willing to work for me by creating more incidents in the development. They were to break into several houses, but not to steal items of value. Unfortunately, the men stole valuables from the first Peach Acres's house they entered and one brother was killed."

Holly stared. "You were responsible for that?"

"To my shame," Elizabeth said. "My intention was to distract the police so the brothers could safely remove Barry's body. There's a cemetery where other members of the Weehawken branch are at rest and where I will someday be myself. I planned to have Barry placed there quietly. Sometime after fleeing Peach Acres, the surviving brother and his helper returned here to town and snuck into the Mather house with tarps and plastic and whatever they needed to remove Barry's body."

Francine gasped. "I saw those things when I went into the house days afterwards. I thought Barry and Grace had planned to paint."

"No, they were for the men. But once they were inside and saw silver pieces, greed once again got the best of them. The police were called because someone saw lights—"

"That was me," Francine said, proudly, "the closest neighbor. Sharp eyes."

"Yes," said Elizabeth with a faint smile. "And thanks to you, Barry's body was discovered despite my blundering." She shifted her gaze to Holly. "And it all was needless because as I've just now learned from you, Mayor, the authorities ruled Barry's death accidental and nobody went hunting for Grace except the three of you, coming to Weehawken, mistakenly believing that I knew where she was."

There was shocked silence all around.

Holly, Toria and Francine stared at Elizabeth open-mouthed.

For the second time that evening, Francine spoke for them all.

"You're telling us that even *you* don't you know where Grace is?"

"Correct." Elizabeth downed the rest of her sherry. "Ever since Grace left me, she has been nothing but a voice on the telephone from a blocked number. Nothing I can say convinces her she will be safe from blame if she reveals herself." Elizabeth looked at Holly. "I can now admit what I was foolishly holding back, why I really came to JumpRope. I did come for Barry's ashes, yes, and also to plan his memorial service. But my plan behind it was that Grace will want to attend, only as I've explained, she will be afraid."

Elizabeth looked around. "Other than the website, I don't know what news she sees about the town. Mr. Mayor, all of you...despite the trouble I've caused your community, I'm now asking you to please help me figure out how to convince Grace that it's safe to come out of hiding."

"I'm getting coffee before we go into this," Francine said, gathering the empty sherry glasses. Toria moved to help. Elizabeth shifted her position. Holly stood to stretch.

Lights swept through the window and across the startled faces in the room.

There was the sound outside of a car door closing.

A moment later, the doorbell rang.

CHAPTER 63

Francine recovered first. "It's after ten o'clock at night! Who comes calling at this hour? My house on Centre Avenue isn't one of those addresses where riff-raff stops and asks for directions." Indignant, she formed a one-woman parade to the entry.

"Yes?" she said imperiously as she swung open her mahogany grand entrance door with its burnished brass fixtures.

A tall, dark-haired, impeccably garbed stranger stood on the stoop.

"Pardon me for disturbing you so late in the evening," he said, "but I was informed by a policeman at the station that the lady at this address would probably know where to find the town mayor—"

Looking past Francine, he saw Elizabeth.

"Auntie!" Relief sounded in his aristocratic voice.

To Francine, he said, "Please, forgive me, but I must—" Stepping past her, he moved into the living room and to the couch where Elizabeth sat. He knelt so that he could reach out to embrace and be embraced.

"I'm so grateful to have found you," he said. "Jade told me you had come here in a rush, but she didn't know why. When have you last been behind the wheel of a car? It had to be an emergency. The only thing I knew that might draw you to JumpRope would be the old Mather Family farmhouse. Some damage, I thought, perhaps a fire."

"Oh, no…." Elizabeth looked appalled. "No, nothing like that. I'm so sorry to have alarmed you. It was just that…well, I had to do *something* and I got this idea."

"Oh, Lord—" His laugh was half strangled. "One of your ideas?"

Francine, who had followed the man in, was less affronted by his abrupt entry than she was flabbergasted by his fine style and excellent haberdashery. Then she noticed his wrist, adorned with a black crocodile strap and a gleaming open works watch.

She gasped aloud. "That's a Breguet." Her eyes stretched wide. "Do you know what they cost?"

Startled, the well-dressed intruder looked down at his wrist. "I do, actually." He rose to his feet and glanced around. "Forgive my manners, bursting in here like this. There is no possible excuse for my rudeness."

Although he was begging forgiveness he easily commanded the room. Extending his hand, he took Francine's. "Allow me to introduce myself. My name is Acer Wolfgang and you, of course, are the noble Francine who knows everything about the people of this town." He showed his charming smile and although not kissing her hand, he managed to give his gesture the same import.

He turned to Toria, who told him her name. "The lovely Toria," he said, holding her hand as he had held Francine's.

"And you—" He focused on Holly, standing nearby. "The mayor of the oddly named town, although—" he held up a finger as if warding off possible protest—"for all we know, the name Weehawken once meant hopscotch. It is a pleasure to meet you."

Acer's firm but not punishing handclasp was met by Holly's equally firm but not punishing handclasp. Acer smiled as if satisfied that he had measured Holly accurately and did not find him wanting despite his smaller stature.

"And now—" he turned back to Elizabeth. "Let us hear your latest plan."

With a stricken look, she said, "I told them everything."

He cocked his head. "*Everything*? After all my efforts to protect you?"

She nodded, looking miserable and stubborn at the same time. "I told them about Grace, how she reacted when Barry died and my plan to protect her this spring when I feared the business about the fallen tree and lilacs would draw interest to the house. And how my plan turned out wrong and needless. I already told them all that."

Acer thought for a moment and then said, "Perhaps I'll be revealing something I shouldn't, but did you happen to mention your plan at that time for Barry's body?"

"That I hired people to break in and whisk it away? Yes."

For a long moment Acer stared at her. Then he shook his head. "Ah, my Auntie Mame…why do I call you that? Let me count the reasons." His sweeping gesture took in Francine, Toria and Holly. "You trust these strangers?"

Elizabeth lifted her chin. "They cared when the authorities didn't. They cared when the authorities wouldn't. Although I didn't want the authorities to pay attention, don't you think they should have at least cared? Yes, I trust these people. And you can't say I'm not a good judge of character."

"Except perhaps with those you hired."

"The exception that proves the rule," she said.

Suddenly smiling, Acer gave a half bow. "I am defeated."

As Acer took a seat beside Elizabeth, Holly said, "I believe you have just referred to the criminals who have surrendered to the police in Brooklyn."

Acer raised his brows as if merely interested.

A cool customer, Holly thought, for in a flash, he had seen it all, seen Wolfgang's part in everything, the reason for his involvement in the pawnshop, the persuasion behind the criminals turning themselves in and the money behind their lawyer—it was all to protect Elizabeth. And, since the thieves and the murderer had been caught and Holly could see no malice, he merely said with a small smile, "From all reports, the criminals stated that coming here to commit crimes was their own idea. They implicated no one else."

Acer nodded calmly. "It's settled then."

"Yes," Holly said, although there were other things he could say, namely that the Brooklyn police had given their police chief Acer's name, but he saw see no point in pressing the matter. Meeting Acer's eyes, he smiled and said, "There seems to be no official interest in following up on anything."

"Ah, satisfactory," Acer said, meeting Holly's gaze with an

acknowledging smile of his own. There was a moment and then he turned to Elizabeth and said, "Please, share with me your latest scheme."

She might have argued with the word "scheme" but she saw the twinkle in his sea-blue eyes. "My plan is simple," she said, and told him how she planned to have Barry's memorial service be a lure for Grace. "By the time she calls me, and I'm sure she will, my new friends here, the mayor, Francine and Toria, will have helped come up with a way to convince her it's safe to return. Perhaps there will be something published, the memorial announcement and a few words about how Barry's body was discovered and making it clear that his death was ruled accidental and that the case is closed."

"I've been following articles about this community in a newspaper called the *Melton Monitor*," Acer said. "They could perhaps be a help in this."

"I know who to contact," Holly said, thinking of JJ Gilbert, and also Pilar, although he wasn't going to say it out loud.

As they talked, it was revealed that Acer, not knowing why Elizabeth had left Weehawken so abruptly, had made plans to stay in a motel on the highway so he would be nearby if she needed his help. He had sent his man there with his things. He had also made arrangements for Jade to come the next day, bringing Elizabeth's wheelchair. Francine, who had another extra bedroom, said she would be pleased if Jade would also be her guest.

Not knowing how she would properly entertain guests if she had duties that took her from the house, Francine said, "There's a banquet tomorrow evening and we will all be tied up. You two, and also Jade, might as well come."

"A formal affair?" inquired Acer.

Toria spoke up. "Some of the ladies will wear gowns, but the men will mostly wear business suits or dress even more casually. Strictly formal might stand out."

"I don't mind standing out," Acer said.

Holly, feeling a responsibility for any guests to his town, said, "I'll see to all your tickets." He always reserved extras to make sure no one was ever disappointed.

Her anxiety reappearing, Elizabeth asked Acer, "So you really believe my plan this time is good? That Grace will respond as I hope?"

"I do indeed." Acer's voice was gentle. "Perhaps by some miracle word will even reach Vivian and your family can be together once again."

"I pray you're right." Tears magnified by her glasses shone briefly in Elizabeth's eyes as she touched Acer's hands. "And I haven't forgotten my promise to you about the land. The more I think about it, the more pleased I am to know the farmhouse will be restored. I'm sure Grace and Vivian will feel the same. And with you at the helm, the housing development you plan on the former farm will be a tribute to our family."

Holly and Toria and Francine spoke in unison as they cried:

"Housing development!"

After a moment of shocked silence, Francine cried "No!"

She spoke to Elizabeth in a tone of horror. "That will harm this fine man, the mayor of this town. You cannot allow it!"

Toria, seeing Elizabeth's and Acer's confusion, said to Acer. "Francine and I found an old business card of yours where you asked Barry about the land. We knew you were interested then, but we didn't know you still were. There's this rumor—"

Francine jumped in again, her tone fierce. "Yes, one that accuses this man, who could have been my stepson, of underhanded dealings!"

"Ah!" murmured Acer, his puzzled expression transformed by understanding. "I learned something of that from a *Monitor* reporter. When the damaged lilacs were cleared away, some jumped to a conclusion about a development. It amused me, fantasy preempting fact." He switched his gaze to Holly. "The result had personal implications?"

Holly explained.

Having listened intently, a sudden light glowed in Acer's eyes.

"I have a plan," he said to Holly. "If you are agreeable to meeting me in your office tomorrow morning at seven o'clock, we shall see what we can do."

CHAPTER 64

When Toria and Holly left, Acer was still inside the house with Francine and Elizabeth.

"Do you have any idea what's going to happen tomorrow morning?" Toria asked.

"No, but it's clear that Wolfgang has something definite in mind."

"Well, after everything I saw about him on the Internet, he's even more impressive in person. Did you see how kind and caring he was with Elizabeth? He's everything I read about him, plus he's nice."

"He has callouses, too," Holly said.

"What? Oh you mean because he knows how to work deals with lowlifes, and I guess, pawnbrokers and lawyers?"

Holly smiled. "He is a canny businessman, yes. But we shook hands. I meant actual callouses. It's not all society events and jet-set meetings with him. He does physical work."

Toria shifted focus. "But can he really do anything to clear up the rumors concerning you? He's meeting you and you agreed. What's it supposed to mean?"

"I guess I'll find out tomorrow," Holly said.

"But it won't change anything," Toria said. "He wants to develop that land and he obviously goes after what he wants. Once he starts his housing plans, I can't imagine what people will say."

"I'm not going to worry," Holly said. "A development doesn't appear overnight. Plus, it seems that Grace and this Vivian must agree to sell and who knows where they are? Elizabeth assumes Grace is in New Jersey because she knew about the interest in the Mather house, but she's not understanding the Internet. Grace could be *anywhere*. Nothing will happen overnight."

"But this business has been bothering you!" Toria said.

"The things you said earlier tonight made a difference."

"When I was teasing you about non-existent kickbacks and such?"

"Yes. It's the sort of thing my father's been trying to drum into my head. People will imagine things regardless. I have to learn to roll with it."

"Because you know you've not done anything wrong."

"Exactly." What Holly didn't say, didn't know he had the words to say, was that knowing that she believed in him gave him the strength to handle problems in a way he hadn't known before.

"Come on," he said. "We have to deal with Elizabeth's car."

Because they had taken her car to Francine's, they had to play auto shuffle—driving back to town hall in Elizabeth's vehicle, then Holly returning it to Francine's while Toria followed in his truck. He and Toria then drove to her house and ended up standing on her porch, each saying they had to call it an evening, yet doing nothing to hasten the end. The August air, although soft and balmy, held hints of autumn. It was perfect for them to linger in her doorway, talking about the night's adventures as well as cuddling and kissing.

Leaning back against her porch pillar, she said, "It's strange that just tonight Mar-see-ah told Francine she would hear a story that wasn't the whole truth."

Holly murmured in agreement. "The remark might have been a turning point for Elizabeth. Otherwise, she might not have revealed the entire story."

"Darlene was told *wealth doesn't always mean happiness*, and she thought it applied to her sister's family, but it could apply equally to the Mathers." As Toria said it, she recalled her own messages from Mar-see-ah about having an adventure. How right that was. Not only a romantic adventure with Holly, but the one in which they worked together to find answers about the Mather house. And it wasn't over yet, at least not until Elizabeth's plan to lure Grace to the memorial service had played out.

Holly nuzzled her cheek and she lifted her face for his kiss, all other thoughts fleeing.

It wasn't until after they had parted that a question unfolded like a delicate blossom in Toria's mind. *"Am I in love?"*

The thought excited and frightened her at the same time. Although she was thirty, she'd been so shy she'd never had a boyfriend. In school she hadn't been like her classmates, always in "love" with this boy or that. She was convinced that true love developed over time. Her mother had fallen for her father and immediately gone to bed with him. She had told Toria that the physical side of their relationship had blinded them to other doubts they might have had. They were still in a romantic haze when they married, yet by the time Toria was born they knew they weren't suited. Still, they had stayed together "for her sake" until she was nearly grown.

In a way, Toria thought, caring for Holly from a distance had been perfect because she had never put her feelings at risk. It was as if she'd finally developed the kind of senseless school-girl crush she'd disapproved of when she'd been younger. But then they had met and she had learned he'd been waiting for the right person too.

Perhaps because of her mother's experience she'd long known that if she ever met the right man, she didn't want to rush into anything. Maybe it was like the thrill of waiting to unwrap a gift, but she didn't want to be a modern girl when it came to love and marriage. She wanted to wait until she really belonged to a man to *belong* to him. Yet now, thinking that she might be in love gave her a moment of trembling pleasure that was almost immediately replaced by anxiety.

What did she really want to do? *Take it slow*, she cautioned herself, and then, as if sending Holly a mental message, she repeated, *take it slow*.

CHAPTER 65

A cer's plan was simple. "Serendipity," he said with a confident
smile, sitting comfortably in Holly's office. He had with him
a packet of papers sent by messenger during the night from his office in
Manhattan to his hotel room, arriving that morning before 6 am. He
shared them with Holly, and then said,

"There's a need in your town, and I had planned an approach
some time ago, but I hadn't yet set the time to use it." He explained,
then finished with, "It's early, but gather what people you can. If that's
successful, I have a few other plans to set in motion."

Holly made the calls, informing committeepersons of an
opportunity for a visitor to make a proposal that would benefit the
community. Although it was Saturday and shockingly short notice,
three committee members agreed to come. By 10 clock, they had
arrived, along with JJ Gilbert, invited at Wolfgang's suggestion.

The group was small enough so they could all sit around a table in
Holly's office in town hall with cups of coffee or tea, plus doughnuts
brought by JJ Gilbert in addition to her notepad and pen.

After introductions had been made, Acer, representing his
company, Wolfgang Engineering and Construction, apologized for
the short notice, thanked the mayor for arranging the meeting and
thanked those in the gathering for their attendance. Standing, looking

every inch the wealthy and powerful man he was, garbed in a grey tropical blend summer-weight suit, a grey on blue pindot necktie with matching pocket square and a white shirt with silver cufflinks gleaming, he spread out his papers. There was just an occasional glint of a stainless steel watch with a white gold bezel. (Not the Breguet, a Rolex.) He wore no rings.

Acer explained he had originally come to JumpRope to help plan the late Barry Mather's memorial service. However, once he was in the town, he decided to take advantage of the opportunity to meet elected officials. Explaining that his company did a certain amount of pro bono work, he took out of the packet copies of the article JJ had written about the recent flooding of the Hitchmile and passed them around to refresh their minds. He said if there was interest, he proposed to study the Hitchmile flooding and to develop, without cost to the community, a plan to correct the problem.

Acer then resumed his seat.

Holly, having carefully reviewed the contents of the packet beforehand, was impressed with the thought Acer had put into the project. The man was serious about correcting a problem that everyone else had complained about but simply accepted as nature at its worst. Holly also saw that if Acer eventually gained the Mather property, the proposed Hitchmile project would give him an advance opportunity to establish himself as a friend of JumpRope. If gossipers still wanted to think that he, Holly, had something to do with the development, fine— let them also give him equal credit for having something to do with correcting the flooding.

His only worry was Reds Burke, one of the three to attend the meeting. Reds, the senior committee member, his hair a carefully groomed crown of white, also wore a summer-weight suit and a white shirt, his with a red necktie, no cufflinks, but a heavy gold band wedding ring on his left hand and a heavy gold ring with a gigantic ruby on his right hand. Reds was outspokenly suspicious of ideas that lacked his advance stamp of approval. Holly, who looked confident enough in his tan sports jacket and Van Gogh sunflower tie, nevertheless feared that Reds would be so negative that his influence would cause the others to close their minds.

After Acer's presentation, Azalea Roundtree, wearing a cap-sleeve black dress with pink roses rambling over her ample form, asked what pro bono included. She said studies always cost so much that there was no money left to get the job done. Acer said his company would absorb all costs of the study. Regardless of whether or not the town wanted to go ahead from that point, the study would cost them nothing. He added that if they did decide to go ahead, his firm would assist financially with grant writing and permitting.

During their brief conversation, Acer learned that Azalea was employed at a local printing and sign design company and he charmingly expressed interest, saying it was good to know of a local establishment doing that type of work.

Hoyt McConnell, jeans jacket over a white T-shirt with a John Deere tractor picture and the words "Keeping it Rural," wanted a suggested time-line for the study. Acer, with sincere regret, said he couldn't answer with any accuracy—it would depend on the difficulty of the study. However, he handed over a report from a completed job his firm had done with flooding in Massachusetts that would give a better idea. With permitting and EPA approvals and such, gaining approval for the entire project had taken a little over two years. A following brief discussion of tractors and heavy farm equipment left Hoyt smiling.

Reds Burke, who had so far not been involved—which must have been killing him—Holly thought, sat forward, his heavy shoulders looking more bull-like as he announced he had started his plumbing company from scratch and that he, a self-made man, had worked hard to educate his two sons to carry on the business in the community. His sons were plumbing engineers, not toilet fixers—they'd designed the water systems of the school addition and of the new Melton Mall. Looking down his nose, he wanted to know more about Acer's credentials.

Holly heard the underlying message in Reds' words: *Who was this smooth big city stranger? Beware of gift horses.*

Unoffended by Reds' patronizing tone, Acer's manner reflected his pleasure that someone in the room truly understood engineering, that they spoke the same language. Holly could see that Reds struggled against feeling complimented but was losing the battle.

Acer drew folders from the packet that showed other projects his firm had completed. He handed them to Reds first, because he would understand, and the following discussion was more involved than what Acer had with the other two members. Acer closed by saying that he would be happy to bring Reds, the other two and the rest of the committee to his Manhattan office to meet his teams and learn more. And, if it was convenient, to enjoy lunch.

Then, gazing around the room, meeting the eyes of each individual, Acer emphasized that his plan would be especially beneficial because his practice was always to use local people and local companies in doing whatever work was deemed necessary.

Brilliant, Holly thought.

At that point, JJ, who had so far said nothing, asked questions of Acer, and then of the committee members, as well as Holly, about the Hitchmile proposal. All expressed interest. Reds, suddenly the most enthusiastic, said it would take more study, and of course, discussion with the full committee and the Land Use Board.

The meeting over, Azalea and Hoyt walked out followed by Acer and JJ. Holly found himself alone with Reds, who, fiddling with a cigar that he would light as soon as he stepped outside, said, "He's smooth and slick, but I'm far from stupid." He arrowed Holly with a pompous know-it-all stare. "He's in with the Mathers and there's going to be houses, but then, you always knew that, didn't you?"

Holly frowned inwardly. Reds was still needling him? Well, he was done with it. Time to stand up for himself.

Holly looked Reds in the eye. "Funny thing about rumors," he said. "Everyone here heard you discuss the plumbing business you turned over to your sons—some might see that as you putting forth their credentials. Now me, I have no business that might profit from a big project involving engineering, water ways, or if houses go up—the extensive plumbing that would be required. But what will people think if your sons end up with the job? It doesn't necessarily mean that deals were made ahead of time, but people will think what they will think and they will talk, won't they?"

Having had his say, Holly cleared the table.

When he looked up again, Reds was gone

CHAPTER 66

It was Saturday afternoon before that idiotic banquet and Jessi was sick of tramping with Arnie along with Pastor over this dreary plot of land with its deserted gas station and rickety barn. Although she loved the idea of presiding over a glossy celebrity restaurant, this tedious business made her look back fondly on the plan she and Arnie had originally—buy it and flip it. All she could do now was grit her teeth. Pastor had not only dragged them there, he had toted along his massive, slug-like son, his stupid mouth hanging half open while his father and Arnie excitedly talked non-stop about going into business together.

Yadda yadda yadda.

Pastor kept including her in the conversation and she pretended to go along, giving all the right answers. The madder she got, the less she showed it. Nobody could ever tell what she was thinking unless she wanted them to. Pastor saw her as an asset. He didn't understand what an enemy he had made out of her with his conniving tricks. He wanted her design smarts? She could work up designs that would knock his socks off. For now, she would appear to play along.

Like attending the banquet. Pastor had the idea that the better standing she and Arnie held in the community, the easier it would be for them to gain planning and zoning approval for their restaurant. Ha! What he didn't understand was that the town boards and committees were filled with jealously-ridden hags. The more they saw of her, the more their envy stirred up. It was like when she bought her ticket the previous night for the banquet. That stubby old school teacher, Francine, had the nerve to ask her if she was going to be "good" that year.

Ha! That nonsense at last summer's barbecue had been a misunderstanding, blown out of proportion by stingy nobodies. They had told her that an 'all you can eat' dinner didn't mean she could help herself to a second take-out meal when she'd only paid for one. She had stormed out yelling it was a good thing because some of the food smelled spoiled. That wasn't altogether true, but nobody cared about her needs. Poor Arnie had to scrounge for his own food that night, but that was okay because he liked to mess with food.

And then, Darlene Gage kept shooting eye-daggers when she purchased two banquet tickets—one for her and one for Arnie. So there! Bleached Blondie Darlene was still being a bad sport over those phony charges she'd filed. Well, she'd withdrawn them, hadn't she? Which is why she'd smiled brightly and said to Darlene, "What's the matter, can't you take a joke?"

So she would go to the blasted banquet. One thing for sure, she would look better than any of them. The evening would be a showcase for her perfection.

She would shine like a star.

CHAPTER 67

The weather that evening was as sparkling as the event. Toria and the others on the banquet committee came through the back door early to make sure everything was ready, as did Holly, along with the other men who were helping with last minute chores.

When the doors opened at six-thirty everything was as perfect as humanly possible.

Guests came in, shoving a little in eagerness. Many were looking for Acer Wolfgang. Once he had known that Holly could assemble sufficient committee persons, Acer had contacted his publicity people. As a result, his engineering proposal to stop the Hitchmile Stream flooding had been on the 10 am, noon and 6 pm TV news. JumpRope's own JJ Gilbert had been discussed as well. She lived in one of the little cabins on the stream and her article in the *Monitor* about the recent flood had drawn this important man's interest. A photo (snapped by JJ) showed Acer, looking big-city splendid, standing outside JumpRope's town hall after outlining his plan to members of the town committee.

There was also a mention of the memorial service for the late Barry Mather. The TV anchor seemed more interested in reviewing the shocking discovery of Barry's body and the mystery of his missing sister, Grace, than he was about the Hitchmile flooding. One waggish resident had quipped, "If it bleeds it leads, but floods are duds."

In any case, a news suggestion that Acer Wolfgang might be visiting for the weekend is what led to guests' hope that they might see this influential man in the flesh.

The crowd found the banquet hall set up with round tables for eight topped with green cloths and decorated with fuchsia and yellow candles set in floral arrangements of tropical-looking flowers. The Teddy Bear mural needed no decoration, but ever since the year the Auxiliary had fashioned Halloween costumes to stick on the bears, inventive decorations were expected. This year's luau theme had paper palm trees nested with tropical birds. The slope-roofed cottages were festooned with paper orchids and the little bears dancing around wore sunglasses and held drinks decorated with paper umbrellas.

But so far, no Acer.

When Slim came in, his eyes landed on the mural. "Those bears with alcohol look underage to me." He spoke to his companion, Lana, the woman from Melton he thought he was getting serious about. He couldn't care less about Acer Wolfgang. His concern was Lana. He feared their relationship was running into the ground. Lana was always giving somebody else a little come-on and she didn't like his sometimes unpredictable hours. Slim thought that if he got a call to leave before the evening was over, he wouldn't have to worry about Lana finding a way home. She'd latch on to somebody quick enough.

A stir near the entrance caused Slim to turn. He saw a smooth-looking customer in a tux, accompanied by an old lady in a wheelchair. Slim recognized him as the big league guy, Wolfgang, who'd been on TV. Slim knew Wolfgang wouldn't be in a burg like JumpRope without an angle. His Hitchmile scheme helped Holly, who had been worried about the development gossip, but Holly's skin was too thin. Slim shook his head. If his skin got scraped by every rotten thing said about him as Chief of Police he'd be worn down to bare bones by now.

He caught sight of Francine hurrying toward Wolfgang. A one-woman welcoming committee, like he was her dear friend—except Holly said she'd just met him when he and a rich lady from Weehawken had come to town the evening before. The lady, who must be the Weehawken one, was in an extra-wide wheelchair—she needed every inch. A younger female navigated them through the crowd. Francine, playing hostess, introduced Wolfgang to those who came forward. He acted pleased to meet them, all suave and gracious. They simpered, delighted to talk to the guy who'd put JumpRope on the map for a few snappy TV minutes. Watching them make asses of themselves was a hell of a lot better than wondering who Lana was making eyes at instead of him.

Moving along, he and Lana followed the crowd to the auction tables.

The tables were parallel to a long wall, a section with a lower ceiling. Big oscillating fans kept the air moving because the space would heat up as the evening progressed. The committee had done a heroic job soliciting donations. The six tables holding them had only just been uncovered. The treasures had been hidden from prying eyes until the last possible moment, the covering sheets now folded neatly. The door prizes, on their own table, were gift-wrapped to add to the suspense. The auction winners were called by number, but people wrote their names on the ticket stubs for the door prizes and their names would be called instead of the numbers. The excited winners would unwrap their door prizes and then show them around.

From the minute the doors opened, Auxiliary members had been selling auction tickets. Buyers thronged the tables making their selections and dropping tickets in the appropriate jars. Wanting Elizabeth and Jade to feel included, Holly bought them strings of tickets, then he was off to meet and greet. Toria, not wanting to stay at his elbow as if she imagined she had an official position, went cruising on her own.

She discovered that the only other man in the room wearing a tux besides Acer Wolfgang, and also looking splendid, was Nero Gibeau. Nero told her it was both a privilege and an honor to be his grandmother's escort and he wanted, quite literally, to suit the occasion. They were seated with Shirley DeGarmo, Ruth Wilson, and Shirley's sons, Kurt with his pregnant wife and Donny with his fiancée, a gorgeous hairdresser from Rancine who worked at a shop at the Melton Mall. She was talking to people at another table so the Colonel had taken her seat and was chatting with Nero, who listened attentively, probably hearing old war stories. Iris, fluttering around with tickets, had probably heard the stories a hundred times. A couple stopped to tell Shirley how wonderful Donny had been helping them when they'd locked themselves out of their car. Donny, chin tucked like a Buckingham Palace guard, strove to maintain a modest expression while his mother clucked and beamed.

Toria joined Holly when he reached his father's and Peggy's table. Holland Sr. wore one of his "head covers," a mixed gray that would have looked entirely realistic if he hadn't been seen in Krupple's Diner that morning wearing one that was all dark brown

They chatted a few minutes, then Holly, with a wink at Toria, went off to do more of what he called, "playing mayor," making light of what she knew was important to him. She returned to their table where Acer chatted with Jade and Elizabeth.

The topic was Elizabeth's other niece, Vivian Mather, who was traveling somewhere in the Far East where it was difficult to be sure she had picked up her mail. Elizabeth wrote letters and Jade handled email, but Vivian had the practice of ignoring family communication for long periods. They had no idea whether or not she had received news of Barry's body having been found or would learn about the memorial service in time.

Elizabeth said with exasperation, "She's just like her father, never content to stay put for more than a minute. A beautiful girl, but she's nearing her thirties and I still don't know what she wants out of life."

Acer replied with something soothing.

Toria, quietly listening, was surprised. She'd heard Elizabeth say that Vivian was the daughter of a much younger brother, but she'd still assumed Vivian was somewhere near to Grace's age. Instead, she was really young. Toria was mulling that over when she noticed Acer's gaze straying across the room. Curious, she traced the trajectory to Darlene, who was still selling auction tickets. Hmmm. It was definitely Darlene who drew his attention. Well, she was deserving of it, tall and slender in a spectacular column of form-fitting blue satin.

Francine, splendid in a Halston-inspired bronze lace, stepped to the podium. She had no doubt that her wealthy out-of-town guests were impressed with the event. She had been particular to have Elizabeth's wheelchair positioned where she had a good view of the action at the prize tables. Acer and Jade sat on either side of her, both attentive to her needs.

People who'd been milling around started taking their seats. Holly slid in next to Toria and murmured, "Take a look off to your left." He gestured. "Is that dress missing its back?"

Toria's gaze found Jessi Spellman. From what she could see through the crowd, it did appear that Jessi wore a backless gown, or perhaps no gown at all.

"Lady Godiva," Toria said. "You'll have to keep a watch on that."

"Me and every other male in the room."

Francine tapped on the podium, drawing attention. She gave a welcome on behalf of the joint Auxiliary and for the help from the Woman's Civic Club members and a thank you to the merchants who had contributed prizes. She reached toward a silver bucket as she announced she would call names for the first two door prizes as the salad course was being served. Accompanied by applause from their respective tables, the two recipients came up, cut the ribbons and wrappings on their prizes and displayed them to their fellow diners. One person won a combination microwave-convection oven from a store in Melton and the other a bronze horse sculpture from a JumpRope antique shop.

"Showy gifts," Holly said, thinking that Toria, his sweetheart, dressed in turquoise chiffon, looked delightfully gift-wrapped herself.

As if their minds ran on the same track, she thought how special he looked that evening. His navy blue suit had a gray stripe and his Cezanne landscape necktie was in shades of blue and pale gray. His shirt was a silver gray. He had told her that he'd debated over it, not wanting to be too daring for the JumpRope mayor.

She said gray wasn't bold, it was classy, and then had whispered, "I had to fight with myself not to wear my red shoes."

He had burst out laughing. "You're always saying things that surprise me."

When the main meal was cleared away and dessert and coffee were being served, the auction drawings began, interspersed with the calling of names for the remaining door prizes. People who had not yet made selections went to the tables quickly before a desired item was auctioned, or bought more tickets for additional chances. Others in the room were content to simply be together and talk. The room was a gentle hubbub, broken by the raucous sound of Francine's loudspeaker and applause from various tables as recipients stood when their winning numbers or names were called.

Slim strolled over by himself and took a chair where Holly and Bob sat. Lana was off somewhere. Slim didn't know where or with who.

Acer, who had returned with fresh beverages for Elizabeth and Jade, took a seat next to Slim and Holly. He found that his attention was again drawn to a lovely looking woman across the room—a mature woman. He liked the way she held her back straight, her head high. Although she was only selling raffle tickets, she moved as if she owned the room.

He spoke to Holly. "That woman with the long blond hair selling tickets. Who is she?"

It was Slim who answered. "The Empress."

"Empress?" Acer's dark eye-brows sailed high.

"Town hall joke." Holly explained. "Her name is Darlene Gage. She's in charge of JumpRope's Property, Construction and Zoning Department."

"Ah." Acer's thoughtful gaze returned to Darlene. "Is she married?"

"Divorced."

"Recently?

"For as long as I've known her," Holly answered. "Interested?"

"I might be."

"To each his own," Slim interjected dryly.

"Are you asking about Darlene?" Iris interrupted. "I couldn't help overhearing. The poor thing's marriage fell apart when her daughter was little. Darlene's a grandmother now. The baby is adorable. You should ask Darlene to show you pictures."

Holly tensed. Not knowing what Iris might decide to share next, maybe Darlene's hysterectomy and the town hall gossip of how she'd possibly gotten a tummy tuck at the same time, he quickly said to Acer, "Would you like an introduction?"

"I'll muddle along on my own," Acer said, standing.

CHAPTER 68

As Acer moved in Darlene's direction, he observed that she was now seated at an empty table. Perfect.

He stepped around people heading for the auction tables because their numbers had been called, and then he paused, watching Darlene for a moment before he moved in and took his place in the empty chair next to hers.

"Good evening."

Jerking her head up, she gave him a look up and down, taking in his meticulous grooming and a fancy watch that had a maker Francine could probably supply in a second. Yes, she had noticed him, all right. Who hadn't? He was just about the only man in the room wearing a tuxedo and entirely comfortable in it. Acer Wolfgang. She'd seen the TV news with him proposing a plan for the Hitchmile. Engineer was the profession he had told the township committee, but that's not all she knew from checking with the Internet.

Acer Wolfgang. *Developer*. Her mind spat out the word like contaminated water and watched it spin down the drain.

"Where's the arm candy?" she challenged.

He smiled. "Pardon me?"

"The bubblegum blonde who accompanies you to affairs like this."

His smile didn't falter. "That's a phase I've outgrown. But I am partial to women with light colored hair." He gave her a speculative look. "You should let it grow out naturally."

"What?" She drew back.

"It would become a silver waterfall. Gorgeous."

"You've got a hell of a nerve."

There was an excited squeal off to one side as a name for a door prize was called.

Darlene reached for her evening purse which lay on the table next to her. She paused, seeing that the ribbon-like strap lay partly under Acer's forearm.

He glanced down and wordlessly shifted his arm.

Had he planted his arm there on purpose? Darlene was sure of it. Mr. Power Play. She reached across him, snatched up her purse and stood. Her midnight blue gown fit closely on her slim and youthfully toned figure and she was all too aware of his admiring gaze. For an instant it crossed her mind that Mar-see-ah had once said something about her meeting a man. For a second, she froze. Then she gave herself a shake. What Mar-see-ah said was nonsense and even if it hadn't been, she wouldn't have meant *this* man, this *developer*.

She was sure he'd discovered she was head of property, construction and zoning. Why else would he come over except to try and buddy up to an official he might someday have to deal with? Well, he had a surprise coming. If they ever met again he would discover he couldn't get around her with his smarmy charm and fancy manners.

He would discover she was one tough cookie.

Towering over his seated form, she said in brusque farewell, "I can't say it's been a pleasure."

His smile, lifting more at one corner, was complacent as he gazed up at her. "It has been as far as I'm concerned."

She made a sound of contempt, but remained in place, as if bound. There was something about his smile that drew her, something about it not being perfect, yet compelling.

He said, "I imagine we will be meeting again."

"Don't make any bets." She tore loose from the invisible connection. Pivoting on her heels, she walked swiftly away.

He watched her retreating form, noticing she allowed her hips to sway ever so slightly as she moved. He liked the way she looked. He liked her attitude.

He lifted the drink he had brought along with him.

"To another day," he toasted and took a satisfied sip.

CHAPTER 69

Francine, done with her stint for calling the names and numbers of the winners, turned the microphone over to Nancy Lou and returned to her seat beside Bob, who was nodding off. He had gone to bed tired and then there had been a call for his tow truck during the night. He'd had only a few hours' sleep and needed to catch up.

"Am I exhausted!" Francine exclaimed. Abruptly, she asked Toria, "Who is that tall man over there. The other one in a tuxedo?"

"You know who that is, Nero Gibeau."

"The drunk? Now he thinks he's a waiter?"

Trying to be patient, Toria said, "Nero is a guest at the banquet. He paid for a ticket and probably for his grandmother's too. He dressed up to honor her."

"Oh."

Toria saw that Francine had caught her tone of rebuke. She felt bad about it, but why did Francine always have to be so disapproving?

There was an awkward pause, and then Francine said, "That's nice, what he did for his grandmother." Her face knotted up and she looked away from Toria and added in a tight voice as if speaking to no one, "My brother had a drinking problem. He hurt someone badly with his car."

Stunned by the admission, Toria realized that this was as close as she'd ever gotten of an apology or an explanation from Francine about any aspect of her behavior. She didn't know how to react.

She was saved when Iris gave a little yelp and cried, "Didn't Nancy Lou just call Jessi's name?"

"Mama Mia!" Slim exclaimed, sitting up and leaning forward. "Bud, get a load of that."

Holly was definitely looking and Toria couldn't blame him. She was looking too.

Jessi's dress might have been backless, but as she got up from her table and started walking, watchers could see that her shining black gown was deceptively modest in front, with a high neck band and a straight fall to the toes of her high-heeled strapped sandals. Both sides of the skirt were slit to the thigh. With each elegant step, there was a flash of shapely white legs. As she rounded a table and the angle changed, the full effect of the backless garment was revealed, exposing the contours of her smooth, pale back from the little band at her nape and straight down her spine almost to the lusciously rounded upper curves of her buttocks.

A spectacular dressmaking achievement on a spectacular little body.

Not everyone in the room was watching at first, but others quickly sensed something going on and soon, every eye in the room was on Jessi.

Delighted with the attention and knowing how hot she looked, Jessi took her time showcasing her way to the place where Nancy Lou stood ready with the door prize and scissors for her to open it.

Darlene watched from behind, peering over Nancy Lou's shoulder.

Ignoring Darlene and thanking Nancy Lou prettily, Jessi, with her jet-black hair fashioned in curving wings on either side of her triangular little face, picked up the scissors and shifted the package a bit—whatever it contained, it seemed solid and had weight to it. She flourished the scissors, making a big display out of every move as she cut through the bright ribbon and colored paper. She was surprised to find that there wasn't any box. The wrapping just fell away.

Still holding the scissors, Jessi frowned, confused by what she saw.

A brightly colored bag. And two books.

She read the label on the bag.

Plaster of Paris.

She read the book titles.

How to Repair Your Ceiling

How to Care For Your Pet Raccoon.

Her head snapped up in befuddled confusion as Darlene moved from behind Nancy Lou and taunted, "What's the matter, Jessi? It's just a reminder of your bedroom ceiling scam at the Apple Corners house. Can't you take a joke?"

With a furious screech, Jessi plunged the scissors into the plaster of Paris bag, tearing it wide open.

Only dimly aware of the firefly pops of lights that meant that avidly watching onlookers had started snapping pictures that they would immediately share on social media, Jessi made a second move.

Hoisting the ripped bag, she hurled the spilling contents directly toward Darlene's startled face. Which was the exact moment when the breezing force of the oscillating fan reached that section of the table. The fine white powder that Jessi had cast into the air suddenly spun back toward her. Momentarily it fogged the air and then it started landing, spatting white particles all over the front of Jessi's jet black dress and jet black hair.

Horrified, she looked down at herself. She looked as if she'd been in a flour fight with a bunch of clowns. Frozen in dismay, she could not allow herself to turn around. Could not allow that crowd of people to see what a mess she looked now....

Arnie!" She screamed her husband's name with a coughing screech as she snatched a folded sheet from the table. Giving it a frantic shake, she slung it crookedly around her shoulders.

By that time, Arnie was there. "Kitten! What…"

"Pick me up!" she ordered fiercely. "Pick me up and get me out of here!"

Obediently Arnie bundled her into his arms, and still not sure what was going on, he hurried her from the room, her comically ruined gown cloaked by the sheet.

Stunned, Slim, watching after the couple as they disappeared, exclaimed, "What in hell did we just see?"

"I'm not sure," answered an equally stunned Holly, "but I think her trick with that sheet and Arnie was the world's slickest save."

CHAPTER 70

It took a while for things to settle down and for the spilled plaster of Paris to be safely swept away. Holly had attempted to go after Darlene for an explanation of what had happened, but she had fled into the ladies room, her closest avenue of escape.

Nancy Lou, who had enlisted Iris to take over calling the rest of the winners, caught up with Holly.

"It was supposed to be a joke," Nancy Lou said. "Darlene set it up and called Jessi's name as if she'd really won a door prize. She thought it would be just between her and Jessi. She's mortified how everyone stopped to watch and the spectacle it turned out to be. I tried to warn her. She should have known Jessi could escalate a card trick into a Barnum & Bailey act. Darlene's done for the night. I'm taking her home."

Feeling helpless, Holly watched Nancy Lou go into the ladies room to fetch Darlene. Figuring it would be better if Darlene didn't see him staring when she emerged, he returned to Toria, who had followed him part way.

Putting an arm around her, he said, "I think I need to find someplace quiet just to sit for a minute." He led her from the banquet hall to a small, dimly lit corner of the lobby that held a table and couch. He pulled her down to sit beside him and after a moment, explained what Nancy Lou had told him.

"I feel bad for Darlene," Toria said. "She'll stand up in court against anybody, but she never does anything like that in a personal way."

"She sure made up for it."

"Yes, and with that man watching."

"What? Oh, Wolfgang? I saw him go over to introduce himself. It looked like she blew him off."

"Was he watching when that happened with Jessi?"

Holly chuckled. "Wasn't everybody?"

"Was he laughing at Darlene?"

"I don't think so." Holly thought back. "I don't know why I noticed him, maybe just the way he stood watching. For an instant I thought he might go to Darlene, but he didn't. Then she ran off. He wasn't laughing—he just looked…interested." Holly chuckled again. "It sure was—interesting, I mean"

"I guess." Toria said. She had overheard when Acer had asked about Darlene. She always looked perfect, but that evening, she had been totally gorgeous, like a woman featured at some prestigious event on a society page. She could understand why a man who didn't know Darlene's vinegary ways would want to meet her. Acer was so handsome and impressive. She thought of how caring he was with Elizabeth. Too bad if Darlene told him to take a hike, but that's how she was. Still, maybe he hadn't been totally discouraged. Not that it would go anywhere, still….

Aloud, she said to Holly, "I'm glad people were taking pictures. It will show that Jessi did the damage to herself."

Holly nodded, "Yes, except I'm guessing we may be right back to Jessi filing charges again. Darlene's a public official. She's not supposed to rig door prize tickets to play jokes."

Toria murmured in understanding and then they stopped talking, no longer interested in anything except themselves. For a long, long time, the two of them simply sat, Holly's arm curved snugly around her shoulders. He thought she smelled really good, like springtime blossoms.

After a while he said softly against her hair, which was flying all over the place as usual and ticking his nose. "It's going to be a late evening."

"Ummm…." She was leaning against him, relaxed and content.

"I was thinking," he murmured.

"Ummm?"

"I was wondering…. We've had several dinners together…. Have you given any thought to sometime sharing breakfast?" He'd thought they could banter about it. He didn't think it would really go anywhere, but he thought they could tease a bit…that it would be a little back and forth that would be…well, fun. Instead, he felt her tense.

She didn't move, but a shock had gone through her. The two of them stay the night together? Of course that's what he meant. Her mind tumbled in confusion. Heat raced up over her chest, burning the hollow of her throat and blotching her cheeks. It was far more than an aurora borealis effect this time, her entire body zinged with solar flares.

When she finally got her thoughts together enough to speak, the stammered words came out shaky. "I—I don't know. I don't think so… it's too soon….. It's…"

"It's okay," he soothed. "*No* for an answer is okay."

But—"

"Shhh," he said, pulling her closer. She tilted her face to look into his eyes, her expression uncertain and worried. He kissed her, warmly, but lightly. "It's okay," he repeated. He held her close, keeping one arm gently about her shoulders.

Gradually, he felt her relax again, her head dropping, her face against the curve of his neck. His sweetheart, his darling girl. He was thinking that if he hadn't so misjudged what he'd intended to be a light remark, the evening might have ended differently than he now knew it would. He would have driven her home confident in moves that would have had her drifting into surrender, but he now understood that even if that had happened, it wouldn't have been right for her. And if it wasn't right for her, it wasn't right for him. Toria was steady, she was true. She was exquisitely special. For the first time in his thirty-seven years he found he was thinking of the future, thinking of the long haul and it was with her. There was no telling what would happen between them as time moved on, but he knew he was going to do absolutely nothing to risk the fulfilling future that he could at long last envision.

CHAPTER 71

When Holly and Toria wandered hand in hand back into the banquet room they were intercepted by Slim. Lana was with him, clinging and gazing up with adoring eyes.

"Taking the girl I brought with me, home," he announced with a grin.

"Don't know what's going on there, but it sounded good," Holly said to Toria as they resumed walking.

"Lana came rushing to him when you talked with Nancy Lou," Toria said. "I think she had been outside crying. Wonder what happened?"

"I'll either hear the details from Slim or I won't," Holly said.

They passed Pilar sitting at a table in a corner writing in a small notebook. Toria smiled to herself, thinking that Jessi's performance would probably make a splash whenever the next issue of the *Jump Rope Jive* was published.

"Whoa!" Holly said when he and Toria reached their table and saw a big basket sitting in the center. "Who's the lucky winner?"

"Me," Jade said. "I bid on this prize with all the tickets you gave me."

The basket was filled with homemade chocolates tucked into plastic containers and decorated with ribbons and silk flowers. Holly was sure they had been donated by Shirley DeGarmo's companion, Ruth. Jade passed them around for everyone to share.

Kurt came up with his pregnant pumpkin bride (her dress was orange). They'd been married ten years and had two other children, but he always gazed at her as if they were newlyweds. They were bidding people goodnight because she was having vague twinges that maybe were the start of contractions.

As they left, a noisy cheer went up at a nearby table as somebody won a door prize.

"You'd think that would be about done," Bob said, roused by the commotion.

"Not quite yet, dear." Francine patted his hand. "Our committee did a wonderful job."

Looking as if he could have done with less wonderfulness, Bob closed his eyes again.

People who knew Bob well were disappointed. Get a few drinks in him and despite Francine's priggish disapproval, he changed from Mr. Sobersides to Mr. Entertainer. It wasn't so much what he said, as it was how he said it—personal experiences related in such a way that his audience would be rolling on the floor and crying for more. But after working half the night with the tow truck, all he wanted was sleep.

Toria noticed Acer watching Elizabeth. She had taken five or six pieces from Jade's candy basket and arranged them on the tablecloth as if studying the different designs on top that indicated different fillings.

The candy had Acer's attention too. Toria couldn't read their expressions. Guarded? Hesitant? Hopeful?

Toria wondered what was so fascinating about the candy. A comment from Francine redirected her attention. "Oh, look. Shirley DeGarmo must have won something."

Across the room, Shirley was getting to her feet. She seemed unsteady as she started to walk toward the auction table—she'd probably been sitting in one place too long. Ruth jumped up and moved to take her arm.

Toria saw Nero give Donny, who had been standing talking to somebody, a nudge, directing his attention to his mother.

Snapping to it, Donny quick-stepped to take Ruth's place.

Toria called Elizabeth's attention to the two women across the room. "See over there? The thin woman, that's Ruth Wilson. She's the one who made the chocolates in Jade's basket."

Elizabeth's head snapped up. "She made these chocolates? Funny, it was always...."

Voice fading, Elizabeth stared tensely across the room.

Toria sensed something odd going on with Elizabeth, but then she told herself that with such thick glasses Elizabeth must be straining her eyes to see.

All at once, the old woman grasped for her four-pronged cane and ponderously heaved herself from her wheelchair and to her feet.

"Grace!" she bellowed across the room.

At the call, Ruth Wilson stood stock still.

Toria thought she looked like a deer caught in the headlights, frozen. And then, when her paralysis broke, Ruth, like a deer, looked ready to flee. But then, after a moment of visible indecision and an inarticulate cry, Ruth stumbled toward Elizabeth, angling around tables and around Francine and Bob.

With another cry, she went directly into Elizabeth Mather's arms.

Stunned, Toria saw the profiles of the two women and the strong resemblance between them. She never remembered meeting Grace, but she knew her description: a heavy woman, big thick glasses, dark hair screwed back in a knot. As if witnessing the unveiling of a conjurer's trick, she looked at Ruth and could suddenly imagine a body made thin by dieting, eyes appearing prominent because of thick contact lenses, hair cut chin-length and dyed a light brown as yet another part of her disguise.

Ruth Wilson, Shirley DeGarmo's companion for almost four years, must actually be Grace Mather.

Grace Mather, among them all this time.

"Grace, my dear little one," Elizabeth crooned.

"Ibbi," Grace sobbed. "Aunt Ibbi—how did you ever come to find me?"

CHAPTER 72

Sunday morning at the Presbyterian Church, the vestibule was filled with parishioners excitedly discussing the previous night's banquet with Grace Mather finally being found—hiding in plain sight, so to speak. The same was surely going on at the Methodist Church, where Holly was attending with his dad and Peggy.

Amy Newton came up to Toria. "Remember the Voodoo Club dinner when you and Francine wanted to know about the name, Ibbi?" Amy said. "I'd seen it on a sampler where I clean house. I found out that Ibbi stands for Elizabeth, only we already know that because we heard Ruth, or rather Grace, blurt it out. It's the nickname, Libby, shortened to Ibbi, with an 'i' on the end instead of a 'y.' Cute, huh?"

Toria agreed, although the name was no longer surprise.

What happened after church *was* a surprise. As the parishioners filed out, they found bundles of the latest *JumpRope Jive* stacked on the steps. People eagerly hustled forward.

Toria thought that Pilar Fanshawe must have been up all night working and then rushed the four page product to an all-night copy center to get this issue of the *Jive* printed for early morning distribution.

The paper would soon be all over town, and then on the Internet. Only the most stubborn would be able to miss it.

Sitting in her tiny kitchen with a second cup of coffee after changing from church clothes to casual clothes, Toria opened the slim publication. Ignoring Pilar's decorating article and another scene from her son, Alexander's, apparently endless play, she saw that Madam Jive's *News and Noose* led off with a birth announcement for Donny's brother, Kurt, and his wife. They had left the banquet and gone straight to the hospital. A little girl.

Nice, Toria thought. She then saw a note that could only apply to her and Holly:

**The Mayor and the Librarian continue
making calf's eyes. Too, too sweet.**

Toria felt herself blush, and then she smiled. This time, she and Holly would laugh together about being mentioned.

Further down on the page, there were lines that clearly referred to Jessi's fiasco:

**Who could guess a banquet prize could explode!
Truth is indeed stranger than fiction. Rest
assured, gentle people, no one was injured.**

Toria shook her head. Jessi had an off and on again friendship with Pilar and Pilar probably wouldn't print anything to make Jessi look really bad—although it was hard to believe that Jessi wouldn't consider becoming a public laughing stock a grievous injury.

Turning to the back page, Toria was startled by an article titled:

**Long Lost Family Member Restored to the
Bosom of her Loved Ones**

With combined disbelief and amusement, Toria read Pilar's take on what had happened the night before with Elizabeth and Grace, combining what little facts she actually knew (not many) with wildly inventive conjecture (a whole lot). Summed up, the article told readers that after the sudden death of her brother, Barry, four years before (a reference was given for readers to look up the previous issue for the

Mather house background), Grace Mather had suffered a prolonged case of amnesia. Drawn back to JumpRope by her unconscious love for her ancestral home, she found employment as the faithful companion of Shirley DeGarmo and remained unknowing of the truth of her identity, even after the body of her dead brother was found and attempts were made to locate her.

The article concluded with: "It was not until after her cousin, engineer, developer and celebrated tycoon, Acer Wolfgang, came to JumpRope's Annual Banquet and Auction with another family member, Elizabeth Mather, that a miracle occurred.

"Elizabeth Mather, aunt to both Acer and Grace, recognized her niece as Grace stood to collect a prize. Elizabeth called Grace's name and in a twinkling, Grace's memory was restored and she ran to embrace her family members. When the *Jive* staff attempted to interview the family for further details, they requested that we respect their privacy during this precious time, which we shall certainly do. However, in an interview with Shirley DeGarmo, we learned that the woman she knew as Ruth Wilson has been a godsend and that she would be grateful to maintain their friendship.

"Now that Grace has blissfully been restored to her senses and to her family, there will be a memorial service for her beloved brother, Barry. There is hope that yet another long lost member of the Mather family, Elizabeth's niece, Vivian Mather, has received word about her beloved Cousin Barry's death and will return home for the solemn occasion. Details of the memorial service will be found in the *Melton Monitor*, which, as a daily, is unlike this publication, which only appears in those golden moments when need and inspiration soar."

My goodness! Toria thought. She couldn't wait to talk this over with Holly. What a mash-up! There were all sorts of inaccuracies. Acer wasn't a relative and Grace never had amnesia—but really, what was the harm? Amnesia wasn't a bad angle. It was in print and people would accept it. As for the authorities, there was no reason they would care either way. As silly as Pilar's newsletter could be, her fanciful explanation had probably done the Mathers a favor. And now that Grace was found, Toria was reminded that there was still an absent Mather family member, Elizabeth's much younger niece, Vivian. But that seemed more of a case of wanderlust than a real mystery. Toria hoped for Elizabeth's sake the young woman would reappear in time for Barry's memorial service.

Toria's doorbell rang.

Toria smoothed her flyaway hair and got up from the table. For some reason, perhaps Amy's earlier mention of the Voodoo Club, she recalled a Mar-see-ah predication to Francine about a mysterious ringing of her doorbell. Mar-see-ah had repeated it twice. It maybe had come true at least once—when Acer Wolfgang unexpectedly showed up at Francine's hunting for Elizabeth Mather. A thrill to think that the prediction could have been right, except, of course, it wouldn't happen to Francine a second time.

Toria laughed as she ran to her own door. Holly! Nothing mysterious—this was wonderful. They were in one another's arms as if they had been apart for days.

"Hi," she said.

"Hi, yourself, Sweetheart," he said. "Where do you want to go and do today?"

Sweetheart. She caught her breath. "I don't know, she said, so happy she couldn't stop smiling. "Have any good suggestions?"

CHAPTER 73

Over on Centre Avenue, Francine was sitting in her dining room, her home all to herself now that her important guests had left. She was disgusted with the Sunday *Melton Monitor*. Not a word about the banquet. JJ Gilbert would probably include a nice feature tomorrow, but Francine wanted something today. She still had JJ's card. She'd call her later and lend color to the article. The woman would be grateful. As to the *Jive*, it did talk about the banquet, but it was all rubbish. You would think Pilar could at least mention how nice the prizes had been. Her *Noose* nonsense about Jessi gave the impression they were all Molotov cocktails. So irresponsible.

She shoved the copy of the *Jive* aside, thinking less about the things it said than about the things it *should* have said. About her lovely dress, for example. And about her house guest, who had brought along a personal maid. And Acer, so cosmopolitan looking! Wouldn't you think Pilar would have raved about him?

The doorbell rang.

Francine didn't know why, but the sound gave her a little chill. For some reason she found herself remembering one of Mar-see-ah's predictions, something about a doorbell ringing, with the mysterious implication that it would turn out to be something or someone important. What nonsense! Still, it took a moment before she could shrug off the eerie sensation and rise to her feet. Stepping toward the entrance, she recaptured her normal annoyance at being interrupted. Really, her house was becoming Grand Central Station.

She opened the door and saw a beautiful young woman with long, dark wavy hair standing on the stoop. Probably still in her twenties, the woman looked unusually accomplished and confident. Her chin was set in a way that proclaimed she was accustomed to dealing with anything or anyone, qualities Francine believed she herself excelled in.

Instinctively bristling, Francine set her own chin.

"Yes?" she said in a lofty tone.

"Hello," the woman said. "My name is Vivian. Vivian Mather."

AFTER

MAR-SEE-AH SPEAKS...

Mar-see-ah laughed softly to herself as her hands moved the smooth river stones, instruments of divination.

Well, now, she murmured to herself.

A new player has come to the little town of JumpRope, seeking answers to the past.

She will find them. Although, the answers may not be what she expects, nor is the price that she might have to pay.

There may be any number of things she does not expect.

Including, perhaps, romance? Oh, my...she will run from that.

How interesting. No wonder the town was so dear to her, Mar-see-ah thought as she reviewed an earlier vision. The sadness and death that she had foreseen had come. Death, sorrow and regret. But healing had come as well.

The oak and the lilacs had indeed been the start of something: bringing together a lonely man and a shy woman who gained the courage to reach for happiness not only for herself, but for him.

Content, Mar-see-ah lifted her hands from the stones.

It was a good place to end.

Coming Soon

Jump into...

DEATH COUNTS
THE GOLDEN COINS
JumpRope Chronicles
by
Ivy C. Leigh

Vivian wanted to keep a promise —

will it cause her to lose her life?

World traveler Vivian Mather comes to the long-established New Jersey community of JumpRope to explore the research of her late cousin, Barry. A notebook recording his study of Native Americans during Colonial times that he had wanted to share it with her is unaccountably missing.

A local psychic warns Vivian that her search for the notebook will lead to danger. Scoffing, Vivian ignores the warning even after discovering Barry's hidden cache of valuable artifacts. The treasure trove is a secret, so how could there be a connection between it and the senseless attack on a young woman of the town and the gruesome murder of a virtual stranger?

When there is yet another attack, suspicion points toward a young war veteran, Nero Gibeau, but Vivian has reason to doubt his guilt. She and Nero draw together as they try to discover the town's hidden evil and the true killer before it is too late.

JERSEY PINES INK

Look for upcoming books
from Jersey Pines Ink
https://www.jerseypinesink.com/

A new horror anthology:
Crypt-Gnats
edited by
Dina Leacock

Death Counts the Golden Coins
JumpRope Chronicles
by
Ivy C. Leigh